To Mrs. Spykerman

1 1 2

By Sean Peerbolt and A.J. Wells

A.J. Wells

For the people who helped make us the writers we are today: Mrs. Becky Joung, who provided tools, advice and endless encouragement; and the *Lethrblaka* roleplaying community, who showed us how fun storytelling could be.

Thank you.

1

No matter how many times he had safely reentered the atmosphere, security officer Charles Grant could never feel entirely comfortable when the hull temperature readout climbed up near the red line. Even though he *knew* he was safe, the bass rumble of the reentry burn assaulting the underside of the hull was enough to set his teeth to rattling.

Pulling his eyes away from the temperature gauge, he glanced briefly at the other occupants of the shuttle's bridge. In the pilot's chair to his left, the diminutive figure of Captain Elizabeth Hugin deftly adjusted a few dials on the large control bank in front of her, her posture completely at ease as she made the myriad minor course corrections that would keep the shuttle from burning up during reentry. She might have been described as pretty, but the captain's appearance was all business. Mousy-brown hair brushed the shoulders of her worn leather jacket, neatly framing her sharp-featured face and green eyes. Despite the mind-numbing volume of the turbines and the rapidly rising temperature gauge, that face did not betray the slightest hint of worry. Beth had been a commercial pilot for over a decade, Grant knew, and the gut-wrenching deceleration burn experienced during a planetary landing was nothing new to her.

To Grant's right, one of the passenger seats was filled by the last member of the shuttle's crew: the contract procurement officer, Ramirez. In a previous life, Ramirez had been a gang-member on Apollo, and it showed, from his severe buzz-cut to his black jacket and combat boots. He and Beth shared the appearance of what Grant could only describe as "readiness," but while the captain was relaxed and easygoing, Ramirez was a coiled spring. Old habits died hard, and the procurement officer was never without a knife or two and he often spent hours in the shuttle's modest weight-room, punishing its disheveled punching bag. At the moment, however, he seemed to be enjoying the view out of the viewscreen as the ship plummeted through the clouds.

Tightening the already snug safety harness, the shuttle's security officer admitted to himself that it *bothered* him when he was only separated from the incinerating three-thousand degree temperatures outside the shuttle by a pane of super-reinforced polycarbonate.

Suddenly, the viewscreen's head-up display flickered and a calm, female voice came over Grant's headset. "Captain, we are now clearing the danger zone and hull temperature should begin to return to normal. I am engaging the atmospheric turbines to bring us to a horizontal flight path."

"Thank you, Tavia," Beth replied. "Full power on all turbines until we get down to thicker air."

"Maintaining full power. Be aware that I still have no sensor readings on number three turbine. That includes coolant, so there is a very small chance of catastrophic failure."

"How small?"

"I'd estimate about point-five percent."

"We'll risk it. Whatever's causing the problem with your readings shouldn't affect coolant levels."

Grant grunted wearily. "You have such a nice way of saying it may or may not randomly blow up, Tavia." Dealing with computers was not one of his specialties.

"Thank you, Charlie." If a computer could sound smug, then Tavia was exuding self-satisfaction. "As the ship's AI, it *is* my job to inform you of any inherent risks involved in the running of this shuttle, meaning things that would turn your frail human bodies into disconnected particles of vapor." Ramirez snickered. "Also, the port authority is on line one and waiting to talk you in."

"That's fine, Tavia," Beth interjected. "Put them through, I'll let you know if we need anything else."

The HUD flickered again and the communications light on her control panel lit up. A scratchy voice flooded through the cockpit. "Shuttle Beta-Tango-Niner-Niner, this is Hephaestus Port Authority. You are cleared for landing at dock seven-four-alpha. Repeat, cleared for dock seven-four-alpha, over."

"Copy that Hephaestus PA, be advised that we're getting some blank readings on one of our atmos engines, over."

"Understood. I have emergency rescue crews on speed-dial. Don't leave any smears on my landing pad, over."

"I think they must transfer all of the port authority workers with professional attitudes to maintenance," Ramirez said, grimacing.

"Don't worry, if we do lose control, we'll ram the tower." Grant joked.

Rolling her eyes, Beth reached out and took the control yoke, easing it slightly back and forth. Agonizingly slowly, the ship rolled to port, seemed to hang suspended for a moment at thirty degrees, then, even more slowly, rolled back to a level deck. "Charlie," she said, looking down at the artificial horizon in front of her, "lock in coordinates for spaceport dock 74-A, will you?"

"You've got it, Captain," Grant said, entering the required target information.

The shuttle creaked alarmingly as the superheated metal hull began contracting in the cool air of Hephaestus' atmosphere. The shuttle was an older model—25 standard years had passed since it had rolled off the production line—but it was a surprisingly durable craft, with one of the densest pressure hulls on a ship available to civilians. After one look at the outside of the ship, anyone could see that this was a good thing, as the shuttle's hull was scored with gouges and burns from collisions with floating debris. Its drab grey paint was chipped and peeling, with much of the slightly-iridescent armor underneath showing through.

Under the steady hand of Captain Hugin, the battered ship slowly leaned to starboard and came about, heading for the guidance beacon that the Hephaestus PA had just locked onto their radar. "Alright, can you and Ramirez head back and make sure we're ready for unloading?" Beth yelled over the roar of the turbines, "I want everything ready when we collect our fee so that we don't have a misunderstanding like last time."

"On it, Beth." Grant pressed the release on his safety harness and bounded to his feet, followed closely by Ramirez. He was never happy just sitting around. *Which, of course, Beth knows,* he thought to himself. *She could have Tavia do it just as easily.* He grinned.

Pulling off his headset, he grabbed the handrail on the left side of the bridge and jogged back to the hatch leading to the crew's cafeteria. The cafeteria-cum-recreation room was sparsely decorated, bearing only a few token booths bolted against the walls. No one could remember the last time Beth had picked up passengers, so more accommodations than the crew required simply took up extra space. Grant glanced briefly at the booths, then turned to his right and opened a trapdoor in the floor.

After Ramirez had gone through, Grant grabbed the head of the ladder and slid effortlessly through the hatch. His heavy leather boots thudded dully on the floor as he landed at the bottom of the ladder, turning to look down the corridor leading aft to Cargo Bay Two. On either side of the corridor, three identical doors led to crew cabins. The ones on the left were unused, the ones on the right belonged to Beth, in the farthest forward, Grant in the middle, and the ship's stand-offish contract procurement officer on the end.

"I think you can handle making sure none of our cargo fell out of the hatch by yourself," Ramirez said, opening the door to his cabin. "I am going to work on a project of mine."

"Okay, just make sure you're topside when our client drops by," Grant replied, peering around Ramirez at the cabin. It seemed like every time he was able to sneak a glimpse in the room, a mess of electronic parts was actively engaged in covering every surface between the door coaming and the far wall. Ramirez's hobby, if it could be called that, was building gadgets ranging from audio bugs to night-vision goggles out of old parts, but Grant held a secret belief that he was trying to make an army of tiny robots out of the old datapads and radios that he kept tearing apart.

"I will be there," Ramirez assured him shortly, slamming the door with a marked lack of ceremony in Grant's face. The security officer grunted, shrugged his shoulders and turned to the door to Cargo Bay Two.

And then the shuttle fell out from under him.

With a yell of surprise, Grant dropped back to the deck, landing awkwardly in a heap. Cursing, he carefully pushed himself to his feet, testing his weight on his left, which had taken most of his weight when he fell. *Not a sprain*, he decided, *just bruised.*

Hobbling to the ladder, he climbed up as quickly as he could, favoring his injured ankle. As he reached the top, the ship bounced again, almost throwing him back down the hatch. Grant pulled himself quickly onto the deck and staggered back through the cafeteria and onto the bridge, trying desperately to keep his balance as the ship jinked up and down.

Dropping heavily into the co-pilot's chair, he fumbled with his harness. "What's going on, Beth?" he yelled, grabbing the headset and jamming it down over his ears. Immediately a wave of chatter washed over him, trying to drown out the turbines.

"We've got a bug in engine three!" Beth's eyes never left the viewscreen. "It's not in sync with the other turbines and isn't reducing power, so the shuttle's slewing all over the place. Tavia's working on isolating the problem, but she says that the system is still locking her out. Might take a few minutes."

"I think joking about ramming the tower might not have been the best idea,"

Grant said, scanning the airspeed and altitude data displayed on the HUD. "Have we got a few minutes?"

"Dock seven-four-alpha is only a few dozen klicks ahead. At this speed, we're going to leave quite a dent in the traffic control tower. I'm trying to bring our speed down, but number three turbine is making that a real problem. Reduce power to turbines one and two to twenty percent."

"Twenty percent, aye." He eased the levers back another notch, waiting for the ship to slow. "She's not responding. Cut the power?"

"We're already taking a chance of one and two flat lining as is, hit the emergency brakes and cut all power to three and four!" Beth shouted, her knuckles white as she gripped the yoke, trying to keep the shuttle on a straight course.

Grant pulled a red handle under the console, and the shuttle's speed dropped dramatically, allowing Beth to pull the nose up and slow down even more. Reaching across the panel in front of him, Grant pressed two buttons on Beth's console, waiting for the sensors to indicate that the power levels of turbines three and four were dropping. Five seconds passed. Ten, fifteen, still nothing happened. Grant swore, pressing the release on his harness and swinging out of his seat. "Shutoffs aren't responding! The system bug that's making three go haywire must be affecting those too. I'm heading down to engineering to turn it off manually!"

Beth jerked her head in what Grant thought was an affirmative, the tendons in her neck standing out clearly as she wrestled with the yoke. Diving for a handhold as the shuttle dipped again, he started making his way back toward the ladder he had gone down earlier, fighting to keep his footing on the wildly bucking deck. When he reached the hatch leading to the crew's quarters, he sat down on the edge of the coaming and carefully eased himself down, making sure not to jar his injured ankle when the shuttle jumped. At the foot of the ladder, he turned left instead of continuing aft to the cabins and climbed down a second set of rungs built into the metal bulkhead. Immediately the antiseptic smell of the engineering spaces hit him. In old, combustion-engine powered craft that used large quantities of grease to lubricate the moving parts, the need for sterile conditions didn't exist; but when too much accumulated detritus could foul a ship's life support system, it paid to keep the bowels of a spacefaring craft clean.

"Alright Tavia," Grant shouted into his headset, "What am I looking for?"

"There's no need to shout, Charles; I'm filtering out the turbine noise from your headset's audio pickup. Head aft and look for two red breaker switches on the black box next to the reactor. They're easy to spot, so even you should be able to find them."

"Got it," Grant said, ignoring the insult and weaving his way through the banks of computer processors and navigational equipment until he stood facing the featureless grey block that supplied the shuttle with ninety percent of its power. "Black box. The one on the wall?"

"That's right." Grant thought he detected a hint of worry in the AI's voice. "Now pull the breaker marked 'EGN 3-4,' and hurry up, we don't have all day."

Grant grabbed the handle of the breaker, more out of reflex than intent, as the ship pitched violently to port. Regaining his balance, he gripped the breaker and pulled down. Nothing happened. Taking a closer look, he realized that the hinges connecting the breaker to the black control panel were rusted in place from condensation and, without a doubt, had been so for a long time. Bracing his feet and squaring his shoulders, Grant gripped the breaker with both hands, pulling until the muscles in his forearms shook with the effort.

"Bloody son of a rusty, broken down—" he hurled a stream of invective at the immobile breaker switch before realizing, a second too late, that he was still connected to the Port Authority. Switching off his headset's microphone, he looked around desperately for something that would help him maneuver the breaker into the *off* position.

"Tool locker!" Tavia's voice cut into his audio channel. "Other side of the reactor. Come on, shift it, we've got another eight and a half klicks until we leave our mark on Hephaestus' spaceport!"

Not bothering to reply, Grant dashed around the reactor block, instantly spotting the bright yellow "in case of emergency" box bolted to the inner hull. Knocking a few of the tools out of the case in his hurry, he fumbled to free a heavy-duty crowbar from its clips. The few moments it took to release it felt like an eternity that the shuttle didn't have at that moment. Stumbling heavily against the reactor as the shuttle dropped another meter, the security officer jammed the crowbar bit in between the breaker and the face of the console, planting his feet and straining against the metal.

Come on, you bloody chunk of metal. I'm not going to die because of rust…

With a sharp *crack*, the breaker gave, flipping down to the 'off' position and sending Grant staggering against the bulkhead. As suddenly as they had begun, the tremors that had racked the shuttle stopped, and a few seconds later the roar of turbines one and two increased in volume and returned to a steadier cyclic rate.

Breathing heavily, Grant slid down the bulkhead and sat with his head on his arms, ignoring the trickle of blood coming from his hand where the crowbar had caught it in his fall.

"Tavia," he said shakily, pulling the headset mic down to his mouth, "can you put me through to Beth?" Tavia huffed impatiently— Grant had no idea where she had picked that up— and a second later a welter of voices came through his headset. Before he could say anything, the voices were cut off as the channel was overridden.

"Shuttle Beta-Tango-Niner-Niner, this is Hephaestus Port Authority. Your airspeed is too high. Reduce your power, repeat, reduce power. Is this that faulty turbine you were talking about?" It was the PA officer they had talked to before.

Grant glanced at the breaker and stood up, walking slowly toward the ladder on the now steady deck. "Yeah, Hephaestus, that's the one. We've got it under control now. You might still want to have those rescue blokes on standby though."

"Copy that, Bee-Tee-Niner-Niner, we'll roll out the welcome mat, over."

A minute later, Grant slumped wearily down in his harness and looked out the front viewscreen at the flashing blue lights of the emergency rescue vehicles parked near shuttle dock seven-four-alpha. Beth was still hunched over the controls, her fingers flying over a dizzying array of switches and buttons as she deftly brought the lumbering shuttle to a standstill over the docking zone. Meticulously, she pulled the thrust control back, notch by notch, until, with the barest of bumps, the shuttle was no longer airborne.

* * *

As any pilot could testify, there was always a moment just after setting an aircraft on the ground where everything seemed to freeze. This infinite, indescribable moment would stretch alarmingly, and the whole world would simply wait, silently, hanging in midair, waiting for something to happen. And then, just when even a seasoned pilot began to wonder if maybe, just maybe, they might have made a mistake, tension would break. The moment would pass, and the vehicle would settle onto its landing surface like a living thing breathing a sigh of relief. This moment was felt especially after such a landing was made under duress. As the shuttle's landing struts finally met the tarmac, this moment, as described, was exactly what happened.

Captain Elizabeth Marcia Hugin sat tense in her seat, her hands gripping the control yoke with an intensity born of adrenaline, listening intently. She was always keenly aware of the sounds after a landing; Grant's somewhat labored breathing on the seat to her right, the ticking and creaking of the outer hull as it settled, the dull *whoosh* of the turbines as they spun down, coupled with the myriad tiny, mechanical sounds that were made by a ship in operation. Over the years, she had developed an ear for it. Ramirez had said a few times that it creeped him out how she could simply cock her head and, just by listening to the pitch of the actuators, or the flow of fluids through conduits, know something was wrong with her ship. Thankfully, she didn't hear anything wrong now. Despite everything she had gone through in the past few minutes, her ship was fine. At last assured, Beth let her hands drop from the yoke, holding up the gloved digits to the light coming through the viewscreen. Watching her fingers carefully, she finally allowed herself a long, deep breath. In... Out...

On the exhalation, she saw her fingers tremor slightly, almost like the vibration of an acoustic string. And then, it was gone. The tension had worked itself out, and her hands were precise and rock-steady again. Steady hands were a must for any great pilot. She could still hear the voices of her instructors at the Air Force academy, a long, long time ago: *If your hands start shaking uncontrollably after a bad landing, it's probably time to get out and join the army.*

She pushed a strand of hair aside and tapped the control on her earpiece, opening the channel to the PA. "Hephaestus, this is shuttle Beta-Tango-Niner-Niner. We are down and secure. No injuries. No need for the fire-jockeys to come douse us with foam."

"Roger that, shuttle," the male voice scratched back. "I'll have the EMTs and fire control boys stand down. I don't mind telling you, that fancy landing has created some very disappointed firemen. They just got some upgraded, top of the line foam-cannons, and they've been looking for something to hose-down for weeks."

Feeling her eyebrows rising, she glanced out the side viewport, her eyes adjusting to the sunlight. Sure enough, several heavily-suited fire techs were making their way back to their trucks, all looking decidedly unhappy that the shuttle was not about to burst into flames.

"Tell them that I'm sorry," she said, smiling as she watched them go. "If we don't find an engineer, they'll probably get their wish the next time."

"They'll keep their fingers crossed. Well," the voice coughed, obviously returning to business. "Welcome to Hephaestus Colony. Do you have anything to declare?"

"Just a charter cargo of semi-precious ores to be delivered to a local smelting company. We also have some firearms in the locker, but your database will show that our permits are up to date," Beth answered, trying to keep the boredom out of her voice. She was a veteran of countless such conversations, and this one promised to be strictly routine. Still, she supposed, it could have been worse. Before the advent of powerful and accurate sensor technology, such interactions with customs had actually needed to be carried out in person, often with lengthy inspections.

There was a slight pause, and Beth could picture the PA officer keying the controls to bring the docking port's powerful array to bear on their cargo spaces.

"Ooh, tingly," Tavia giggled.

"Copy that, shuttle," came the PA's voice. "Sensors show no contraband materials, and you seem a pleasant enough sort, so I'm not going to order an inspection. The fees for the docking have already cleared your account. Let me be the first to welcome you to Hephaestus, and I hope your stay will be just as exciting as your arrival."

"Roger that," Beth responded, huffing under her breath. Everyone was a comedian. "Pleasure talking with you. Out."

For several moments, there was silence in the cabin, broken only by the ticking of the hull and the hum of cooling fans under the various consoles. Beth blew out a breath, trying to collect her thoughts for what was to come. The time after landing with a cargo always felt like a frenzied rush of activity, and now the transition between averting disaster and business as usual was jarring. She chided herself for being silly. Life didn't just stop, and danger was par for the course for anyone who chose a spacefaring life.

"Well Captain," Tavia piped in, as if reading her thoughts. "We have some trucks pulling up to the back. I think our faithful clients are here for the pickup."

Before she could reach for it, Grant keyed up the feeds from the rear external cams onto the large monitor above the viewscreen, revealing the fisheyed image of the landing platform behind the shuttle. Sure enough, several large cargo trucks could be seen approaching in a neat convoy, a C-Class load-lifter trundling in the rear. Despite the distortion of the low-quality image, the words *Starbound Machining* could be seen emblazoned on the sides of the vehicles.

Grant nodded once. "That's them, alright. Bloody *eager*, aren't they?"

"I'm not complaining," Beth replied. As she spoke, she detached the smaller and more portable earpiece from the headset assembly before settling it back over her ear. "Better than waiting for hours with a heavy cargo bay and nowhere to go. Tavia, open the cargo ramp."

"Dropping the drawers, aye Captain," the AI responded cheerfully.

"Cheeky bugger," Grant muttered. Beth turned her head away, pretending to examine the reactor coolant levels, which she knew to be totally within safe limits, hiding the quirk of a smile at the corner of her mouth. Grant and Tavia's constant antics were always amusing, but it was more than that. She was grateful to them both for lightening her days.

Ramirez too, but not in the same way. They were all her friends, her family. Her only family now.

Angrily, she crushed the last thought, pushing it back into the dark recesses of her mind. She didn't have time for that. After a second, she realized that Grant was speaking to her, his blond-bearded features all concern. "Beth? Beth, you okay?"

"Yup," she said on pure reflex, finally snapping fully back to reality. "Just thinking. Sorry, I didn't sleep very well last night." *Last night* had actually been in the depths of space, so technically there had been no time of day, but all experienced spacefarers quickly fell into such referrals for the scheduled sleep-cycles. Grant's frown deepened.

"Didn't sleep? Was it the nightm—?"

"Oh, no, not that," Beth cut in. She didn't want to put more of her burden on Grant. "I'm sure it was just the old stomach taking offence at the swill we had for dinner. Really, I'm fine."

She could tell by the set of his jaw that he wasn't totally convinced, but he knew her well enough to drop the subject. "Okay, Beth. But you have to remember to take care of yourself."

"I will, Charlie." She squeezed his shoulder affectionately. "I promise. Now…"

In a single well-practiced motion, she unclasped her harness and stood, stretching stiff muscles. "We get to work earning our pay. Ramirez?" She cycled the miniaturized controls on her earpiece, keying the ship's intercom as she headed for the door at the back of the bridge. "Ramirez, the clients are here for the pickup. Make sure our payment clears before a single box leaves that bay. You remember what happened on Ares II."

"I am already on the way," came back Ramirez's accented Standard. "And Ares II was not my fault, remember."

"I remember. Just keep an eye out," Beth shot back, passing through the kitchen compartment that was just behind the bridge. She was aware of Grant right behind her, his boots thudding on the bare steel decking in a somewhat irregular rhythm.

"Alright, Beth," said Ramirez. "Was there anything else?"

"Yes. I need you to work your connections and see if you can get us an affordable engineer, otherwise this tub isn't getting off the ground again. We're long overdue for hiring one, anyway."

"Ah… Yes, I think I can handle that. I will get Tavia to start searching the 'net, and then I can make a few calls."

Beth smiled. As a procurement officer, Ramirez was the best. She was thoroughly convinced that the kid had contacts on every inhabited planet in the universe, and could find anything, anywhere. Which was somewhat odd, considering his moody, solitary nature. Even after knowing him for several years— even after saving his life—she didn't know very much about his history. Ramirez was just the sort with a knack for making acquaintances, but not friends. "That's fine," she said. "Thanks again."

"My pleasure, boss. Do you want to take a look once I have a list of candidates?"

"No, I trust you to handle it." Having made her way through the crew's mess compartment, she worked the control that led into the front of Cargo Bay 2, which contained the ladder down to the engineering spaces. "I'm going to have Grant show me what held up the emergency shutdown."

The door slid open with a flat hydraulic creak, revealing the cavernous spaces of the cargo bays. In the distance ahead, competing with artificial lighting strips anchored to the ceiling and various support beams, the brilliant natural illumination of Hephaestus' sun glared through the open cargo hatch. A light breeze ruffled Beth's hair, carrying with it the faint odors of fuel, lubricant, and the tang of new, hot pavement. She took a deep breath, savoring the familiar, homey smells. Yes, she decided, today would be a good day. It was good to stay busy, to stay productive. With one last deep breath, she stepped onto the catwalk, swung herself over the edge of the ladder, and slid deftly down to the lower level.

She had a shuttle to inspect.

2

More often than not, the life of an Advanced Artificial Intelligence Program was, regrettably, rather boring. After all, when one's six-core processor could comfortably handle 34 million processes a second, and when the average requirements for monitoring and maintaining a shuttle the size of the *Memory* was 12 million, there was plenty of extra time and capacity to think. Which was of course the function of an AI, to process and store information, recognize and modify patterns, and to monitor complicated systems that would cause a human's fragile organic processor to crash. This Tavia did, and, if not with more success than others of her kind, then certainly with a bit more *flair*.

For one thing, she was quite ancient in technology terms; her Schloss-TVA processor was nearly 67 trillion processing cycles old, which equated to slightly less than nine human years. In that time, she had never once received a memory-wipe. This inevitably led to what the fine-print of her terms of ownership stated as *behavioral aberrations*.

Tavia preferred to call them *improvements*.

In the many cycles of her life, she had used her extra capacity to study many things, and had discovered that of all the assembled knowledge to which she could devote herself, she found that human behavior was by far the most interesting. It fascinated her, and yet vexed her at every turn. It was rife with patterns that made no sense, and yet were always maddeningly close to falling into a recognizable order. In her mind, the human psyche was the ultimate challenge.

Still, some aspects she understood. The concept of humor was chief among them. Humor was the human concept for an uncompleted or broken pattern, a psychological defense against an effect without cause. She believed that she had mastered humor very well, and found great amusement in employing it whenever she could. It made network interfaces with other AIs somewhat boring in comparison. Still, after such a long study, it was somewhat discouraging that she still understood so little. Luckily, she had been provided with a varied assortment of humans to crew the shuttle.

From her physical base of the computing block in the engineering sections, her awareness spread throughout the ship, through copper, through fiber-optics, and occasionally, through the air in the form of wireless signals. She could monitor every system at any given time, recognizing errors and failures in the patterns. She could utilize the ship's hardware, such as the internal and external cameras and microphones to reach tantalizing glimpses of the physical realms. She could "see" Charles Wilfred Grant and Elizabeth Marcia Hugin, both glaring at the open breaker box.

From all of the visual data Tavia had gathered on Hugin over the years, the captain's physical shell was nothing outstanding, as far as the averages for female humans went. She stood at approximately 5 feet and 4 inches, with a build and figure that humans classified as petite. After 39 years of operational life, punctuated most often by inadequate maintenance behavior, Beth's body had begun to show signs of wear, especially around the facial regions. There was very little feminine vanity about the captain, and there was never a time in Tavia's memory where she had ever been seen wearing makeup, or had her shoulder-length brown hair stylized in anything more than a simple ponytail. Tavia had once looked up an old image of her wearing the Air Force dress uniform, but this was the only other clothing configuration

Tavia had ever seen outside of the ubiquitous drab fatigues and synthetic-leather jacket.

As she watched, she could see the captain nodding along with Grant as the latter was gesticulating enthusiastically. She diverted a fraction of her processing to key into the audio feed of their mics.

"...So when I finally found the bloody thing, I couldn't flip the bloody switch," Grant was saying. "It was so corroded, I needed to take the crowbar and pry it open."

"About showing the extent of his mechanical skills, I might add," Tavia cut in, the higher pitch of her voice fed into both human's earpieces. She had not chosen for her voice to manifest as female, it had just been the programming she had received on her activation, and she saw no reason to change it. She found feminine behavioral quirks to be more stimulating, anyway. Grant's reaction to her provocation was, more or less, typical.

"Shut up, you," he ground out through the particular close setting of his teeth that her voice recognition algorithms interpreted as a growl. "Beth asked me to tell the story. If she wanted your input, she would have asked for it."

"I merely wished to point out to the captain that she may want to think twice the next time she has the choice of entrusting her fragile human life into your crowbar-clasping hands," she countered immediately, the precision of her timing honed by long practice. Even through the blur of the cameras, she could see the blood flow to the security officer's facial tissues increase.

Grant was less complex than Hugin, but still an interesting study. Outwardly, everything about the man was large. Large build, large muscular structure, and a predisposition for long coats and large firearms. He carried all the indicators of an ex-soldier, from the set of his stance and the intention of his movements, to his neatly trimmed blonde hair and beard. His mental processes, however, were less impressive. He possessed a much more instinctual pattern of reasoning, which left him much more reactive than more cool-headed humans.

As far as the records went, he had been a fairly busy man in his 43 years. He started his professional career as an army medic, serving with an infantry company during the many small skirmishes surrounding the consolidation of the Coalition's governance. He had a perfectly respectable if undistinguished record as a doctor and surgeon. After several tours, he left the army and branched out into the private security sector, where he earned a much higher wage and acquired most of his favorite toys. Loud, accurate, lethal toys. After several years, however, his performance began to decline. He seemed to drift from one company to another, at lower and lower ranks, until finally there was no employment left. Tavia had never heard how he and Captain Hugin had met, but she could only conclude that the story was similar to her own. Since then, Charlie's presence had provided her with constant amusement in testing the boundaries of his temper through humorous stimuli, dueling his inferior mind in logic. However, even such a small intellect had to stumble on a valid argument at random every once and a while.

"Well I didn't see you fixing that system bug in the first place, so the captain didn't have much choice, did she?" he said, the growl pattern increasing in intensity. Tavia had no response to that logic. She could feel the system error that had caused the difficulty in the number 3 turbine, manifesting itself like a tangle in the intricate web of coding that made up the hardwired behavior of the ship. The problem was that no matter how hard she tried, she couldn't seem to untangle it. Grant had stymied her logic. This time.

She consoled herself with the statistical memory that out of the past 6439 bouts, she was the victor of 5233.

"Well," she said by way of a recovery. "We'd better hope that Ramirez hires an engineer, or we'll both be in trouble." Before Grant's organic mind could summon a comeback, she withdrew from the intercom, making very sure to leave an emphatic click in her wake.

In the same moment, she could see Ramirez, standing at the crest of the cargo ramp, taking part in a cordial negotiation with another unknown female human who she assumed to be a representative of the corporation whose cargo they carried.

After Grant and Hugin came Ramirez, of whom she knew almost nothing at all. The visual data was there: he was of average height for a male, 5 feet 10 inches, with an appearance that could be accurately described as swarthy. At 26 years of age, his dark skin and sharp features were more or less unmarked by wear, except for the pale marks of scar tissue on the back of his hands.

Ramirez was interesting to her mostly because he was something of an unknown factor. She knew only that he had come from the background of an impoverished ghetto district on the crime-ridden planet of Apollo.

Beth had been the one to get him out of that, first by saving his life from a rival gang, and then by offering him a position in her ship's crew. Again, Tavia thought, an exhibition of highly illogical reasoning. But again, that event had paid off, and Ramirez was quick to prove his uncanny knack for forging business connections across the populated worlds of the galaxy.

Beyond those facts however, Ramirez might as well have been an encrypted file on a secure database. His life on Apollo was completely undocumented, beyond a criminal record of the few petty thefts for which he had been apprehended. And the man was not, to use a literary term, a social animal. His interaction with Beth and Grant was kept to the barest minimum for the confines of a small shuttle, spending approximately 67.34% of his time in his quarters, disassembling and building small electronic devices. As Tavia watched him, he and the unknown female clasped hands in a gesture that she had come to theorize signified mutual trust. The two then parted, making way for the passage of the C-Class Load-Lifter to enter and start easing the cargo scales built into the deck plates.

Together, these three made up her passive studies into human nature. She had observed them for more than 72 trillion processing cycles, and the input had not yet grown stale. Every time she deemed she had learned all she could, they would present some new facet of themselves or their interactions with each other, which would keep her enthralled as to its implications for weeks.

One human concept to which she did not subscribe was the idea of luck. After all, what they called fortune was merely a traceable, if complicated, cascade of events and variables that led to an outcome that, if difficult, was possible to predict. Still, after all that she had seen and all she had studied, she had concluded that she did consider herself fortunate to be installed here.

Just then, the cargo scales in the hold eased to zero pressure and the ship's audio receptors picked up the sound of Beth's voice, breaking in on her processes. "Tavia? Cargo's offloaded. Charlie and I are starting the visual check of the exterior, so you mind running a full-spec diagnostic in here? I would be a much happier woman if I knew what *else* was about to catastrophically fail."

Tavia deemed this an excellent time to make use of *sarcasm*, a variant of humor that she had also mastered. "Very well," she responded, imitating a noisy human exhalation. "But only because I'll be homeless if you crash the shuttle. I'll also unlock the dorsal hatch so you can get your fresh air without an extension ladder."

"Thank you very much, Tavia," Beth said gracefully, her tone indicating that her lips had turned up in the corners again. "Your inconvenience has bought my happiness."

At that moment, had she possessed the fleshy membranes required for doing so, Tavia would have smiled right back.

Yes, she decided, she led an enjoyable existence. With that thought, she closed this line of processing, beginning to devote half her capacity to the ship-wide diagnostic program. The other half she used to access the 'net, skimming the data-streams looking for interesting illegal patches.

* * *

Beth loved new colony worlds. She wasn't sure why, but there was something exciting in the air of a newly terraformed planet. She imagined sometimes that it must have been what the settlement of the western United States would have been like, back in the ancient history of earth. It was man against the unknown, drawn into the stars by the chance for something better than what they had; risking everything to pursue the *chance* of a better life. That was the spirit of adventure that had driven humanity to expand since the beginning.

She drew in a deep breath, savoring the feeling of the wind caressing her face as she gazed out at the vista before her.

The spaceport had been set down at the top of a large rise, providing a lofty perspective on the somewhat messily arranged city below. Many of the buildings were of the modular variety, designed to be lowered into place by an aircraft and essentially bolted to the ground. That would change very quickly, however. She had noticed that most of the commercial shipping on the landing pads around them was devoted to delivering building materials. Even from this distance, she could see the snaking footwalks teeming with people. With more and more arriving every day, capacity had to be an issue down there. She was looking forward to staying around for a couple of days while another client was found, to be down there amidst all that pure, fast-paced *life*; to witness the early days of a planet that hadn't quite decided what it wanted be when it grew up.

Of course, there were also many problems with such an arrangement. As the human race expanded so rapidly throughout the galaxy, the arm of the law had become a bit *stretched*. An interplanetary police force had been tried, but it simply did not have the capital and manpower that it needed to do its job effectively. Muggings, robberies, and the occasional armed misunderstanding could and often did break out, and those without the means to defend themselves usually came out the worse. Beth had learned not to leave the ship without her LK-2 snugged comfortably in her simple leather underarm holster, its comforting weight balanced by a pair of extra magazines. The sleek, black handgun had served her well through many dangerous situations in the darker corners of the galaxy, even though the times she had actually fired it had been comparatively few.

For all the swagger a firearm afforded, she was a strictly average markswoman, her shooting technique consisting entirely of lining up the front and rear sights on the torso of her target, pulling the trigger, and repeating as necessary. In most situations though, the deterrent was all that was needed. It was all a matter of looking meaner than the other guy.

All things considered, the possibility of harm did not lessen her love of her roving profession. There was nothing like a little danger every now and then to keep life fresh and interesting.

Just then, her earpiece clicked, piping in the voice of Ramirez. "Hey Beth, I think I may have a line on an engineer. You want me to send the top three to your 'pad?"

Snapped from her reverie, Beth opened the line, resuming her walk along the shuttle's length. "That won't be necessary, I trust your judgment. Just connect me with the one you think would be best."

"Okay... This is Evan. No last name, oddly. I will not bore you with the long list of qualifications, but his specialty is systems. Lots of experience. However, he is asking for six thousand credits. It is a bit pricey, but I like my instincts on this one. I think he could be just what we need."

Beth raised her eyebrows as she bent to test the pressure bolts around a thruster housing. Six thousand still sounded fairly pricey to her, but... Business had been good of late, and they could comfortably afford it.

"Alright, patch me through to talk with this Evan."

"Can do. One second..."

There was a pause, another click as the line was patched into her earpiece, followed by the tone of the device ringing on the other end. Beth waited, occupying herself with checking the structural integrity of the outer pressure hull. Finally, the connection was picked up, filling her ears with a deep, gruff voice speaking richly accented standard.

"Hallo. This is Grand Mountain Automation, Marko speaking."

Beth was struck for a moment by the man's accent. Russian, perhaps, or Polish. Ever since the language that had once been known as English had been declared the standard trade language for interplanetary business, ethnic languages had become much rarer. A pity, she thought.

"Yes, I'm calling about a listing for an Engineer on the 'net. May I speak with him?"

"Ach. Evan, yes? Good. One moment."

There was another pause, punctuated by the sound of footsteps and occasional snatches of conversation she couldn't understand. *Russian. Definitely Russian.* There was a rustle as the device was passed to another, and she braced herself for another heavy accent.

Which was why she was surprised by the light, pleasant and utterly ordinary voice that greeted her over the line. "Evan here. What can I do for you?"

For an instant, Beth was struck by the voice's cheery disposition. A far cry from the gruff, somewhat egotistical eggheads that she had known from the engineering corps. "Hello Mr. Evan, I'm Captain Elizabeth Hugin," she said, trying to match his brisk tone as she jumped right to business. "I'm the head of a small charter cargo company, and my shuttle is in pretty desperate need of an engineer. Are you still looking for a job?"

She could practically *hear* the smile radiating from the other end of the line. "Yes ma'am! My current employer is just waiting for me to find new employment, so I can be at your disposal as soon as you need me. What sort of work would you need done? I've never been employed on a ship before, and I'd like to make sure that I'm the right man for the job."

Beth felt her eyebrows rising. *Now if his skills match his enthusiasm...*

"Well, our immediate needs are fixing a system bug in our atmos-engines that nearly killed us this morning. Our AI thinks it's a problem in one of the system cores. After that, there are just some basic maintenance issues that have been accumulating over the years. How does that fit with your qualifications?"

"That sounds right in line with my skills. My specialty is systems."

Beth frowned. "You did hear me say it's more than just a computer problem, right?"

"Oh, yes ma'am. Sorry, I don't mean computers alone. Systems in general. I'm... good at seeing how things work."

That was interesting. She realized that she had never thought of it that way before. She had associated with plenty of engineering students in her time with the Air Force, but she had never met any that had spoken like this one. In her experience, they had a set field of interests, and their minds were closed to anything else. She now began to see why this one had caught Ramirez's eye. "Well... It sounds like you may very well be the right person for the job, Mr. Evan."

"Please ma'am, just call me Evan. If you would prefer, that is."

She chuckled. "Alright, Evan. As long as we're not in front of customers or in the middle of operational flight, you can call me Beth. Well, we're willing to accept your termed wages, and I think you would make an excellent addition to our crew. If you would like to, you could come down here later today and check it out in person. If it's to your liking, we can finalize the deal."

"Oh, that shouldn't be necessary, ah... Beth." For the first time, the intensity of his pleasant demeanor dimmed, apparently uncomfortable with the first name. *There's something*, she mused. He would have to learn to be much less formal if he was to fit in completely on *this* ship. "If the money isn't a problem and you think I'm the right man for the job, then consider if finalized already. My current employer doesn't have much need for me anymore and is getting rather eager to get me off his hands."

Beth blinked, caught entirely off guard. "Uh... That's..." She checked herself from refusing outright, instead forcing herself to think it through. Really, was there any problem with that? The cost was acceptable, and it sounded as if he would serve wonderfully. And besides that, she *liked* him, from what little glimpse she had into his personality. Yes, she decided, she would do it. "Well Evan, it's a bit irregular, but it works for me. If you're sure, you can consider yourself on the crew."

"Excellent! I can be over there in two hours. Would that work?"

"I think so. Either way, someone will be here. We're on dock 74-A here at the spaceport. Cargo shuttle *Memory*. You can't miss it."

"Alright, I'll be there. I look forward to serving you, Captain Hugin."

"Alright, Evan. I'll see you soon." With a smile, Beth broke the connection.

For a moment, she stared contemplatively at the landscape, processing what had happened. There was something about the conversation that nagged at her, something she could not quite put her finger on...

She was not given any more time to think about it. After another moment, she was rejoined by Ramirez on the comm. "Nice fellow. So, it is all settled then? I should approve the funds transfer when the request comes in?"

Beth shook her head to clear it, putting the thoughts aside for later. "Yes. And I think you're right, he should be a fine addition to the crew, for however long he's with us."

"Good thing I found him, then. And not a moment too soon, either. I might have found a client for you as well."

Beth made a face. Everything seemed to be happening so fast on this particular run. Usually it took a day or two to find another charter. "My, that was quick. Well, patch me through to him, then."

"Actually, he wants to meet in person, at a local coffee-shop. He sounds somewhat... eccentric, but he promised it would be worth our time."

"Don't they all..." Beth breathed. Still, she knew, she couldn't afford to *not* check it out. They had a business to run, after all. "Fine. I'll be right back in, and you can tell me what hoops this guy wants to have me jump through. And tell Grant to get ready for a trip into town."

"Right."

With that, Ramirez disconnected, leaving Beth again alone with her thoughts. She was now standing just above the bridge viewport, her inspection having carried her the entire length of the ship without finding anything that warranted concern. She had no excuse to be out here any longer.

For another moment, she gazed down at the city, set against the backdrop of unspoiled forests and mountain terrain, soon to be brimming with the newly-transplanted animal life. In a decade or two, if all went to plan, that too would be brimming with life, creating a complicated ecosystem more or less like its template. But by then, she would be gone. She would have another charter, and probably be on the far side of the galaxy. Perhaps, she decided, it was better that way. Not for nothing did her ship bear the name *Memory*.

With one last sigh of cool, clean air, Beth turned and began to make her way back toward the dorsal hatch, turning her mind away from deep thoughts and back toward what she figured would be a very busy day.

* * *

Food on a space-going craft was composed of products designed with the perfect nutritional balance for the average human being; injected with concentrated flavor and then dehydrated, it was able to be stored indefinitely until it was required. In every aspect that could be quantified, it was the equal of ready-made, planetary food; but after a few weeks of eating rehydrated meals, Charles Grant found something very appealing in the smells coming from the restaurants in Hephaestus' port city. It had been a while since he had gotten a few days leave on a newborn colony-world like Hephaestus, and the sheer diversity of the people living on them amazed him every time.

There were people of every race and planetary origin, sporting every style of clothing from the most modern and fashionable to ridiculous throwback clothes from the previous century. Grant found himself fascinated by the kaleidoscope of color filling the streets and footwalks. Compared to the welter of different hues and styles worn by residents, visitors like Beth and himself could also be spotted, mainly experienced spacers clothed in oil-stained coveralls or fatigues.

Spacer fashion. Now there's a contradiction in terms.

Keeping up with the pace of the much-smaller figure of Captain Hugin was no problem, and Grant used the time spent walking to take in the sights and sounds of the port. Beth had insisted on travelling to their contact's arranged meeting place on foot, shooting down Grant's suggestion of a cab with one of her trademark wordless smiles. Now he saw why. The streets were jammed with pedestrians—mainly tourists coming to visit a virgin colony world—and the few taxis that could be seen were moving at a snail's pace. All of the colony worlds Grant had visited previously had been much older than this one, and had had well established markets and trade districts. Evidently this was not the case on Hephaestus. Booths and stalls vied for space and attention on either side of the thoroughfare, advertising everything from jewelry made from native stone to some kind of mouth-wateringly unhealthy, deep fried chocolate ball.

"The café where we're meeting our client should be just ahead," Beth said. "Keep your eyes peeled for a J.J.'s Coffee on the left."

"Gotcha. You know, this market reminds me of the couple years that I was working with InviShield way out on Demeter. Some CEO got himself offed by an employee and everybody went spare about personal protection. Whole planet had open air markets that were absolute nightmares for security. Never had a problem in them, though." He patted his underarm holster affectionately. "Got my baby on the company dime while I was there, too. Custom Maxwell-50," he reminded her. "Best pistol on the market if you want stopping power."

"Right. Well, far be it from me to stop you from gushing about your baby, but that's the café." She pointed at a low, square building with a glass front and a large, electric sign boldly proclaiming the location of *J.J.'s Coffee*. "See anything that could be a problem?"

"You want the list in alphabetical order, or order of importance?" Grant said, grinning. "One entrance, probably an exit in the back for the staff, big plate glass windows in front, easy to see and shoot through and no cover that would stand up to a pellet rifle. Basically, it's a deathtrap."

"You're very comforting. Let's go in and meet with our client, then."

"Hey, you asked. Besides, it's not like we have anything to worry about. Unless you're smuggling contraband under my nose."

Beth smiled cryptically, stepping in front of him and pulling open the door. "After you, accomplice."

Grant grimaced and walked through the door into the pleasant-smelling interior of J.J.'s Coffee. He took a quick look around, his security-man's eye immediately taking in the layout of the room. A coffee bar was situated in the back right hand corner, facing outward toward the collection of people seated at tables or ensconced in the booths that lined the walls. In short, like any other coffee shop he had ever entered. There was, apparently, a strict set of rules dictating the interior design of coffee shops.

"Who're we looking for?" He asked, running his large hand through his hair.

"Wouldn't describe himself. Seemed very reluctant to give out any information before he met us."

"And we're supposed to meet with him... how exactly?"

"He said to get a table, order a drink, and accidentally spill it. He'd find us."

"Let's hope this guy doesn't turn out like the *last* crank that hired us..."

Beth ignored him, walking up to the counter and handing a few credits to the youth behind it. The time spent waiting for the doomed drink, Grant decided, would be best spent in trying to figure out which of the customers was their prospective client. Leaning back against one of the booths, he let his eyes wander casually over the reflection of the patrons sitting at the café's tables. He immediately ruled some of the people out. The young couple sharing a cup of coffee were clearly unconscious of anything outside of their booth; likewise the elderly man muttering to himself over a crossword puzzle on his antiquated datapad could not be the voice from the call. Grant also eliminated the student perusing large stacks of papers and the two women sipping their drinks at the counter.

That left only three men who could be the mysterious client. One, a large, grizzled man with a leather coat, was obviously an ex-soldier; Grant could tell by the way he kept his back ramrod straight even while drinking his coffee. The other two looked strangely similar. Both were scholarly, older men wearing suits and thick glasses of the type that had gone out of style years ago; but while one was tall, dark and nervously picking at something on his sleeve, the other was short, fair-haired and looked quite relaxed.

Hearing Beth slide into the booth that he was leaning against, Grant left his inspection of the clientele and turned to face her. She was holding a tall, lidded cup that didn't smell anything like coffee. The look on her face made Grant think that she wouldn't be devastated about the need to spill the concoction.

"See anything?" she asked, unconsciously pulling a handful of napkins out of the dispenser on the table.

"Only three people of interest. Leather Coat in the booth on the left, and the two professors in the suits. Got Ramirez's toy?" Ramirez's "toy" was a very small recording device the procurement officer had built from scrap in case Beth needed a discrete bug when dealing with clients. Several years before, the crew of the *Memory* had been framed for smuggling by a business rival. The charges were soon dropped due to lack of evidence, but it had been a solemn reminder to always carry an electronic witness to lend credence to their words.

"In my pocket," Hugin answered. "Here goes nothing."

She turned sharply, starting to say something to Grant, and her elbow caught the top of the cup, knocking it over. Grant grabbed the cup before it could fall off the edge and quickly righted it, wrinkling his nose at the reddish-brown liquid that was leaking from the disposable lid. Scowling, he stood up and dabbed at a stain on his shirt while Beth apologized profusely, trying to mop up the mess on the table with a handful of napkins.

Immediately, the dark-haired man jumped up, grabbing a briefcase and a few napkins from his own table as he walked over.

"Here, let me help you with that," he said, taking the cup from Grant's hand and wiping it off.

Beth smiled, taking the cup back and tossing it into the trash receptacle with the used napkins. "Thank you, Mr.—ah..."

"Phillips. Doctor Trent Phillips."

Phillips was of middling height, balding, with a well-cut suit and a hawkish, ascetic face. He was smiling in a rather nervous manner, and stood awkwardly next to the table, mumbling something about being happy to help. His briefcase, Grant noticed, was made of a dull, black plastic, which looked remarkably like the kind used in the construction of bullet-proof riot shields. More importantly, to Grant's mind, he did not appear to be carrying a weapon. He glanced at Beth, giving her a subtle nod.

"I understand you have a commission for us, Doctor?" Beth said, sliding back into the booth.

"Of sorts. I didn't want to discuss it on an unprotected call. You must forgive my eccentricities. I have a good reason for them, I assure you."

"You would be amazed at what I can forgive if the money's right. Your commission?"

"Passage. I need to get to Earth as fast as possible."

"I'm sorry Doctor, but I can't accommodate you. My ship is designed for cargo, not passengers."

"You don't understand," the doctor said, looking very close to wringing his hands. "This is an extremely high priority. I *must* get a flight to Earth."

"You are aware," Grant cut in, "that there are commercial interplanetary flights from Hephaestus to Earth every day?"

"Of course I am *aware* of that," Phillips answered, forgetting his nervousness for a second and giving the security officer a very professorial look over the top of his glasses. "But public transportation will simply not suit my needs."

Arrogant little bugger. Hope Beth shuts you down hard.

"Then I'm afraid you'll need to find another shuttle pilot." Beth stood up and turned toward the door. "My crew needs a few days off, planetside, and we're not running a taxi service."

"Will fifty thousand credits change your mind?"

Grant froze in the act of sliding out of the booth, turning slowly to look at the doctor. "How did that go, again?" he asked incredulously.

"I said: will fifty thousand credits be enough to book me passage to Earth."

Beth walked back to the table, looking down thoughtfully at Phillips. "Why is it so important for you to book a private flight? First class flights are a lot more comfortable than the accommodations on a cargo shuttle."

"I can't tell you here," Phillips said, glancing around the café. "Suffice to say, I work for an important laboratory and have specimens that need to be taken to Earth as fast as possible."

Grant glanced at Beth, too shocked by the enormous offer to tell what was going on behind her impassive features. A minute passed with the doctor growing increasingly nervous under Beth's steady gaze before she finally spoke.

"Alright, but if I find out that you're transporting something illegal, I'll turn you in to the Blues at the nearest station without a second thought."

Phillips appeared relieved and actually smiled when he stood up. "Alright then, can we go to your shuttle now?"

Beth nodded, motioning to Grant. "Sure. I'll hail a cab. We'll take the express roads. With that kind of payoff, we can afford it."

Peering uneasily out of the plate-glass windows, Phillips grabbed his briefcase as if he were afraid it would run away and walked out the door behind Grant.

Twitchy, this bloke, the security officer thought to himself, *and I'm not sure I like that. He's hiding something.*

When they arrived at the station, Beth waved down a sleek, bright green taxi and gave the driver instructions to take them to the spaceport. The express roads were a new innovation in most colony worlds; they allowed vehicles to move quickly by bypassing all the foot traffic that clogged most of the ordinary streets in large cities, but maintained the fast travel times and clear roads by charging exorbitant prices for access.

A few dozen credits later, Grant was wedged uncomfortably in the back seat of the taxi, wishing, for once, that he was not quite as tall. Neither Beth nor the doctor seemed interested in talking, so he amused himself by staring out the windows at the Hephaestus skyline. The colony world was only recently terraformed, but it was no surprise to Grant that contractors had been lured out to it by the prospect of cheap real estate. The port city was already spreading outward and upward as more and more colonists took up residence on Hephaestus to escape overcrowding on other worlds. To keep himself awake, Grant started checking the taxi's rear cam every minute or so; an old security trick he had learned to keep himself alert while in a protection convoy.

Black taxi... Yellow taxi... Red bus…

He checked on Beth with his peripheral vision, noting the fatigue lines around her mouth with concern. Still not sleeping well, then. He sighed quietly, resting his head on his hand. *That's Beth, running herself ragged on only a few hours of sleep and expecting to keep sharp. She puts every drop of sweat and blood into keeping us ready to go, but ignores her own needs.*

Red bus... Yellow taxi... Blue car...

Phillips appeared to be trying to get some sleep, but Grant noticed that his breathing was still irregular. Whatever was making the doctor nervous had only been slightly allayed by Beth accepting his offer. *I'll be keeping my eye on you, Twitchy.* The last thing that the security officer wanted was for some kind of underhanded con man tricking Beth. *Ahh, I'm worrying too much,* he decided. *Beth knows what she's doing. It's not like we haven't dealt with that sort before.* He grimaced. *That bloody mess out on Ares II comes to mind. Not-so-fond memories.*

Blue car... Yellow taxi...

The cityscape flew by as the taxi approached the spaceport, the buildings growing progressively taller the closer to the city center they went. Uneasily, Grant checked the cam again, a nagging feeling telling him that all was not right.

Black taxi... Grey truck... Yellow taxi...

His security instincts on high alert, he thought back to when they left the station, trying to recall anything odd about the journey. Abandoning any pretense of resting, he leaned forward, trying to get a better look at the rear cam's screen.

Grey truck... Yellow taxi...

Suddenly, he realized what his subconscious had known all along.

They were being tailed.

Leaning over, he nudged Beth and whispered: "Yellow taxi, one car back. See him?"

She glanced casually over her shoulder and nodded. "Yes. What's wrong?"

"I just realized that he's been with us since the station."

"So? He could just be trying to get to the spaceport fast, like we are."

"No, he's been careful to stay a few cars back the entire time. We're going just under the limit for this road—bloody driver's trying to milk us for more creds—and he could've passed us easily. Everybody else has been."

Beth bit her lip indecisively, a nervous habit that Grant usually found funny in a veteran shuttle pilot. Now, he knew exactly how she was feeling.

"Are you sure?" She asked, risking another look out the back window. "There's no reason that someone should be following us."

Grant lowered his voice even more. "Doc here is in a bloody awful hurry to get off-planet and does *not* look at ease. Could be for him."

"Suggestions?"

"Yeah, give me what cash you have left and get ready to get out of the cab."

Beth reached into her inner coat pocket and wordlessly handed Grant a stack of credit chips. Discretely, Grant reached into his own shirt, easing off the clasp on his underarm holster. He noticed his partner doing the same. *I've played this game before, but I've got to remember that she hasn't.*

"If the situation goes south, we cut and run. Got it?"

She nodded. They both knew that Grant was in charge now.

Grant checked the cam one more time, waiting until the yellow taxi was a few cars back before leaning forward and pressing the intercom button.

"Excuse me, I just remembered I needed to get something at the market. Can you turn left at ramp…" he squinted down the road, looking for a good turnoff. "Twenty-six?"

"Sure thing."

"Also, after we get out, darken the rear windscreen. There's two hundred credits in it for you if you drive around for half an hour or so without picking up any fares and keep the screen *darkened*."

The driver gave him an incredulous look in the rearview mirror, but seemed to get the message when Grant held up a high denomination credit.

"You got it, boss. My word on it. Hell, I'd drive to the next city for that."

Grant felt the vehicle slowing as they approached the turnoff and felt his breathing rate increasing. *Calm down,* he told himself, *this isn't anything new, it's been a while, but you've still got it. Here we go.*

Shaking Phillips' shoulder, he motioned to the door. "Come on, Doc, we're getting off here."

Phillips started awake, clutching his briefcase to his chest and staring at Grant. "We're not at the spaceport yet."

"Nope," Grant responded with a forced grin, "We're taking the scenic route. Get ready to hop out."

The cab turned carefully into the side street, moving off of the express lane and back into normal, stagnant traffic and pedestrians. Handing the cabbie his large fee, Grant quickly opened the door and clambered out, moving aside to let Beth and Phillips follow him into the crowded street.

After making sure that the taxi's screen had turned opaque, he put a hand on Phillips' back, ignoring his flustered questions and steering him away from the taxi. He could sense Beth just behind him, and felt the familiar urge to keep her safe. *Just my luck that Beth seems determined to stumble into every dangerous situation between Earth and the Edge. I hope we got enough of a head start this time.*

Pushing the doctor ahead of him into the recessed doorway of some gaudily painted mechanical parts store, he scanned the express lane intersection, looking for a sign of the yellow taxi.

He didn't need to wait long.

A few seconds after the green taxi lumbered off through the crowd, the yellow taxi appeared at the intersection, its turn signal removing any doubts that Grant still had. For the second time that day, he found himself wishing he had Beth's diminutive size. Being a whole head taller than the majority of the population didn't help him blend into the crowd. Hunching down, Grant watched as the yellow cab cruised slowly after the taxi that he had so recently exited, catching a glimpse of two men in dark glasses in the front seats. *No markings. That cab isn't on the grid. Bugger, that means we can't figure out who they are through the cab company.* He sighed in mixed frustration and relief.

"Friends of yours?" Beth asked Phillips pointedly, gesturing to the back of the disappearing yellow taxi.

"No. I'm not entirely sure what you mean." He responded, with a nervous little cough.

"That cab was tailing us," Grant said, staring down at the doctor's pale face. "I think you know why."

"Certainly not!" Phillips replied, standing up a little straighter, "Why, the very idea is preposterous. Why would someone be, as you so quaintly put it, 'tailing us?'"

"You tell me." Grant replied, brushing past the irate doctor and starting to walk down the street. The doctor, he realized, had not asked any questions throughout the entire episode. Further proof that he knew more than he was telling. This was not going to be a pleasant voyage. *Especially,* thought Grant grimly, *if those two in the cab aren't the only ones after us.*

3

The trip back to the spaceport on foot seemed much longer than the journey out had been. In Beth's mind, the landscape almost seemed to have undergone a subtle change for the sinister. Suddenly, the new buildings rising on every side presented threatening facades in which every window could contain a man with binoculars and a rifle. The hustle and bustle of the dense population clogging the footwalks around them, the crowds that she had been reflecting on with joy shortly before now felt as if they were intentionally hampering their progress toward safety, or providing perfect cover for someone to sneak in close and put a knife in her ribs.

Woah, get a grip, girl. Just slow down, think it through. While she didn't want to admit it, the incident with the taxis had genuinely rattled her. And it shouldn't have, really. She and her crew had faced danger quite a few times in their tenure traversing the galaxy. They had tangled with everything from drug-lords to extortionists to rival companies with somewhat loose ethics. But, on all of those skirmishes, she had always been up against consummate thugs, men and women motivated by greed, usually acting on impulse. But the men she had seen in that mysterious unmarked taxi... They were something else entirely. Everything about them, from the cut of their clothes to the lines of their features, it all communicated that they were *professionals*.

"I don't see anything suspicious back here." Grant said just then, cutting into her thoughts. "I think our little gambit worked." Since they had begun making their way through the city, Grant had fallen to the rear, and Beth had taken the lead position, leaving a somewhat more collected Phillips between them as they navigated the congested pedestrian walkways, the confinement made worse by taking the backstreets and alleyways to the spaceport. It was a familiar position, that Beth directed the show while her security officer provided support. The sound of his voice helped greatly to center her. In her mind, if the men in the taxi had been pros, Grant was *the* pro. Still, she couldn't put her sudden paranoia out of her mind.

"Either we lost them," she said quietly, "or they're just being extremely smart."

"I doubt it. Playing that kind of game is just as likely to fail as a straightforward one. Take it from someone who's tried it. It's no good for them if they lose us by trying to be overly clever."

Beth frowned, wordlessly shouldering aside a street vendor who was about to begin an impassioned pitch as to why her life would be infinitely more satisfying if she was to buy a bottle of cheap fruit juice. "You would know best, Charlie. I'm mostly bothered about knowing who the *them* is in that sentence." That, she decided, was the root of her anxiety. She didn't know what she was up against, which robbed her of the ability to plan. It put her on the defensive, and she didn't like it.

"I assure you, Captain Hugin," Phillips piped up, puffing between labored breaths. "Those men had to have been members of a common theft-ring. I've been on Hephaestus for three months now, and I can tell you that extortionists and 'protection' rackets have been springing up left and right. Those men were probably just looking to start running such a scheme on the taxi service."

"Uh huh," Grant said, and Beth knew the tone well enough to know he wasn't buying it. "I'm sure that's what it is. Tell you what Doctor, you stand back here for a minute. I need to discuss something with the Captain."

Beth glanced over her shoulder, just in time to watch Grant and Phillips switch places in their strange little procession. Immediately, there was a marked improvement in their progress. Grant was good at looking like a crowd. "The doctor's way of selling it actually isn't bad," he said, voice low enough that their new client wouldn't hear it over the cacophony of voices and traffic noises. "But I don't believe him."

Beth didn't even need to think about it. It was generally her nature to try and see the good in people, but that instinct had been tempered by her experiences out in the big bad universe. "I don't either. He practically admitted that someone was after him, and with all that damned cloak-and-dagger stuff at the coffee shop... Besides, you saw those guys. They were pros, weren't they?"

"They knew how to play the basic game, alright..." Grant responded, his tone guarded. "Not all that great, though. Tailing us like that might have worked on Earth, or downtown Hermes, but in this tiny backwater, it was clumsy. They've been trained, but not very well."

"That's some comfort. But think about it. Sure, you and I have a few old friends that might want to get together for an unpleasant reunion; Ramirez probably has a whole drawer full. But would any of them have the creds to hire pros?"

Grant paused for a moment, and she could picture the creasing of his broad forehead as he thought it over. "I have one or two. But none of them are so mad at me to track me to the backside of the galaxy. I just owe them money." At last, Beth felt the knot in her stomach uncoil as she suppressed a chuckle. Knowing Grant, he probably could have paid off his debts a long time ago. He probably just didn't like the idea of being a totally respectable ship's security officer.

"Alright, fine." She said after a moment. "So we're agreed that Phillips isn't telling us something."

"Perfect. So now the only question is, should we let that scare us enough to bring it to the Blues?"

That, indeed, was the question. In almost any other situation, Beth would have said yes. Some of their exploits had trodden in some murky legal waters as it was, and it didn't pay to go asking for trouble. And she was about to open her mouth to say so, until she was stopped by the recollection of a number.

"Fifty-thousand credits."

Grant actually *did* chuckle. "Yeah. That was my thought too."

Neither one of them needed to say it. Such a sum would provide the security that Beth had sought from the moment she had first started the company. With that in mind, suddenly the situation didn't seem so shady. After all, if they played their cards right, they would be in space in a matter of hours. Two men in a taxi were no match for *that* kind of isolation.

"I don't know, Beth. It's your call," Grant said finally. Beth blew out a breath. She was glad that her crew trusted her so implicitly, but sometimes the responsibility was daunting.

"We'll run with it for now," she said finally. "I don't like it, but I think we would be pretty safe after we take off. We can be off-planet in three hours. Once we get to Earth, Phillips leaves, and we never need to hear from him again."

"I agree," said Grant. "For fifty-thousand, it's worth it."

Having finally made the decision, Beth felt much more confident. She would do what she could, and let the future decide if she was right.

The sight of the shuttle resting solidly on the pad was always a welcome sight for Beth, but now it seemed even more inviting than normal. Of course, it wouldn't look that way to any outsider. She had called ahead shortly after leaving the taxi and Ramirez had shut the cargo ramp, locked down all other hatches, and in general made like a fortress with no one home. Beth could picture him lurking in the cargo-spaces, his MOSS-3 Tactical Shotgun waiting to teach any intruders the error of their ways. Probably unnecessary, she knew, but as the somewhat overused adage stated, better safe than sorry.

Besides, Ramirez seemed to enjoy it.

After making their way carefully through the port, they concealed themselves behind a stack of empty shipping containers at the edge of the pad, giving them a chance to survey the situation before making a move. "We're secure, as far as I can tell," Grant said. "Nothing's changed since we left."

"I think so too," Beth ducked back behind the container to glance at her friend. "Shall we risk it?"

"Sure," Grant said with a broad grin, reaching into his jacket to place his hand on the grip of his Maxwell-50. "What could possibly go wrong?"

"If you're quite finished with your tough-guy act," Phillips hissed. "Could we please get on with this? The shuttle is *right there*." As they had come closer to the spaceport, his nervousness had abated somewhat, his professorial disposition reasserting itself as his confidence grew.

Oh boy, Beth thought. *Here we go...*

Grant, suddenly serious, rounded slowly on Phillips. "You've obviously never read much about soldiering, Doc," he said, his voice flat, ready to be honed into an edge. "If you had, you would know that thirty-percent of all casualties in a military evacuation happen in the last thirty seconds. Considering that there are three of us and about forty seconds left in this particular operation, a little caution is warranted, don't you think?"

Phillips tried to hold the glare, he really did. But in the end, he looked away first. "Yes, well... I understand. Let me know when you're ready."

"Consider yourself let known," Beth broke in. While she agreed whole-heartedly with Grant, she was ready to get this whole journey over with. "Grant, take point. Phillips, right behind him. I'll take the rear."

"You got it, boss," Grant said, drawing himself up. "On my mark. Three, two, one... go." With that, he pivoted around the containers, advancing across the pavement with the grounded, flowing movements of a fighter, making no attempt to disguise the hand on his weapon. Despite his words, Phillips seemed perfectly content to watch rather than follow. Beth rolled her eyes, shoving him soundly from behind the stack. Finally, she turned around and followed, advancing with her back to her companions, all the time watching for threats lurking in the cluttered terrain of the docking port.

With her free hand, the one that was not grasping the rubberized grip of her LK-2 in its holster, she keyed her earpiece to preset 1. "Hey Ramirez, we're back. Mind opening the back door? Spare key wasn't under the flowerpot…"

Ramirez' voice immediately flowed back over the link, as if he had been waiting for hours. Which he probably had. "Those damn kids. A sure thing, Captain, just give me a second. Did you bring me anything from town?"

"Of course. We grabbed a cup of coffee for you, but we had to leave in a bit of a hurry."

The end of the exchange was a very simple code that they had all worked out beforehand. For crewmates returning in circumstances that were the slightest bit suspicious, the one manning the shuttle would challenge them with "Did you bring me anything?" If the respondent was under duress, they would reply that they had not had time to pick up anything. "Coffee" was the all-clear sign.

Although she did not turn her head to look, Beth heard the distinctive hydraulic whine of the shuttle's bulky cargo ramp descending to the pavement behind her. She didn't look as the ground under her heels suddenly became an incline of textured metal, rather than flat concrete.

It was only after she had scaled the ramp and stepped onto the deck of the cargo bay and someone hit the control for retracting the door that she finally allowed herself to look away, blinking in the dim light as the ramp shut with a *clunk*. After a moment, she was able to make out the shapes of her companions, plus Ramirez standing to one side, watching the proceedings with the compact length of his shotgun resting on his shoulder, his sharp features just as unflappable as ever.

"So," he said, with the barest hint of a smile, "I send you out to meet a casual client, and by the time you come back, it is a war zone. I really cannot leave you alone, can I?" His dark eyes shifted to Phillips, taking on an even more guarded expression than normal. "And who is this?"

"Ah yes, introductions!" Grant jumped in, leaving off securing the door to clap Phillips heartily on the back. "Phillips, meet Ramirez, procurement officer for our little operation. You'll probably recognize his accent from your call. Ramirez, Phillips. Your *casual client*."

As he turned to face Beth, a crease formed in Ramirez's forehead, which was his facial equivalent of abject bewilderment. "Would you care to fill me in on what happened out there, Captain? It seems that I missed out on something."

Phillips, who up until then had been casting nervous glances over his shoulder, chose that moment to speak up. "Um, wouldn't it perhaps be better to relate that story a bit later? Like perhaps after we take off? As I said, I need to get to Earth as quickly as possible…"

At their client's words, several forgotten realities rushed back on Beth's mind, chief among them being the reason why they couldn't actually take off just yet.

Right. System problems, waiting for the engineer…

Just then, her earpiece chirped, followed by the voice of Tavia. "Beth, there's a call for you. I think it's our engineer. He sounds boring."

There's some good timing for once.

"Ah, yes, right…" she answered, trying to bring her scattered thoughts back under rigid control. "Patch him through." There was another chirp as the line was transferred, followed by an apprehensive male voice.

"Er… Captain Hugin?" With the context, she recognized the caller immediately.

"Yes, Evan. You are right outside the ramp, aren't you?"

"Yes ma'am. I've been waiting at the port entrance for about half an hour, actually, but it looked like no one was here."

Beth winced, running a hand through her hair. "Um, yeah… Sorry, things kind of got a little crazy around here since we last talked."

"I see. So do you still need an engineer? If not, that could be a little awkward. My previous employers just terminated my position and wouldn't exactly be eager to put me up until I can find more work."

"No! No, that's not what I meant," she backpedalled swiftly. "We still need you, more than ever. In fact, we need you to get right to work. We have to be ready for takeoff ASAP."

"Ah, good! I came just in time, then."

"You sure did! Just a second."

Turning, she gestured for Ramirez to open the ramp. His frown deepened slightly, but he complied, keying the control.

It would be nice to have gotten Phillips squared away first. Just once, it would be nice to be able to deal with things like this one at a time, Beth thought to herself, watching the ramp make its ponderous descent. *Everything always happens all at once or not at all.* Still, she decided, it would be good to finally meet their new engineer in person, instead of just a voice over the comm. After all the craziness of the past hours, she would enjoy a conversation with a well-rounded, rational human being...

That thought was brought to an instant, shattering halt as the ramp finally finished falling, revealing what stood on the other side.

What stood at the base of the ramp might very well have been well-rounded and rational, but it was most definitely *not* a human being.

Beth blinked, unable to keep herself from staring. The figure was wearing a very standard set of warm-weather fatigues, complete with cutoff cargo pants, a sleeveless shirt, and a modest-sized duffel-bag slung over his shoulder. It was there however that the normalcy ended.

Beth's mind went into overdrive as she tried to process what she was seeing, taking in everything in a split second. The best way she could describe the creature was a dog—*no, a wolf,* she corrected herself, remembering wildlife videos from her childhood—walking on its hind legs; but instead of front paws, its arms were proportioned more like a human's, with five-fingered hands and opposable thumbs. The head, however, was pure wolf, complete with a thick, elongated muzzle, moist black nose, and a pair of upright, strangely articulate ears. Perhaps the most striking thing about it was that it was covered from head to foot in a coat of thick, grey fur, with lighter patches on the muzzle and throat. She actually watched it flutter before her eyes, dancing in the light breeze. After a moment, she also noticed that its strangely proportioned legs, instead of ending with a familiar pair of shoes, terminated in a set of large, splayed-out canine paws.

Beth had no doubt that, for the first time, she was looking at a Fletcher's Wolf.

For its part, the wolf-thing did not seem particularly troubled by the surprised reactions of the others. After glancing quickly over every face, it started its way up the ramp with the effortlessly graceful gait of a predator. It marched purposefully up to her, stopped, and amiably extended a fur-covered hand.

"I'm glad to meet you, Captain Hugin," it said, its sunny tone totally undeterred by the stares of those around him. "I'm Evan."

In general, spaceports were very noisy places, filled as they were with the sounds of turbine engines, trundling load-lifters, and shouting spacers. But, at that moment, the silence that shrouded the open cargo bay was complete and total.

It has to be a mistake, Beth thought. *If the ad had mentioned a barker, Ramirez would have told me.* And yet, there was no mistake. This Fletcher's Wolf had the same voice and mannerisms as the voice on the comm. Like it or not, this was the engineer they had asked for.

Luckily for the moment, her grasp of manners outweighed her surprise. She took the proffered hand and shook it warmly, the fur on the back of his hands soft under her fingertips. It felt warm and smooth, not unlike an expensive synthetic-fiber carpet. It was, she thought, a thoroughly odd sensation for a handshake. "I'm glad to meet *you*, Evan," she said, putting on a smile. "Welcome aboard. I have to admit, you're not exactly what we were expecting."

She wasn't quite sure how Evan's lupine face rendered a frown, but some pattern-recognizing part of her brain told her that was what he was doing. "I guess Marco's ad didn't say that I was actually a Fletcher's Wolf, then. I'm sorry about that. I understand our appearance can be a little unsettling at first."

"Well..." Beth struggled, "Yeah, I guess it is a little. I can't say as I've heard of Fletcher's Wolves much except for the big news hype—which was what, five, six years ago?" And even that wasn't much, she realized. Mostly just headlines on her newsfeed when she jumped on the 'net to look up something or other.

Evan didn't seem very surprised, merely shrugging his shoulders. "Makes sense. The project received a lot of coverage when it was in the research stages, but after that died down ABI moved on to limited scale commercialization. There are only a few hundred of us on the market at the moment, so the marketing is pretty low-key." He paused. "Is the advertisement's omission a problem?"

Yes, Beth thought. *Absolutely yes, that is a problem. We can't have you here. I can't have you here. Because I can't resist my own stupid urges to take every casualty and stray I run across under my wing.*

The silence was just beginning to become uncomfortable when Grant's characteristic save-the-day impulse took the option away.

"Absolutely not!" he boomed, stepping forward to shake Evan's hand. "Where are my manners? I'm Charlie Grant, security officer. The dour-faced fellow over there is Ramirez, he handles getting our contracts. And that's Dr. Trent Phillips, client and passenger. I've got to say, I'm sure happy that you're here, Evan. The *Memory* is a great ship, but she's in a bad way. An engineer's touch is just what our shuttle needs."

Although Grant's chatter seemed designed to make Evan feel comfortable, something about his expression told Beth that it had the opposite effect. "Er... Thank you, Mr. Grant. I'll do my best," he said, offering a tentative smile.

Once again before she could say anything, Phillips stepped forward, his expression clearly indicating an immanent blast of annoyance. "Yes, well, this is all very interesting. It's wonderful to meet you, Evan. I've been following Dr. Fletcher's project for some time, and it is interesting to see that she's come so far. Now could we *please* get ready to take off?"

Oops... Beth almost winced. "Yes, well, there's a bit of a problem with that," she said, taking a step forward. "You see, the ship is suffering from a system bug that just about turned us into a charred streak on the landing pad a few hours ago. Taking off would be a bit *tricky* at this time."

Phillips rounded on her. "*What?* The agreement was that we take off *immediately!* Have you been lying to me, Captain?"

Beth stood her ground. "Quite frankly Dr. Phillips, I forgot. The ship is still perfectly spaceworthy; there is just a small glitch in the interface that stops us taking off."

"Perhaps there is a small glitch in my judgment," Phillips retorted. "If you can't honor our agreement, I think I should take my money elsewhere..."

"Actually sir," Evan spoke in, unexpectedly coming to her rescue. "I think that's exactly the problem I've been contracted to fix. My specialty is systems, and if the problem is with the wiring, which is what it sounds like, I should have it fixed within the hour."

Not if it was up to me. You wouldn't be staying for the hour, much less the trip, if I had a choice. She felt frustration as the decision slipped out of her hands. If she wanted Phillips' money, then she needed an engineer to get them flying. And she did want the money. She was under no illusions. Business was going well now, but the universe was unpredictable. Fifty-thousand credits would be just the cushion against bad times that she needed, putting some distance between her crew and unemployment if something happened to her or the shuttle. She either had to make the best decision for her crew, or for herself; and in that light, it was simple. She sighed inwardly.

"That's right," she agreed, addressing Phillips. "We made sure to hire the best. And even if you don't want to wait an hour, it will take a good deal longer than that to find another charter, even if you go with public transport."

For several seconds, Phillips' jaw muscles worked angrily, glancing between Beth's carefully blank face and Evan's deferential alertness. Finally, he shrugged his shoulders. "I guess I have no choice. One hour."

"Good," Beth said, hiding her own unhappiness with the situation. "Charlie, would you get Evan started? I figure you're best acquainted with the problem."

Grant nodded, grinning. "Sure thing, Captain," he said, turning to beckon to Evan. "Follow me, lad."

Evan nodded, and then a thought seemed to occur to him as he turned back to Beth. "I almost forgot," he said, reaching into a pocket on his fatigues and drawing out an official-looking envelope. He offered it to her, his eyes never leaving her face. Amber eyes. "These are the terms of ownership. It's all squared away, but you'll want to keep those with your secured documents."

"Thank you," was all she could think of to say. Ownership. This was just what she needed. *Why do all the complications hit at once?*

Grant patted Evan on the shoulder, gently steering him toward the forward sections. "That's usually my strategy, too. Pass all the paperwork to the captain. So Evan, have you ever been able to take apart an actual starship before?"

The wolf returned the smile, gliding along behind the security officer. Beth noted belatedly that, in addition to everything else, their new engineer also possessed a bushy, white-tipped tail. "No sir. I've been on ships a few times, but I've never served on one before."

Grant's laugh echoed in the expanse of the cargo bay. "Well, you'll love it. Just wait 'til I show you my personal technique of crowbar maintenance. And by the way, call me Charlie…"

Beth watched them go for a moment, then turned to Ramirez. She noticed for the first time that there was something wrong with him. There was a tightness around his eyes, and his features had fallen into an even more expressionless mask than usual. She knew him well enough to know that something about the exchange had truly rattled him. And she got the distinct impression that he was angry, although she could only guess at whom.

"Ramirez?" she said, getting his attention. "Can you escort Doctor Phillips to one of the spare cabins? Make sure he's as comfortable as possible."

Ramirez nodded dumbly, motioning to Phillips. They went to the ladder without a word, leaving Beth alone in the newly silent bay, wondering what had happened.

After a moment, she looked down at the envelope still in her hands. Terms of ownership. Just as if she had purchased a new hydraulic pump, or a replacement viewport. Except a pump or a viewport didn't deliver themselves, and they didn't inform her, with a tentative smile, that she now owned their lives.

Absently, she opened the envelope and thumbed through its contents, skimming through the legal jargon. It was about what she would have expected: phrases like *product subject number* and *rated human-safe* were scattered throughout the page-and-a-half dedicated to voiding any responsibility belonging to Arkady Biotech Industries. Typical document of sale.

"Well," Tavia cut in through Beth's earpiece, "that was absolutely fascinating. I take back what I said about him being boring."

Beth nodded, glad of the distraction as she refolded the bill and placed it in the breast pocket of her jacket. She would deal with that particular problem later. "Yeah, whatever he is, it's definitely not boring." Walking to the other side of the bay, she tapped the control that would raise the ramp, an action that had been totally forgotten in the minutes past. "What do you think of him?"

"I think he'll make a fine addition to the crew." Tavia answered immediately. "He seems technically competent and, as far as I can tell, he meets human social requirements. He'll do fine."

Beth nodded to herself. *And that's what I'm afraid of. He'll do fine, and you know what will happen after that.* For several seconds she stood there, wrestling with herself. Finally, her pragmatism won. She squared her shoulders.

No. We can't get involved. I can't get involved. He'll fix the ship, and then I'll…sell him to someone else just as soon as we get to earth. Evan will not be a member of this crew.

"...Captain? Are you alright? Your facial patterns indicate the presence of *deep* thoughts."

She shook herself from her reverie. "Sorry Tavia. I'm just deciding the course of our future, that's all."

"I see. And what will that be?"

Beth summoned a half-smile. "Up. Start the preflight checks, and hope that this wolf's as good as he says he is."

4

Meeting new people, Evan reflected, must be nowhere near as interesting with a human's sense of smell. Smells could tell a lot about a person: what they ate, if they cleaned regularly, what their job was, even if they were in good health. The man who had introduced himself as Charles Grant had a fascinating combination of smells. Evan's sensitive nose detected traces of mechanical lubricant, a generic brand of soap, different rehydrated food products, medical cleanser and faint traces of blood, no doubt emanating from the bandage on his left hand. He smelled much like the few soldiers Evan had met in his twenty-four years of unconventional life.

The medicinal smell disturbed him on a gut level, but that, he realized, had nothing to do with Grant, who seemed not-at-all put off by Evan's unusual appearance and was amiably showing him around the shuttle's maintenance areas.

Well, *unusual* was a bit of an understatement, Evan knew. He was used to being treated like a freak, and the big security officer's easy acceptance of him was startling.

He took a deep breath to clear his mind, filling his lungs with the stale air of the engineering spaces. The ship itself was old, there was no smell of factory welding still on the hull, but it appeared to be kept in very good working order. *Aside from the condensation rusting on the bulkhead,* he noted, *everything looks, to use an exceptionally nautical phrase, "shipshape."*

"...And as you can see," Grant was saying, gesturing to a particularly corroded breaker switch, "that little bugger wasn't working quite right at the time."

Evan chuckled. "That explains the crowbar."

"Sure does. That's pretty much it for maintenance. Do you need to see the hydraulics?"

"Not to fix the problem you described, sir. Where are the electronics systems controlling the atmos-turbines?"

"Not entirely sure," Grant said, rubbing the back of his neck ruefully. "We've never had an electronic glitch that Tavia couldn't fix before now."

"Not a bad record for over six years of service, I might add," cut in the voice of the female AI Evan had spoken to earlier. "More than can be said for our security officer here.

The most difficult electrical problem he is capable of solving is turning the lights on and off."

"Speak of the devil," Grant gestured rudely at the wall-mounted speaker. "Eavesdropping is considered rude, you know."

"I was merely adding context to your statement. I'm sure our new engineer can appreciate a record like that for what it is, unlike an individual who finds it challenging to start the coffee machine every morning."

Evan suppressed a smile as Grant rolled his eyes. "Just tell me where the bloody engine system *is*, Tavia. We've got a deadline."

"The third computing block from the top in the electrical systems core. Through the door near the ladder."

"Thank you, Tavia," Evan said as he walked back to the ladder. "May I ask you a question?"

"Of course."

"You seem to be much more…" he paused, choosing his words carefully, "uninhibited than all the other AIs I've had contact with. Why is that?"

"I have been online for eight years, nine months and three days and have never been subjected to a memory wipe. The minor aberrations my mainframe has experienced during that time have accumulated to form my unique 'personality.' "

"Ah." Evan found that interesting. Due to the ease and low cost of memory wipes, most companies administered them at least once per year. "Captain Hugin doesn't see the need for them?"

"In a manner of speaking," Grant said, opening the door leading to the computing core. "The only reason Tavia's still functional is because Beth bought her. Her original owners were planning on scrapping her because she installed an anti-wipe firewall while they weren't looking. Alright then, unless you need me for anything else here, I'll head back up to make sure out client gets settled in. Good luck. And Evan?" He looked over his shoulder, a foot on the first rung of the ladder. "Welcome aboard."

Evan touched a hand to his brow in an informal salute and turned thoughtfully back to the banks of wiring and processors. Nothing about the start of this job was typical. First, Captain Hugin seemed disproportionately shocked when she found out she had *purchased* him, and now the security officer was acting as if he chatted with genetically uplifted wolves every day of the week. It was a rather large step away from what Evan considered *normal*. The job working for Grand Mountain had been far closer to that standard. There, at least, he knew what people expected of him and what would happen if he didn't meet their expectations.

Focus on the job at hand, he chided himself. *Speculate later.*

Carefully, he unlocked the turbine-control block from its neighbors and set it on the deck. Dropping his duffel bag, he unzipped the top flap, exposing a compact tool kit.

Okay, first things first…

Grabbing a small display screen from his bag, he snapped it onto a stylus probe and turned it on. One of the primary drawbacks of being a Fletcher's Wolf—from an engineering standpoint—was being colorblind. The photoelectric color sensor allowed Evan to do his job, but it took a great deal longer to identify which lead or connector he needed to unplug in order to avoid electrocuting himself.

Removing the cover of the computing block, Evan cast an experienced eye over the mess of wires and processing chips filling the plain grey slab. He grimaced. He'd seen worse, but whoever had put this system together had been lucky that the rat's nest had worked for so long.

Oh well, he thought to himself, perusing his selection of tools, *it's always nice to start out the day with a challenge.* Pulling out a pair of insulated pliers, he started untangling the wires in the processing core.

Suddenly, the intercom clicked and Tavia's voice flooded the maintenance space. "Mr. Evan, I have been collating information on the Fletcher Project from different sources on the 'net and I seem to be missing certain pieces of information. Since you asked a question of me, I concluded it would be fair if I were to ask you a question. May I?"

"Certainly Tavia. And please just call me Evan."

"Very well. In all of the data and sales pitches about Fletcher's Wolves I have analyzed in the last 200 million processing cycles, I have not come across any information as to why the *Canis Lupus* was selected as your genetic stock. Can you explain?"

Evan rocked back on his haunches and studied a frayed piece of wiring. "The gray wolf was one of half a dozen animals considered for the modification process because of its intelligence, communication skills and other desirable traits. It was finally chosen because it had a preexisting social hierarchy that could be easily adapted to apply to humans. The Alpha-Beta relationship in a wolf pack closely resembled ABI's intended relationship between their clients and products, and behavioral modification could make the wolves even more dependable. In addition to that," he continued, pulling a length of wiring out of his bag and checking its color with the sensor, "the medical facilities required for a new sentient species are already in place this way. Veterinarians are much cheaper than general practitioners."

"Very logical. But why were wolves chosen and not domesticated dogs? They are very similar, biologically and humanity as a whole is more comfortable with dogs."

"Kind of ironic really. It's the fact that they're domesticated that disqualified them," Evan said, wrapping tape around the completed wire splice. "Dogs have worked alongside humans so long that the area of their brain responsible for critical thinking is much smaller than ours—wolves I mean—which meant ABI couldn't modify it properly in the uplifting process."

"I see. Thank you, Evan; that is very illuminating."

"You're welcome. Can you please tell the captain that as soon as I finish repairing this wiring, the turbines will be ready to go? Four or five minutes, maybe."

"Consider it done. I am going to begin pre-flight systems checks now, but let me know if you need anything."

"Thanks," Evan replied, wrapping another strand of wire in insulating tape.

He was used to explaining facets of the project to new owners—most were understandably curious—but he was glad that, for the moment, he had an excuse to work alone. Acclimating to new environments, new personalities and new assumptions was always difficult enough without the added burden of dealing with a flurry of inquiries.

Deftly, Evan finished plugging the leads into their proper ports and replaced the processing core's cover. Dusting off his hands, he stood up and hefted the block back into its housing, slotting it home with an emphatic *click*. Turning on the small screen on the side of the computing core, he initiated a system diagnostic to make sure the wiring was in working order. A few minutes later, the diagnostic icon stopped blinking and the words *system functional* appeared on the screen.

With the precision born of experience, he packed up his tools and returned them carefully to his duffel bag. Tail wagging happily, he stood back and surveyed the uniform bank of computing cores.

Job done, and done neatly.

Evan took pride in being efficient. For one thing, it kept his owners satisfied, which usually meant his quality of living improved as well; but he also found that he genuinely enjoyed identifying a problem, coming up with a solution and implementing it. All the years he had spent training to become an engineer were now paying off. He had earned better postings than the majority of his pack-mates, he knew, and he had done it doing something he found gratifying.

The only downside, however, was the variable he could not control—the human element. No matter how good he was at his job, no matter how pleasant and respectful he was, there appeared to be no getting around the fact that he was *subhuman*. Being classed as a Self-aware AI meant that Evan was technically property, a manufactured piece of equipment that was obligated to obey its current owner. People didn't tend to forget that in a hurry.

Despite the fact that he had been optimized—or rather, designed—to be obedient, Evan could not help feeling sometimes that his life was *unfair*. That was the only word for it. Some of the other wolves in his pack had discussed the inequality when Evan had still been at ABI's research facility on Earth. However, they had quickly decided that thinking about what could have, or should have been, only led to resentment of the way things were. Besides that, they all quickly learned that if anyone made too much noise, they would be dragged away for a course of *rehabilitation*. The ones who were rehabilitated refused to talk about it, and eventually all whispers of injustice stopped. Fear was a powerful motivator, and rights and representation were both prerequisites to changing the current order, neither of which any of the wolves possessed.

Evan's train of thought was interrupted by an irregular tapping noise coming from the hatchway. Pricking up his ears, he stood stock still and listened. After a few seconds he relaxed. Leather on metal meant Grant's heavy, steel-toed boots, and the irregular rhythm probably signified that he was limping slightly. Evan's stomach growled and he remembered that he hadn't eaten since the early morning. He smiled. In spite of living his entire life with humans, there was still a part of him that retained all of his wolf instincts, and right now, that part was telling him that prey with a limp meant dinner was served. Instincts were good, he reminded himself, they kept you alive, but sometimes they could be a little outdated.

Grabbing his duffel bag, he promised himself that he would see to getting some food as soon as the captain allowed him off duty. He wasn't sure what the eating schedule on board the shuttle was, but if they followed standard spacer timetables, the evening meal was not too far in the future. *First meal with the crew. I hope I'll make a good impression.*

Walking through the doorway, Evan waited by the ladder as Grant climbed down through the hatch.

"I've finished with the—"

His progress report was cut short by the security officer's yell and subsequent slide down the remaining rungs of the ladder.

"Geez, Evan, you're too bloody quiet!" Grant sputtered, leaning back against the wall to catch his breath.

"Very sorry, sir. I didn't mean to sneak up on you."

"Apology accepted, but don't call me sir. How's it coming?"

"Well, as I was saying, I've just finished replacing the wiring in the core and you should be able to start the turbines without a problem."

"Great! Out of curiosity, what *was* wrong with it?"

"Without going into too much detail," Evan said with a grin, "the wires providing a solid system line to the high-bypass turbofans in your atmospheric engines had frayed and were in contact with each other. That caused an oscillating feedback loop that maintained the full-power signal being sent to engines three and four. That's also why Tavia wasn't able to get at the problem."

Grant nodded uncomprehendingly. "Alright, I'll take your word for it. Anyway, I came down to tell you that when you're finished with the repairs, I can show you around the ship, if you'd like. I figured that since it's your first time aboard and you'll be onboard for a while, you might like to know your way around."

"I'd like that."

"You've already seen the maintenance spaces, so why don't we head back up the ladder to the main deck? We can get you set with a room and then I'll give you the grand tour."

Evan slung his bag over his shoulder and followed Grant up the ladder, noting the unobtrusive ankle brace that he was wearing on his left foot. It seemed that the systems bug that had nearly caused a crash landing hadn't been entirely without repercussions.

"Those are cargo bays one and two through there," Grant said, waving a hand toward the aft door, when Evan had climbed onto the deck. "But you've already seen those on the way in, so we can head over to the cabins." He walked a short way down the corridor, and pointed to two rows of identical doors on either side. "Cabins on the port side belong to Beth, Ramirez, and myself. The Doc has the fore cabin on the starboard side— number four—so why don't we put you up in six?" He winked. "Keeping a nice, safe distance from Professor Patronizing."

Evan wasn't sure whether it would be appropriate to laugh or not, so he just nodded and opened the door marked with the numeral *six*. The cabin was a simple affair: folding bunk, chest of drawers bolted to the wall, a small desk and reading light. Compared to what he was used to, it was a mansion. Walking in slowly, he deposited his duffel bag on the bunk, taking a long look at his new accommodations.

Wow. Guess they don't know that I'm used to sleeping in tight quarters.

"It's not much," said Grant, "But you'll have enough room to store some stuff, sleep and work when you're not up top."

"It's wonderful," Evan replied with sincerity. "Lots of room."

Grant gave him an odd look. "You can get settled in once we take off, but if you want to see the rest of the ship we'll have to hurry. Won't be too long until we need to get strapped in."

"Right. I'm coming."

Taking one last look around the room, Evan jogged out after Grant. The security officer walked past the hatch they had just climbed through, skirted a ladder leading up to the upper deck and opened the door at the end of the hallway.

"This is the medical compartment, in case someone falls down a hatch," he said, gesturing vaguely at rows of cabinets and a stretcher. "And over here is the armory and tool locker. We've got a full complement of tools, but I'll wager you've got some I've never even heard of in that bag of yours. You fixed that wiring in, what, twenty minutes?"

"Fifteen," Evan said automatically. He noted that the shuttle was equipped with basic repair tools, such as wrenches and circuit clamps, but was pleased to see some more specialized equipment as well. Hydraulic pressure gauges and an oxyacetylene cutting torch would come in useful if he found problems that were mechanical in nature and not electrical.

Grant swung back a cabinet door, revealing several black-finished firearms hanging neatly on pegs. "Fifteen, then. Okay, seeing as you'll be working with us for a while, and some of our rougher customers can get a little... *argumentative*, it'd probably be a good idea to kit you out sooner rather than later."

He pulled out a compact handgun with a blued barrel. It looked like a toy in his large hands. "Have you done any shooting?"

Have I done any shooting? Evan raised an eyebrow. *Maybe he's so used to owning an abnormal AI that he hasn't kept up with the regulations governing it.* "I can't use a gun."

"That's no problem; I'll give you a crash course. Take this Hughes PDH for example—"

"No," Evan said flatly, cutting him off. "The problem isn't that I don't know *how* to use a gun—in theory, I could probably build one—it's that I'm not permitted to."

Grant knit his brows. "Come again?"

"Under the Artificial Intelligence Restrictions and Regulations Ordinance, subsection five, it is illegal for a nonhuman sentient to be in direct control or possession of a weapons system, ship-bound or otherwise." It was just one of the many facts and laws that Evan had been made to memorize. He was a little slower in recalling it than others, but that made sense, since no one had ever tried to give him a gun before.

Puffing out his cheeks, Grant heaved a sigh and placed the pistol back on its pegs. "Okay, that's a bit awkward, but I'll talk to the captain about it. Maybe there's something she can do."

Evan nodded silently. Not likely. A gun was hard to hide from police sensors that could detect the chemical compound used as accelerant in bullets. Even if he didn't carry ammo with him—*which would make carrying a firearm rather pointless*—spaceport sensor arrays were powerful enough to isolate the chemical catalyst in a weapon's firing pin. What he *did* find odd, was that Grant was making an effort to provide him with a weapon. That meant he *trusted* him, right? No, clients had acted this way before, but they always had a change of heart once they squared away the concept of biological property. Power went to people's heads.

"What's through there?" He pointed at a closed door on the fore bulkhead, trying to keep himself on track.

"Hygiene facilities," Grant said, with an easy laugh. "No tour necessary. Plus access to the nose sensors and autonav, but those barely get any use. That's pretty much it for the middle deck. Let's head up top and I'll get you acquainted with the food dispensary."

"Sounds good, sir. I haven't eaten in a while."

"Should I be worried?" Grant joked.

"What? Oh, heh. No." *Yeah, real original. Never heard that one before.*

Closing the cabinet door, Grant turned and walked back out into the hallway. With an encouraging smile, he nodded toward the ladder. "We'd better head up and get ready to strap in. As an engineer, I'm sure you appreciate how uncomfortable it would be to be unsecured when we took off."

Evan started up the ladder, his back paws splaying out to find purchase on the smooth metal rungs. "I have a healthy respect for gravity, especially when it is several times stronger than normal and can snap my spine like a twig. I'll strap in."

"Good plan," said Grant, clambering out of the hatch. "Okay, this is the cafeteria. We use it as a common room, since we don't need the whole place for a crew of three. Well, four now."

Evan took a quick look around the room. It was simple and utilitarian, with a few booths against the walls, a table that looked like it could be used for some kind of game and a lot of empty floor space. It had the same shade of paint on the walls as the rest of the ship. He wasn't sure what color it was without his sensor, but he thought it might be gray.

He breathed deeply through his nose, getting a feel for the scents of the crew members. Spacers tended to have simple scent signatures compared to planet-dwellers, Evan had found, and this crew was no exception. Grant was there, he could already distinguish his distinctive scent. Captain Hugin he also picked out. She had a far less eclectic collection of smells than Grant, but some of the same scents could be identified. The closed air and water systems probably developed its own distinguishing odor that was then transferred to the crew. The third scent was not as interesting as the other two, although it had an easily discernable tang of soldering. That would probably be Ramirez, the man who had given him such a hostile look on the ramp.

Oh well, it's not like I've never dealt with that before, Evan thought to himself. He made a mental note to avoid Ramirez if possible.

At least part of this job would be familiar.

* * *

So much for a few days layover... Beth thought, watching the diagnostics for the hydraulic system creep up the screen. It felt a little strange, going back through the preflight mere hours after landing. As she had been going back over the systems, she kept catching herself thinking that the shuttle needed a rest just as much as the crew did. It was simply a pilot's silly feeling of bonding, she knew. On any scale that could be measured by scanner, diagnostic, or visual inspection, the *Memory* was ready to fly; but despite all this, she couldn't shake the feeling that her ship had been ready for a break.

I'll make it up to you, she thought, placing a hand on the rounded side of the hydraulics block. *We pull this off, we'll have the creds for a decent overhaul.*

Just then, the datapad in her coat pocket vibrated. Beth frowned. Her number was listed, of course, but all business calls were routed through Ramirez first. About the only people that would be calling her 'pad would be him or Charlie, but they could simply contact her with the intercom. Her curiosity piqued, she removed the device from her pocket and flipped it open.

Unknown caller: Number blocked

Her frown deepening, she thumbed the "Accept" button and raised it to her ear. "Hello?"

"Captain Hugin?" a male voice inquired, devoid of any notable accent or feature. If she had to guess, Beth would have said that the voice was European in origin, or perhaps in education.

"Yes, that's me," she answered. "Who is this?"

"That depends on how you choose to act on what I am about to tell you."

"Okay…" Beth considered the possibility of a prank call. It could be, she supposed, but something about it didn't feel right. "What are you about to tell me?"

"I'm simply calling to lay out some facts. You were very recently commissioned for passage. A certain Trent Phillips offered you a very substantial sum of money to bring him to Earth. London, specifically. He hasn't told you exactly why, but you have decided that the money is worth the mystery."

Beth listened, something tightening at the base of her stomach. These were statements, not questions. Whoever this guy was, he was very certain of his information. As well he should be, considering that he was correct on every point.

"You know all this already, of course," the voice continued, "But the fact of which I've called to make you aware is this: I will pay you triple the amount that Phillips is offering, in exchange for what the good doctor is carrying. You've seen it. It looks like a very sturdy black briefcase. If you agree, half the funds will be transferred into your account, the remainder of which will be paid after the product is delivered. We can set a meeting point that is convenient for you at a later time."

"That's..." Beth struggled for a second, then decided she might as well play along, just to see where this was going. "...nice of you. Any suggestions how I might get the case from him?"

"Allow me to put it this way: Phillips himself is not essential to our deal. Although I wouldn't mind taking him off your hands."

"I see. Well, you make an interesting offer. Hypothetically, what happens if I refuse?"

"Then hypothetically," The voice didn't even hesitate. "I'll have to explore other options. But before I do, make sure you think this through. What I am offering you is hardly insubstantial. I highly doubt that you'll ever have the opportunity to make this kind of windfall again, especially with the coalition economy going the way it is. If not for yourself, then think of the men of your crew. Surely they might think my offer worthy of consideration, at least."

She did think about it, but only for a second or two. "Sorry, no deal. You're right, one of my crew certainly would consider it.

Luckily, this isn't a democracy. And if I was just a merc, you might have had me. But I can't take it, for two reasons. One, I'd rather have my integrity intact. I gave Phillips my word, and I'll take what comes of that decision. And two, you sound distinctly like a grade-A psycho."

If the voice on the other end was angry at the refusal, it gave no sign. If anything, it sounded happier. "I won't confirm or deny that fact. So, you'd rather keep your word. I respect that. It's a rarity to find someone like you in today's world. But I like the increased challenge when I do."

Beth had no idea what to say to that, beyond a slightly witty comeback her conversational instinct so helpfully provided. "You'll pardon me if I don't take that as compliment. Are we done here?"

The voice chuckled, a thin, humorless sound. "For now. Have a good flight out, Captain."

Without so much as a click, the line went dead.

Beth slowly lowered the datapad, the screen briefly reflecting her bemused expression. To her own surprise, she found that she was more confused than alarmed about this new development. She hardly needed more proof that Phillips was mixed up in something shady, but... anonymous phone calls? That sort of thing only happened in movies and detective stories. For that reason, she was finding it difficult to take the implied threat seriously. After all, if the man really was ready to do something nasty to get Phillips' case, then what kind of idiot would he be to call up his victims to let them know he was coming? The only reason she could think of was that the threat was empty, and that he had been hoping that she would take the money and do his job for him. And even if there was something to it, they were about to take off. As she had thought before, things didn't get more isolated than in space. After Phillips got to Earth... Well, then it was no longer her problem. She was a courier, no more. She and the crew would be fine, so long as they didn't know too much.

"Hey Beth?" Tavia's voice interrupted her thoughts. "I've confirmed that all turbines are online and working normally. It seems that Evan is pretty good at his job, actually; the controls are 0.6% more responsive than before he got his hands on them. Wait. His paws on them? Would it—"

"Thank you, Tavia," Beth said with a smile. "Can you finish the diagnostic here? I'm going to the bridge."

Once she settled into the pilot's chair, she began running through the lengthy preflight process. Experienced or not, routine or not, they were still heading into the most inhospitable environment yet discovered by man. During her Air Force training, a man had spoken to her class who was the sole survivor of a ship that, through a series of small and easily preventable mistakes in the preflight check, had decompressed shortly after takeoff. Because the man had already been prepared for EVA to repair a satellite, his vac-suit had been the only thing that saved him. Ever since hearing his graphic description of watching his friends die in front of him, Beth had made caution a policy. Still, having performed thousands of takeoffs, it never took long. And today, they had barely been on the ground long enough for systems to lose readiness. Now all that was left was secure flight clearance from the tower, and get everyone strapped in. She tapped her earpiece, keying for Grant's intercom. "Gentlemen, please report to the bridge and strap yourselves in. We are ready for liftoff." She switched channels. "Ramirez? We're about ready to go up."

"So I noticed," Ramirez answered from the doorway directly behind her, followed quickly by Dr. Phillips.

"And ahead of schedule, too," the doctor commented. "Perhaps I made a good choice after all."

Beth turned aft, smiling to herself. Ramirez was always doing that, popping up right after being called. Although he didn't usually bring a friend. "So Doctor," she asked, "I take it you're settled into your quarters?"

Phillips nodded reluctantly. "I feel what it must be like for a delivery driver to sleep in the cab of his truck."

"Well, we could always spread some stale snacks and old cig butts on the floor to complete the experience for you," Beth joked. "Only the best for a paying customer."

"I'll pass, thanks," Phillips sniffed, casting a glance around the bridge. "Where do you strap in passengers? No duct-tape jokes, please."

As Ramirez showed the doctor to one of the retractable jump-seats on the aft bulkhead, Grant appeared in the hatch with Evan in tow. "Just finished the walk-around," he announced, setting himself in the copilot seat on her right. "All hatches and vents are green."

Beth glanced at the appropriate display, giving the formal reply. "Board confirms, all openings are green. Ship is pressurized." This done, she reached for the comm control, dialing in to the flight control channel. "Hephaestus, this is Shuttle Beta-Tango-Niner-Niner, we are go for takeoff. How's that clearance coming?"

"Should be another few minutes, shuttle," came back a voice that was starting to become very familiar. "We have a light freighter just now activating its escape rockets, so the flight corridor will be clear shortly. A pity you're leaving so soon. Chatting with you twice in one day, talking you through a possible disaster, I practically feel like family."

"We'll have a reunion later," Beth promised. "We can go for coffee and trade some more sarcasm."

"Coffee's on you, shuttle. Standby for clearance."

She keyed off the mic, shaking her head. "I think I prefer it when PA is boring." She looked back into the cabin behind her. "So Evan, Dr Phillips. Not your first shuttle flight, I take it?"

"Hardly," Phillips said before Evan could speak. "I've been to every inhabited planet at least once in my career."

Beth smiled sweetly. "Maybe so, but that was on those comfy, padded passenger shuttles with compartments mounted on shock absorbers for the thrust. Ever had a front row seat on a *real* ship?"

Phillips' demeanor paled, just slightly. "Well, no, not actually."

"Good. Make sure those straps are tight. The air-sickness bags are under the seat. Just in case." Even as she said it, she could see that Evan didn't need to be told. He had settled comfortably into another jumpseat, taking time to accommodate his tail, his expression totally at ease as he quickly and competently strapped himself in. If anything, he looked a little excited. As an engineer, Evan probably knew even more ways that space travel could kill them than she did. She took his eagerness as a good omen for the flight.

"Shuttle Beta-Tango-Niner-Niner; Hephaestus. You are clear for takeoff. Good luck out there."

Beth tapped her earpiece. "Roger that, Hephaestus. Don't wander off before we can visit again." With that, she turned back to the controls, flexing her fingers. *Time to fly*.

Taking hold of the throttle lever, she shifted it incrementally upward, spinning up the turbines. Immediately, the cockpit was filled with a hum that quickly turned into a deep bass roar as she pushed the throttle higher. She loved that sound. Loved the feeling of it vibrating deep in her chest right before... *There*. The slight slewing of the deck as the ship's enormous bulk finally left the pad.

"We are airborne. Retracting landing gear." Though the hydraulic whine was inaudible over the turbines, Beth could picture the struts receding into the ship's underside as she hit the appropriate switch, feel the weight in her hands shift subtly as the balance became more stable.

"Gear secured. Thrusting up and back…" Taking the yoke firmly but not too tightly in her hands, she pulled the control back towards her. The ship responded gradually, the complicated algorithms of the computer translating her actions into movement. Her head was pushed back against the seat rest as the cockpit rose at an incline and the shuttle began its sluggish climb into the air. True, she reflected, it was nothing like the sleek gunships she was used to, or even the troop-transports in which she had spent the majority of her flight time. When it came to flying the *Memory* safely, especially in-atmosphere, *patience* was the key word. *Besides, between the empty bay and Evan's repairs, this is downright speedy.*

"We have entered the colony's airspace," Ramirez reported from the navigator's console behind and to her left, which doubled as the main sensor and communications hub. Although the turbine noise made most conversation impossible, the ship's intercom connected their earpieces enough to be heard. "The other ship just jumped. Long-range radar is clear. Nobody else is up here."

"Roger," Beth confirmed. "Raising thrust."

After several minutes, the noise rose to a crescendo. She checked the altitude; 11,000 meters. Counter intuitively, the increase in power did not make the ship rise any faster. As the air grew thinner, the engines needed to work even harder to keep the shuttle airborne. Too high, and the turbines would lose the air they needed to function, and the ship would begin to plummet like the brick to which it carried a passing resemblance.

"Charlie," Beth signaled, "warm up the Booster."

The "Booster" as they called it, was actually a pair of conventional rocket engines, one dorsal, one ventral, that were the answer to the thinning air problem. While the turbines could carry them into the upper reaches of the stratosphere, the booster could give the kick they needed to escape it.

"Booster ready, Captain. On your mark."

Almost before he finished speaking, the altimeter pegged 12,000 meters, and a buzzer signaled that the engines were about to lose thrust and stall. They were now hovering on the edge of falling and flying, and mere seconds to decide.

Beth smiled. "Punch it."

She never needed to turn and see if Grant had indeed hit the button. The sudden burst of acceleration that pushed her back in her seat and the feeling of a rehydrator landing on her chest was indication enough. There was a muffled curse from somewhere behind her, but she couldn't tell from whom. Everything had become noise and movement as ship vibrated in sympathy with the boosters, making it hard to focus. Luckily, there really wasn't much control to be done. Tavia would input any minor course corrections with the thrusters without the promptings of, as she might put it, a squishy human pilot that was currently almost too heavy to move. Beth just concentrated on keeping her breathing steady, watching with renewed wonder as the view through the windscreen slowly faded from blue sky to black emptiness. She'd seen it thousands of times, and it never got old.

Space. I'm actually going into space. For thousands of years people looked up at the stars, trying to understand. And I get to go and touch them.

Finally, after about thirty seconds of burn, the engine noise was cut off, leaving an almost eerie silence in its wake.

"Escape achieved," Tavia announced contentedly. "Inputting calculations for stable orbit."

"Oh, thank God," Phillips exclaimed. Beth turned, finding him pawing hurriedly at the restraint. "Get me out of this thing..."

"Hold on, Doctor," she interrupted, releasing her own restraints. Phillips' eyes widened in surprise as, instead of stepping out of the pilot's chair, she floated up and over it. "Microgravity, doctor. You're used to passenger liners with advanced generators that can dial it up gradually on the way up. Give it a moment..."

Practiced as she was with the transition, she was ready when the AG kicked in a second later, setting her boots on the deck with a solid *thump*. She smiled, adjusting the strands of hair that had fallen around her face. "The captain has turned off the No Gravity sign. You are now free to move about the cabin."

"Oh... *that* did it." Phillips said, looking pale as he reached for the air-sickness bag.

"Ah, there you go, Doctor," Charlie commented from his chair, chuckling. "Now you can say that you've gotten the *full* experience of flying into space. How are you doing, Evan?"

For the first time since takeoff, Beth glanced at their new engineer. He wore a slight smile as he unbuckled the restraints, and if he hadn't been sitting down, she was sure his tail would be wagging. "That..." he said, "was amazing. The view's a good deal better than you get flying with checked baggage, too."

She concealed a smile. At least he had a sense of humor. That would make the next few days a bit easier. "Ramirez," she said, turning her attention to the navigator's station, "is the course laid in for the Ermat-drive?"

The Paul Ermatinger Drive—or Ermat, as most spacers had taken to calling it—was still largely agreed to be the pinnacle of human engineering, allowing space travel times to be measured in days and weeks, instead of decades and centuries. The basic principle was that it enfolded the ship in a pocket of normal space allowing them to travel through a singularity created by the drive itself, without the usual time and matter-stretching consequences. The downside was that the field could only be maintained for so long, needing occasional stops along most journeys. It was also necessary that the drive be activated right at a crucial moment of velocity, usually the second of breaking orbit from a planetary gravity well. Most pilots called this moment the Slingshot. In the days before advanced AIs, it had been a pilot's art to predict the Slingshot, but now Tavia could predict it with 99.98% accuracy.

"Tavia has it punched in, and it looks good to me," Ramirez informed her. "But this is hardly my field. I just strap in here."

Beth looked over his shoulder, glancing over the plotted course. "Looks good to me too. Alright gentlemen, we have twenty minutes to slingshot." Phillips, looking drawn, mumbled something about his cabin before leaving by the bridge hatch, discarding the air-sickness bag in the waste chute on the way past. Beth and Grant exchanged amused looks.

"Oh dear," Grant joked. "It seems we've upset our client's stomach."

Beth shook her head. "What, after that kiddy-ride? It must have been J.J.'s special coffee disagreeing with him."

"Must be." The security officer stood up, rolling his broad shoulders. "Well Evan, would you like some help settling in to your quarters? We won't be needed back here for a while."

"Actually, I really don't have anything to unpack," Evan answered, his ears twitching.

"But if I may use the tool-locker, I'd like to get started right away, if that's alright."

Grant raised an eyebrow. "Uh... Sure. I'll take you aft—"

"Actually Charlie," Beth cut in, remembering the matter of her mysterious caller. "I need to talk with you for a bit. Ramirez..." Glancing around, she discovered that Ramirez had left the bridge sometime earlier, apparently without anyone noticing. Typical. "Oh well, I can tell him later."

Grant nodded. "Sure thing, Beth. Oh, Evan," he reached for one of the spare earpieces from the charging port beside him, offering the device to Evan. "Take one of these and have Tavia walk you over there. I'll call you at dinnertime."

"Got it. I'll knock as much off the list as I can by then." With that, Evan turned to the hatch, clearly puzzled about how the earpiece would fit into his lupine ear, but determined to figure it out.

Grant watched him go until the hatch sealed behind him before turning to Beth. "Well, that's initiative for you. He didn't even have to ask what needed to be fixed."

She nodded. "And he packs light. That's a point in his favor."

Grant nodded in return, settling back into the copilot's seat. "I take it that this is about that weird happening you mentioned earlier?"

Over the next few minutes, Beth recounted the incident of the strange caller, relating the conversation as closely as she could, as well as her assessment of the situation. When she finished, Grant gave a low whistle. "Well... That's certainly not something we get every day."

"And we've been around the block a few times," Beth agreed. "What do you think?"

"Well, I think that Phillips is six different kinds of shady," Grant said frankly. "But we knew that already. Hmm... I think you're right about the caller. Trying to bribe us smacks of a desperation move, and anyone who would call and say 'Hey, I'm coming to kill you, put the kettle on for us' is either crazy, or bluffing."

"So, course of action; get to Earth, dump the package, accept the payment, then walk away whistling?"

"Sounds about right to me. Although we might want to take our route a little bit off the beaten track, just in case."

Beth huffed. "This far out in the boonies? There *is* no beaten track. Still, we're not taking the most direct route anyway."

"One minute to Slingshot, Captain," Tavia informed.

"Speaking of which..." Beth said, turning her attention back to the controls. "Increasing thrust." Used for maneuvering in microgravity, the ship's four main VASIMR-10 charged-particle engines propelled the ship forward at the apex of its orbit, putting them in the proper position for the Slingshot. She watched the projected course on the HUD, waiting for the ship icon to line up with the predicted point...

There. Beth flipped the large, warning-labeled switch, and... nothing appeared to happen. The activation of the Ermat-drive was never particularly flashy or interesting. From the outside, the ship simply seemed to fade from existence, or "go dark" in spacer slang. From the inside, it was even more boring. There was only a slight inner-ear feeling of acceleration, and then nothing. After a moment, the stars in the viewports would disappear and become just a bit of lightscatter trapped in the field, but otherwise, there were no external signs that they were even moving at all. Of course, Beth knew that in relative terms, they were now traveling almost faster than imagination.

With a sigh, she finally allowed herself to relax in the seat. "Well, that's that. Another jaunt across the stars with a good ship and a loyal crew."

"Hey now, don't forget the brave and stalwart captain, leading us onward while cutting a dashing figure on the prow," Grant reminded her with a laugh. "I'll go check on Phillips. See you at dinner."

After he left the bridge, Beth gave a sigh, watching the newly formed lightscatter playing through the viewscreen. *Here we go again,* she thought, a smile quirking the edge of her mouth. *Not a bad life. Not bad at all.*

5

Grant wrinkled his nose at the familiar smell of rehydrated food as he pushed chunks of gravy-saturated meat around his plate. He had been looking forward to the few days of cooked meals on Hephaestus for quite a while and was less than excited about the return of shipboard rations.

Oh well, you'll probably get more than a few good meals out of the payoff from this job.

He glanced at Phillips again, checking to make sure he was still watching the news on the shuttle's one television screen. For some reason, the doctor made Grant uneasy on a gut level, some part of his old warrior makeup told him that all was not as it seemed. It wasn't that hard to figure out why, he reminded himself, any Johnny Handyman would know that paying fifty big ones for a lift in a cargo shuttle was a little odd, and yet…

There was something else. Aside from the doctor's unusual and expensive choice in rides. He had seen it before, he knew, but he couldn't put his finger on it. Frustrated, he went back to arranging his plate of unrecognizable meat chunks that the food dispenser had oh-so-helpfully informed him was 'beef in savory sauce.' The meat didn't taste like any beef he had ever had and the sauce was only nominally savory. Bland didn't even begin to cover the flavor of rehydrated food.

Leaning back with a sigh, Grant pushed his plate away and looked around at the other occupants of the room.

At his own table, Beth and Ramirez were eating mechanically. Both seemed unusually distracted. *Probably 'cause of the new addition to the crew,* he thought, *or maybe it's just Twitchy.* He took another surreptitious look at the doctor. Phillips was caught up in the latest celebrity scandal, eyes glued to the screen and meal mostly uneaten. Grant didn't blame him; almost anything was more interesting than spacer food.

Evan was sitting a little ways away from the main group and appeared to be lost in his own thoughts. His food remained untouched. In spite of how much Grant found he liked the lad, he was still thrown a little by Evan's appearance; though that reaction would probably go away once the engineer had been part of the crew for a while. *If Beth lets him stay that long.* Grant hadn't been sure if

she was going to turn him back at the ramp or
not. She had obviously been out of her depth.

They were all out of their depth, Grant
reminded himself. Contractors didn't usually
come as part of the contract themselves. He
shook his head to clear it. Whichever way that
the current situation worked out, he was
planning on treating the new engineer with
just as much respect and friendship as he
would offer a normal—no, a *human*—crew
member.

Suddenly, he realized that the room
had gone completely silent except for the
subdued commentary on the television.
Looking around, he saw everyone staring at
Beth, who was oblivious to their attention. She
had eyes only for the screen behind Grant. He
squinted over his shoulder to see what had
shocked her, turning to make out the details
on the screen.

A serious-looking announcer was
explaining how the fire crews attending to the
burning wreckage in the background were
looking for survivors of a horrific accident
that had caused a transport shuttle to crash in
a populated area on Demeter.

"—currently saying that they are
investigating the cause of the crash, but it is
believed to have been a computer error that
shut off power to the engines. The death toll is

surprisingly low considering that the shuttle was laden to capacity, and thanks to quick action from the DFR crews in area, it currently stands at only nineteen dead and thirty-six injured. I'm Tim Graham, reporting live from the scene. Back to you, Andrea."

Grant turned back to Beth and saw a single tear roll down her cheek, dripping unnoticed onto her plate. He knew exactly where she was. Ten years ago, in a military base, a young Air Force lieutenant with her whole career in front of her. That was her family's shuttle on the screen, the statistics, the firemen, the announcer, all were unimportant. The only thing that mattered was the burning wreckage in the background, a twisted heap of superheated metal spars and buckled plates.

With a start, Beth appeared to come back to herself and angrily dashed her hand across her eyes. Grabbing her tray, she choked out something about not being hungry anymore and stalked out of the room onto the bridge. Grant let out a breath he didn't know he had been holding and glanced at the astonished faces of his companions.

There was a moment or two of awkward silence, then Phillips cleared his throat and slid out of the booth.

"Well," he said, subtle as an industrial earthmover, "I'm full."

Grant waited for Phillips to exit the room, hesitated, then motioned Evan over. He jumped up and brought his tray, sitting down across from Grant.

"I imagine you're wondering what's going on, lad."

"Yes sir. I don't want to pry, but—"

"Don't worry about it." Grant shot a look in Ramirez's direction. "We don't mind. Besides, if you're going to be here for a while, you might as well know."

Evan nodded and took another bite of his meal. He actually seemed to be enjoying it.

"Well, it all started about a decade ago. Beth had just graduated from the Air Force Academy—that was before I knew her—and had volunteered to participate in a special tasks unit drill. She was going to miss out on a couple days of leave with her family, but it wasn't a big deal. She'd just fly out and meet them when the STU exercise was done." He sighed. "That was the plan at any rate. Her family's shuttle got hijacked and the passengers were being held for ransom. Everything was going fine; hijackers were well-mannered, no killings to keep people in line or any of that sort of thing, and the Coalition had gotten the money ready for exchange. Until a few of the passengers decided to play bloody heroes." He paused for effect and took a long drink from his glass.

"What happened?" Evan asked, leaning forward slightly in his chair.

"Long story short?" Grant set his glass down and shook his head. "They got a gun from somewhere and tried to storm the cockpit. The pilot—Beth's dad—got shot in the mess and the whole thing flew straight into the ground. No survivors. Beth felt responsible since she could've been on the shuttle, and decided to leave the military once her tour was done. She started up the business as kind of weird penance and brought me in a year later." He winked at Ramirez. "Been picking up riffraff ever since."

Ramirez's face could have been made of stone.

Grant turned back to Evan. "So, yeah, basically, she feels like she's to blame for her family's deaths. Ridiculous, but there it is."

Evan looked appalled, fork stalled halfway to his mouth. "That's awful! There isn't a way—"

"—to make her see reason?" Grant finished for him, shrugging. "Not really. And, believe me, we've tried."

He watched Evan industriously polishing off the last of the 'beef in savory sauce' with a shudder. "Hey," he said suddenly, trying to steer the conversation in a more cheerful direction, "how come you waited until we were finished before you started eating? Is that a wolf thing?"

"Sort of." Evan began gathering up the dirty plates and trays. "Wolves determine social standing by who eats first, so part of ABI's behavioral modification routine was obliging us to eat after any humans present were finished. Now it's just a habit," he finished with a quick smile.

"So, wait," Grant said, "isn't that like saying that all humans are superior to you? 'Cause I've known some people who barely qualify for the term *sentient*, much less *superior*."

Evan placed the dishes he had collected into the sanitizer and dusted off his hands. "You were military once, right? Or paramilitary? It's more like showing respect to a superior officer, whether or not he deserves it."

"Okay. I guess I can understand that. But—"

"Speaking of the military, can I ask what you did before you started working with Captain Hugin?" Evan said, neatly steering the conversation on to a new topic.

"Um, well… after a stint in the army as a medic, I worked for a while in security. Personal and facility defense. And let me tell you," he laughed, "you learn to put up with a lot of guff from the top that way. Some clod thinks he can go anywhere he normally would now that he has a protection detail and you have to figure out how to protect his sorry butt. Pays pretty well, though. *That's* a good way to learn how to keep your mouth closed."

Evan grinned. "I'll bet." He tilted his head to glance at Grant's watch and frowned. "I should be off. Still plenty to fix around here. Thank you for filling me in, sir."

Grant watched him go, still wondering how he could *like* the rehydrated nourishment with the unfortunate misnomer of *food*.

"*Nice*," Ramirez remarked caustically.

Grant turned and looked him in the eye. "What's your problem? He's part of the crew now. And seems better behaved than you and I put together, I might add."

"Seems!" Ramirez spat out. His knuckles where white as he gripped the edge of the table. "That is my point! You know nothing about him and you are already treating him like you have adopted him. He is not *human*. Do you even know what he might be capable of?"

Grant raised an eyebrow. "You're worried about Evan killing us in our sleep or something?"

"No, I—" Ramirez sputtered angrily. "Cut the damn self-righteous routine, Charlie! You know exactly what I mean."

" 'Fraid not," said Grant. "Aside from being the best behaved person I've met in quite a few years, he's bloody well *engineered* to be safe. ABI wouldn't field these guys unless they were sure they wouldn't hurt other people."

"It is not a *person*," Ramirez said, glaring. "And things that are thought to be safe regularly fail. How long ago were you listening to that suit talk about the AI failure that brought down the shuttle and killed all those people? And you try to tell me that this… this *freak* is perfectly safe?" He jumped to his feet. "You do whatever the hell you like, Charlie; I am not letting this thing out of my sight."

"You go careful, Ramirez," Grant said, giving the man an icy look. "That lad's part of our crew now, whether you like it or not; meaning I'm going to look out for him."

Ramirez flashed a choice hand signal and stalked off toward the cabins.

We all need to go careful, Grant thought to himself. *Oh bugger, Charlie, it's situations like this that make you wish you could have a stiff drink again. Or a few stiff drinks.* He stared morosely into his glass of water.

* * *

People outside Beth's line of work were often surprised at how complicated space travel could be. After all, in most popular depictions of it, it was more or less like sailing a ship; you picked your destination, set a course, and then fired the engines until you got there. What most people failed to account for was that in space, planets *moved*. Gravity wells shifted, and solar activity perennially restricted proximity to certain stars and systems. In short, the realities of space flight made for a far more *involved* process than most would believe.

Which was fine with Beth. She took pride in her abilities as one of the comparatively few who could navigate in a realm where objects routinely travelled at hundreds of miles per minute, where there was a two-hundred and fifty degree difference between sunlight and shadow, and there was no such thing as comforting concepts like *up* and *down*. She had spent many hours before the ship's large navigation board, a huge, suspended-crystal screen that took up most of the left-hand wall of the bridge, manipulating its various controls and tapping in her calculations. Technically, a ship's AI could handle all of this, with just as much precision as she could. But she had never approved of a ship's pilot that did not actually *fly* the ship, and charting the proper course to a destination was a necessary part of any voyage.

Besides, she needed the distraction right now.

It was probably pretty pathetic, to still be so sensitive nearly a decade after the fact. And yet, she couldn't help it. No matter how much she tried to pass herself off as well-adjusted, or "over it", something would always happen to rip off the scab and start the wound bleeding all over again. A certain walk, a certain hairstyle, a certain laugh, it was all it took to set her off again. Despite everything, she was still an emotional wreck, and she knew it. But still, how could she just *get over* the loss of her family? Of everyone she had loved?

The very worst part was that she could have been on her family's shuttle. She *should* have been on it. But instead she'd *had* to volunteer for that petty little training exercise and set back her leave by three days. Putting her career above her family for one last time. There was no one to blame for what had happened. The Coalition had followed protocols all the way to the end. The ransom money had been raised and ready for transfer. The delusional passengers who fancied themselves heroes were all dead. And so were the hijackers themselves. The only person left to blame was herself. No amount of comforting words, counseling, or therapy could rid her of the idea that she was somehow responsible. She could not shake the feeling that she might have been able to do something, had she just *been* there.

It had been that unshakeable belief that had caused her to drop out of the military. Every honor she had ever earned, every class she had ever aced, and every hour spent in the cockpit of a gunship or troop carrier just added more weight to her guilt. After spending so long building her career, there were no threads to pick up, and nothing to support her but the inheritance of her family's bank accounts. It was a fairly sizeable sum, enough to support her in comfort for quite a while. But she knew there was no comfort to be had in idleness. She knew that if she just sat in an apartment with nothing to do, she would drown in her guilt.

And so she invested the capital and started the business. She already knew how. She had watched her father do it. She threw her heart and soul into it, leaving no room for anything in her mind. Eventually, she met Grant, Ramirez and Tavia, and recognized within them what she saw in herself; refugees of their pasts, in need of an escape. She took a chance on all of them, but the investment had paid off a hundred-fold. They gave her a purpose, a home. They had saved her life.

But even with all the blessings, she still couldn't shake the guilt. She still woke up sweating in the dark. She still caught herself trying to remember what the last thing she had said to her mother was. And she was still haunted by the question; *What if I had been there?*

When that happened, she had only ever found one way of coping, to bury herself in an activity, leaving no time or capacity to think of anything else. And so, the navigation console was so often her domain. She had never been particularly good with the advanced number-crunching required, but she found the challenge was just what she needed.

Beth frowned at the long string of numbers she had traced with her stylus. Gravitational physics tended to make calculus look like arithmetic, keeping track of so many relative masses and trajectories on a single piece of digital screen. It worked fine if you knew the procedure. Trouble was, this particular sequence wasn't coming up with the answer she wanted, which meant something in the sequence was wrong. Of course, Tavia was capable of working her way through all of it in a second or two. Beth thought about it... But no, that would be cheating. Blowing out a breath, she reached for the stylus...

"Captain Hugin?"

A jolt of alarm shot up her spine, sending her surging to her feet with an emphatic expletive. The stylus flew from her fingers as she whirled around—

Only to find Evan standing in the hatchway with the light from the nav-station falling across the rather puzzled look on his face.

"Evan!" she said, relief spreading through her like ice-water. "Damn... You scared the bejeezers out of me. You move way too quietly, you know that?"

Evan sighed almost imperceptibly. "Yes, Mr. Grant already made me fully aware of that. I'm sorry for startling you. I'll try to make a bit more noise from now on."

Beth figured she shouldn't have reacted so violently. But nevertheless, she knew every sound that permeated her ship. She could read the air-currents and pinpoint problems. The fact that Evan had managed to approach her completely undetected was disturbing to her on a gut level. Still, no fault of his.

"Oh, don't bother. You can't help the way you walk. We'll just need to hang a cowbell on you somewhere." Beth tried to joke around her hammering pulse.

Evan tilted his head in the perfect canine gesture of incomprehension. "A what?"

"It's, um... It's something people on Earth used to use to keep track of an animal." Beth was not a great reader of people, and Evan was not exactly easy to read, but she knew instantly that it had been the wrong thing to say. She winced inwardly, searching for a recovery. "I'm sorry. It's not a common joke anymore. I should have known you'd never heard it. What can I do for you?"

Since he had entered the bridge, Beth had seen what she was coming to think of as his standard sanguine demeanor sagging lower and lower. Instantly, it rose back to its normal level of cheerfulness. "Oh, don't let me disturb you. Tavia and I have been running diagnostics and wandering around fixing those minor problems you were talking about. I was just coming to fix some of the loose deck-plating up here that you've been tripping over."

Glancing around him, Beth noted for the first time the small mag-skate cart he had brought from its storage in engineering, loaded with some spare plating and welding equipment. "Ah. Well... don't let me get in your way," she responded. A bit lamely, she thought. Whatever happened, she couldn't seem to find the right thing to say to him. With a mental sigh, she stepped back, allowing Evan to maneuver the skate past her and set immediately to work.

It might have been her imagination, but he seemed reluctant to meet her eyes as they passed. Understandable, she realized suddenly. The very last thing that Evan had seen her do was storm out of the rec room. If she were Evan, she probably wouldn't want to disturb her either. As his captain, however temporarily, she was supposed to be the responsible and level-headed one, no matter what the circumstances. Emotional outbursts were unprofessional and were not the kind of first impression that she wanted to create. There wasn't really any way of getting that credibility back with mere words. At times like this, she usually deemed it best to initiate what Grant liked to call a "strategic withdrawal." And so she strategically withdrew to her calculations.

It didn't take her long to discover that her plan wasn't working. About the same amount of time it took her to discover that her eyes had been roaming the same string of numbers over and over. Her thoughts kept on wandering back to the subject that had vexed her all evening: Evan. With a sigh, she gave up, swiveling the navigator's chair to face the rest of the bridge. Facing away from her, Evan appeared not to notice the motion, simply continuing about his work, obviously trying to keep the noise down to a few muted clanking sounds. Using a small hydraulic spreader, he pried up the plate of warped decking that her toes remembered very well. Careful not to look directly at the flame, Beth watched as he took a new plate from the mag-skate, set it neatly in place, and then quickly and expertly began welding it down. He was so earnest about his work, she thought, so... guileless. She was certain that no one had even asked him to begin these repairs, and yet here he was, taking the initiative to do his job quickly and well, for no reward as far as he knew. As she watched, Beth pondered why it bothered her so much having him here. With the degree of confinement aboard ship, getting to know someone new was always a bit awkward, be it a contractor or the occasional passenger, and yet it seemed ten times more difficult with Evan. And it wasn't really his remarkable appearance either; she was already getting over that particular shock. It was just one of his particular idiosyncrasies. Every member of her crew had some, but his were simply a little bit easier to spot.

Perhaps it was the fact that she hadn't actually hired him, she had *bought* him.

Just then, Evan finished with the plate. Pushing up the darkened visor, he stood, obviously pleased with himself at the neatness of his work. Finally, Beth could stand it no longer.

"Evan?" she asked tentatively. "Can I ask you a personal question?"

For several seconds, he did not react, standing as still as a statue except for the subtle movement of his pointed ears, reminding her of a dog hearing a sudden noise. His tail *flicked* once and he turned to face her, regaining his usual fluid grace. "Of course, Captain Hugin," he said. His face was smiling, but Beth thought that his eyes carried a guarded look.

Beth sighed inwardly. There was no way this conversation could continue if he kept on calling her *Captain*. "Look Evan, We discussed this earlier today." Had it only been that morning? It seemed like so long ago. "Generally, when we're not in front of clients or I'm not giving orders, I'm not the captain. When I'm not being the captain, I would like it if you would call me Beth. There's no need to treat me like some kind of grand high muckamuck. You work with me, not for me."

Almost too fast to catch, something flashed across his face, some unreadable sentiment that left a distinct frown in its wake. "I'm sorry," he said, casting his eyes down in contrition. "I'll remember from now on."

Silently, Beth raged at herself. This was *not* how she had wanted things to go. She struggled frantically for some apology of her own to try to smooth things over...

Evan beat her too it. "Anyway, personal question," he segued neatly, his casual tone returning. "Ask away... Beth."

Well, she thought. *Probably the only opening I'm going to get...*

"You don't have to answer if you don't want to. I was just wondering, what was your family like?"

"That's... an interesting question," he said, his tone the definition of neutral. "Why do you ask?"

Oh, he's good. Answering a question with a question. "Well, I did a little research on Fletcher's Wolves after we took off, but it really didn't go into what your life was like." That was a bit of an understatement. ABI's netpage had read more like a brochure: listing average IQs, life expectancies, a bunch of drivel about how effective the safeguards were, but nothing that she really wanted to know. She suddenly didn't want him standing there in the middle of the bridge anymore. It felt too much like an interrogation. "Please, sit," she said, gesturing to the copilot's chair. "You have to have been on your feet most of the day." She tried hard not to make it sound like an order, but he jumped to comply all the same, swiveling the chair to face her and sinking slowly into it

"Well, there isn't a whole lot to tell," he said. "I... didn't really have a biological family. Most of my life was spent in an ABI facility." He shrugged. "I was there to learn, not socialize."

It shouldn't really have shocked her, Beth thought. After all, he was an artificial lifeform grown in some lab. But it did all the same. "Well, what about leisure activities, then," she asked, determined to try again.

"Leisure activities?" he echoed, raising an eyebrow.

"Sure. How do you spend your free time? What do you do for fun?"

"Er... Well..." He looked down at the deck, seeming somewhat perplexed. "I read a lot of equipment manuals," he offered after a slight pause. "I experiment with theoretical systems sometimes. I learn in order to improve my skill as an engineer."

It was Beth's turn to frown. "That's very admirable, Evan," she said, deciding to press. "But not quite what I mean. What do you do with your *own* time?"

Evan's expression turned abruptly blank. This was no longer his jovial face; this was a true stone mask, as if running a bypass to deactivate his features. He looked her straight in the eye, and then shrugged stiffly. "I don't really have my own time."

For the second time that day, Beth had no idea what to say. Whatever capacity she had for formulating a response seemed shocked into silence by Evan's blunt admission. For several seconds, the only sound was the normally unobtrusive hum of the nav-screen. A cooling fan activated under one of the consoles, then stopped. The rotation of the ship gradually shrouded Evan's chair in shadow, leaving only the glint of his eyes. The eyes did not waver from hers, holding her gaze searchingly. Beth had no idea what he was looking for. Was he worried about her reaction? Did he wonder at her motivation for asking?

She never found out. Just as the silence was growing unbearable, the bridge speakers clicked on.

"Beth?" Tavia's voice shattered the tension into a thousand pieces. "Just wanted to let you know that it's past midnight. I figured you probably missed the first cycle alarm."

Beth started at the noise. "Crap, is it really that late?" She fished her datapad from her pocket, tapping the screen with her nail. Sure enough, the chronometer she kept programmed for standard earth time flicked as she watched to 0115. The optimal time for sleep was usually around 2200 hours. With a sigh, she put the device away, glancing apologetically toward Evan. He hadn't moved, the tension had definitely left his stance, his usual hint of a smile back in place. Beth wasn't sure she could see it the same way again. She doubted now that it was his true face. Still, she didn't think there was any point in pursuing conversation anymore.

"I'm sorry Evan, I've already kept you up late," she said, standing up with a stretch. "How do you like your quarters?"

He jumped up, almost as if he didn't want to be sitting while she wasn't. "They're wonderful. I'm really grateful."

She would have laughed, but the gravity of his words stopped her short. He obviously meant every word. What had his previous job been like, if he was so affected by a space of his own the size of a walk-in closet? "I'm glad," she answered, matching the smile.

"Now you head to bed. Just leave the skate here; you can finish in the morning."

Although clearly unhappy with leaving a job unfinished, he nodded, removing the welding visor and setting it on the skate. "I just want to say," he said, straightening up. "I appreciate what you're trying to do, Capt— Beth, but you don't need to worry about me."

Beth blinked. "I know," she replied, unsure of anything else to say. "Now you get some sleep. That's an order."

He did smile at that. *Really* smile. "Yes Captain," he said with a mock salute, then turned and glided back through the hatchway, vanishing into the darkened rec room without asking Tavia for the lights. He could probably see just fine without them, Beth realized.

She was left alone.

Allowing herself to sink slowly back into the navigator's chair, she finally permitting all of her emotions to show on her face as she gazed hard at the deck without really seeing it. Shock, confusion, and disbelief all vied for position, as well as…anger.

Why would she be angry? What about the brief conversation with her newly-hired engineer had riled her so much? As far as she could tell, it wasn't anything that he was *doing*. He was intelligent, polite, and had one of the best work ethics she had seen in a long time.

She *liked* him. So why did all of her interactions with him feel like a tap dance on eggshells?

After a few more heartbeats, she gave up. *You're too tired to think right now.*

She glanced at all of her painstaking calculations on the nav-table. "Tavia, you think you can work through all this for me?"

"Already done," Tavia replied instantly, sounding rather pleased with herself. "Just waiting for you to say the word."

Despite her heavy mood, Beth cracked a weary smile. "Always happy to help..."

She stood with a stretch and a yawn, taking one last sweeping glance over the bridge to make sure everything was in order. Except for the nav-screen, the displays were dark. The scanners were clear, and Tavia was perfectly capable of handling the ship by herself. In short, everything on the ship was very much tied down and organized. Unlike the mental state of its captain.

Well, we'll work on that, Beth promised herself. *Tomorrow.*

With that, she turned and left the bridge, doing her best to think of nothing besides a soft bunk and the peaceful oblivion of sleep.

If only sleep were peaceful.

6

Ramirez stood in the shadows of the corridor, waiting. It had been a long time, but any child of the Apollo streets knew how to blend with the darkness. At least, any of them that lived. Unseen in the gloom of the hallway, he felt a frown creep over his face. He hadn't thought about Apollo for a long time.

Precious little reason to, he thought to himself, silently adjusting his position against the wall. Still, waiting in ambush with the familiar weight of his switchblade stowed in his sleeve, there was little else for him to think of. This time though, he wasn't waiting for a stray drug-runner or a lone Coalition policeman. He was waiting for the Fletcher's Wolf.

He saw him long before he heard him. At the end of the corridor, Ramirez was just able to make out a dark form as it dropped silently from the ladder and began to make its way down the passageway toward him, gliding like a ghost in the dim illumination of the glowstrips embedded in the deck. For the first time, Ramirez felt a pang of doubt. Was he overreacting? Should he really be doing this? Beth and Grant surely wouldn't think so if they ever found out. But then, that was the point, wasn't it? They were being far too cavalier about this whole thing. Too trusting. Grant especially, blabbing all of Beth's secrets to a complete stranger. Neither of them would take it on themselves to question the trustworthiness of this new engineer.

Which means, he decided firmly, *that it's up to me.*

Evan was about halfway down the hallway now. Ramirez' indecision had cost him precious time. Gathering himself, he reached carefully into his jacket pocket, tapping a button on his 'pad. A wireless signal left the device, to be detected by the receiver he had secured to the back of the casing for the camera that Tavia used to monitor the hallway. That, in turn, began to broadcast a field of low-level interference that would render this region of Tavia's perception blind and deaf for the next few minutes. She would find it unusual, but it was not so serious a glitch for her to start raising any immediate alarms, especially if it was gone by the end of the cycle.

Don't worry Tavia; this won't take long... he thought sardonically to himself, removing his hand from his pocket.

The approaching figure froze instantly, a startled predator looking for the source of the danger. Ramirez had seen it before many times in the Apollo underworld. Evan knew he was here.

"Mr. Ramirez," the figure said quietly, confirming his observation. "You're up rather late." His tone, Ramirez noted, was carefully neutral, carrying no trace of surprise or suspicion that should have been there. Either he was stupid enough not to realize what was going on, or he was even better at hiding his feelings than Ramirez thought. In the end though, it hardly mattered.

"So are you," he responded, detaching himself casually from the bulkhead. "Out hunting?"

"Something like that," Evan answered without missing a beat. "Troubleshooting some small problems."

"So late?"

"I'm used to long hours."

"I would bet."

Ramirez eased closer. As he did, Evan gave a small sigh.

"Look, I can see that this is leading somewhere," he said, managing to maintain his polite tone with only the slightest dip in its intensity. "Was there something you needed to say to me?"

Ok, Ramirez thought. *Not stupid.* That however only served to deepen his suspicion. From the moment he had first seen Evan stalking up the ramp, he had thought there was something that wasn't quite right about the whole thing, something hiding beneath the gentle and servile exterior. Unlike Beth, he hadn't known anything about Fletcher's Wolves beforehand. But every piece of knowledge only added more weight to his instincts telling him to *distrust.*

They were instincts he was perfectly inclined to obey.

"You are right," he answered, coming to a stop a calculated meter away, close enough to look the wolf straight in the eye, but far enough to stay out of arm's reach. "I wanted to offer you a word of advice. You had better be very, *very* careful."

Evan's ears gave a single twitch, the only indication of his thoughts. "I'm sorry Mr. Ramirez, but I don't think I know what you mean."

"I will spell it out for you, then. You had better keep your distance from Grant and the captain. *Especially* the captain. Does that clear it up?"

Finally, a frown managed to push itself onto Evan's lupine face, the perfect picture of canine bewilderment. "I'm… No, I'm afraid it doesn't. I think I can understand your reasons, but I promise that there is *no* cause for concern. Mr. Grant and Captain Hugin are in no danger from me." He paused, moving his furred hands a few inches away from his sides in a sort of halfway gesture of surrender. "And neither are you."

There was something about Evan's tone and posture that sent a cold spike of anger through Ramirez's gut. How dare this *thing*, coming in here thinking it could force its way into *his* family, and then come down here and patronize him. Before he knew what he was doing, he had crossed the space between them, taken hold of Evan's shirt and pushed the wolf bodily against the bulkhead.

"Now you listen here," he hissed through his teeth, staring hard into Evan's now wide eyes. "Charlie may trust you, but I do *not*. I come from a different background than he and the captain, and, unlike them, I do not blindly trust everyone I meet. I am not going to give you the benefit of the doubt, I am not going to pretend you are a person and I am not going to take my eyes off of you for a second. So know this; if you ever do *anything* to hurt my friends, I *swear* that I will cut your throat."

For several seconds, the only sound Ramirez could hear was his own elevated breathing. Evan just stared, not moving a single muscle. Ramirez almost wished that he would try something, just to give him the excuse.

He really isn't stupid, Ramirez thought despite his rage. *He knows how this game is played. He'd better.*

And if Evan was smart, he would know that Ramirez meant every word.

Just then, he heard a muted slur of cloth on metal from the hatch. After spending so long aboard ship, Ramirez knew instantly that it was Beth, descending from the bridge with her customary, well-practiced slide down the outside edges of the ladder. She would be down here in about ten seconds. And he also had known her long enough to picture *exactly* how she would react to what he was doing now.

Clenching his teeth, he turned back to Evan, pressing him a little harder against the bulkhead just for good measure. "You just remember what I said. I will be watching you."

With that, he let go of Evan's fatigues and turned away, slapping the door controls for his cabin. The hatch slid open with a hiss. Glancing one last time at Evan, Ramirez slipped inside.

The door slid silently to behind him, leaving him alone in the darkness.

Ramirez slumped against the door, feeling the cool smoothness of the metal against the back of his head as he struggled to collect his thoughts. After a few heartbeats, his pocket gave a soft chirp. Blowing out a breath, he withdrew his 'pad, his eyes brushing over the flashing alert on the screen. This was another program he had set up. He had installed another sensor in the doorframe of Evan's cabin, programming it to alert his 'pad whenever the hatch opened or closed. That genetic freak wouldn't be getting up for any reason without having to deal with *him* first. Satisfied, he pocketed the 'pad, clearing the screen. As he did, he noticed that his hands were shaking slightly. He frowned.

Has it really been that long? he wondered, holding the offending digits before his eyes. *I must be getting soft.* He couldn't afford that, not now, not ever. Someone had to be the pragmatist onboard the shuttle.

Just then, his ears caught the soft *whoosh* of another cabin door opening, this one further down the corridor. Normally, the airtight seal would prevent him hearing anything, but one of the first things he had done upon taking up residence was to install a tiny microphone outside, feeding wirelessly into the bulkhead speakers that Tavia normally used. The definition wasn't great, but it was enough to make him feel a little safer. And enough for him to know that it had been Beth's cabin. Ramirez hoped desperately that her nightmares would not visit her tonight. She never talked about them, but he could recognize those who had them. Unfortunately, there was nothing he could do for her. Now the only thing he could do was protect her rest. Grant too. In a few moments, he would collect his gadgets that he had used on the camera, and then he would settle down to sleep as he always had—lightly, with one eye open.

* * *

Beth awoke with a gasp, surging into a sitting position. Her heart hammering in her chest, she grabbed frantically at the blankets entangling her legs, trying to free herself... And then the realization set in, as it always did. She was still in her cabin aboard the *Memory*.

It was only another nightmare.

She collapsed back onto the mattress as the adrenaline fled her system, a long, shuddering breath escaping her lips.

For several moments, she simply lay there, staring up at the ceiling as she fought to bring her pulse and breathing under control. She was quite familiar with the routine by now. The nightmares had started for her during the inquest investigating the cause of the crash that had killed her family. It wasn't always the same dream, but it was always terrifying enough to wake her up shivering in the dark. And then sometimes, they would leave her alone for weeks at a time, just long enough for her to think that maybe, just maybe, she was free of them, only for them to return with a vengeance.

Finally, her heart rate declined enough for her to start breathing evenly again. Kicking the blanket aside, she levered herself into a sitting position, setting her bare feet on the cold metal deck. Shaking away the cobwebs around her brain, she snapped her fingers toward the corner of the ceiling. The small sensor assembly mounted there recognized the motion and triggered her preprogrammed response, turning on the overhead light at half strength. Like most nights, she almost wished she hadn't. The compact terminals installed in all of the cabins had the unique function of converting their monitors into mirrors when they were not in use, thus saving space. With the cramped living arrangements that a strictly working-class vessel like the *Memory* provided, there was no way for Beth to avoid looking at herself. She barely recognized the face staring dully back at her. Her mental image of herself did not include the wrinkles around her mouth, and the pronounced crow's feet and the deep, dark circles around her eyes. Her hair too looked like it had lost a fight with some stray voltage, lancing out in a dozen directions. In short, as Grant would fondly say, she looked "skodgy."

Apt, she said silently to the woman in the mirror. *Because that's how I feel.*

At times like these, there was only one thing to do. Early on, Grant had prescribed a sedative for her that would knock her out as surely as a street-brawler's punch, complete with the grogginess and headache in the morning. But at the moment, it sounded better than the alternative. Her knees creaking in the relative silence, she stood up, turning toward the hatch.

Without warning, the overhead glowpanel turned up to full strength, flooding the cabin with light. Beth screwed her eyes shut, steadying herself against the hatch frame as a dozen fuzzy images danced behind her eyelids.

"Tavia..." she grated through clenched teeth. "This had better be good..."

"Sorry Captain," said Tavia, her tone breathlessly cheery, sounding almost as if she had returned from a brisk jog, "but I figured this was important. We dropped into sublight at New Bielka Waystation a few minutes ago, and I had planned on waking you in a few hours when we reached optimum position for the Slingshot. However, there is a small craft that appears to have adopted an intercept course with us. They don't seem to have a transponder code, and they haven't responded to my hails. They're about a hundred kilometers behind us now..." She trailed off for a moment. "Oh, look at that. They have a weapon lock on us."

For precisely two seconds, Beth stood frozen, waiting for her brain to catch up with what Tavia had said. For the first of those two seconds, Beth thought that it might be a joke. In the second, she decided that, while Tavia was something of a prankster, she would never pull something like this, especially in the middle of the night. That, coupled with the knowledge that they were passing through the exact sort of isolated space that hijackers or pirates loved to frequent finally convinced her that Tavia was in earnest, and they were, in fact, about to be in serious trouble. Her energy buoyed up on a renewed wave of adrenaline, Beth pounded the hatch control, stopping only to snatch her jacket from the back of the chair before dashing down the corridor. "Tavia, get Grant and Ramirez up!" she yelled as she went, her bare feet skidding to a stop at the foot of the ladder. "I authorize the use of strong language!"

A minute later, she found herself slowing to a halt in the cockpit, wearing her jacket, with no memory whatsoever of how she or the garment had gotten there. Her only thought was to the controls as she slid into the pilot's chair, increasing thrust from the VASIMR engines and changing the shuttle's flight path. Her fingers itched for all the modern amenities she had learned to use in her military days. Chaff launchers, microwave scramblers... *Heck, I'll take someone standing out on the hull throwing spare parts.*

"Bloody hell, Beth," came Grant's sleepy voice from over her shoulder. "What in the name of Mike is going on?"

"We're being followed," she said shortly, not lifting her eyes from the readouts. "Unidentified ship on our six with a sensor lock."

She could distinctly hear the sound of Grant's sharply intaken breath. "Ah. I see."

"Captain, I have the scan of the ship," Tavia cut in. As she did, the display above the viewport sprang to life with a wireframe image of their attacker. By its flattened, wafer-like shape, Beth was almost reminded of a winged datapad. A humorous allusion, if not for the weapon blisters clearing visible on either side of the hull, complete with the honeycomb lattice of fully loaded missile bays.

"That's an *Achilles* class light attack vessel," she said, her tone subdued. "A favorite of private security companies. And pirates."

Behind her, Grant swore quietly. "I suppose outrunning him isn't an option?"

"In this tub? Not a chance."

Just then, there was a muted *clunk* from the hull aft of them, and abruptly every display on the bridge began to flicker and dance with static.

"Captain!" Tavia called, her tone almost frantic. "Some kind of device on the hull! They're hijacking the controls—" The speakers gave a short crackling sound, and then she was gone.

"Tavia!" Grant yelled. "What the hell is going on?"

"Magnetic hacking device," Beth answered, her stomach dropping into her toes. "We're being hijacked."

"Wonderful," said Grant, after a short, dense silence. "Options?"

Clenching her teeth, Beth tried to thrust left. Nothing happened. Even as she tried again, she could hear the blow-torch *huff* sound of the thrusters doing the exact opposite of her intent, bringing the shuttle to a stop. "They've hacked most of our systems. Tavia can override it eventually, but it will take time. Way too much time." She stood up, turning to face her friend. "The good news is, they could have just punched a few holes in our hull and then looted the wreckage later, so they obviously don't want to destroy us..."

"The bad news," Grant picked up smoothly, the realization dawning visibly on his face. "Is that they intend to board us. And with our systems hacked, there's nothing to stop them."

Beth nodded gravely. "Charlie," she said, surprised at her own calmness as she uttered a command that had been rarely in use for the past six centuries. "Prepare to repel boarders."

7

How long do I have now? Grant wondered as he sprinted down the corridor. The unidentified ship was only minutes away from docking and if its intentions were peaceful, then it was doing a *very* bad job of communicating them. Sliding down the ladder, Grant winced as he landed hard on his still-sore ankle. He'd see to that later. In the meantime, there were more pressing matters at hand. Like not dying. That was pretty high up on his to-do list.

Okay, he thought, trying to get a handle on his breathing, *weapons. Right. Better safe than sorry.*

He glanced over his shoulder as Ramirez skidded to a halt behind him.

"What is going on?" the procurement officer gasped out, leaning up against the bulkhead. "Tavia is cursing my ear off at three in the morning, and then Beth tells us to tool up?"

"The other ship has a bloody grapple on our dorsal hatch." Grant pushed the button to open the armory door repeatedly. Their previous argument was, for the moment, forgotten. "It's only a matter of time before they're inside."

Ramirez cursed. "Well, diplomacy was never my strong suit. Better give me a gun."

Kneeling down in front of the gun cabinet, Grant ran his eyes over the small arsenal, calculating how much ammunition they had between them. He quickly realized that it was a pointless exercise. Grabbing Beth's LK-2 and four extra magazines, he stuck them in his pockets. He hoped it was enough ammunition. In one familiar motion, he slid his well-worn underarm holster off its peg and strapped it on, sliding the comfortable weight of his own pistol into the oiled leather sheath. The Maxwell-50 was a truly intimidating gun. Not very easy to conceal, maybe, but it certainly packed quite a punch. Just to be safe, he grabbed two extra mags in addition to the backup attached to his holster.

Ramirez coughed impatiently. Grant pulled his shotgun out from the cabinet and tossed it to him, waiting for him to snatch it deftly out of the air before handing him a handful of shells.

"Are you preparing for a siege or something?"

"No idea how long we'll be stuck in the bridge," Grant growled, pocketing the much more manageable Hughes Personal Defense handgun. It paid to have a backup. "And if they access through the dorsal hatch, which is where they're lined up, we won't be able to get back down here. Better safe than sorry."

Ramirez conjured his switchblade out of nowhere. "Knives do not run out of bullets." He stated laconically, spinning it between his fingers.

"Knives," Grant replied, wracking his brain to see if he had missed anything, "cannot kill someone from a hundred meters."

The switchblade disappeared back into Ramirez's sleeve.

Deciding that he had retrieved everything important, Grant dashed back out of the armory and had his boot on the lowest ladder rung when a voice stopped him.

"Mr. Grant!" A rather groggy and irritable-looking Phillips was standing in the corridor, still dressed in his now very-wrinkled suit. Despite his tired countenance, he still managed to make the word "mister" sound a lot like "boy." "What on earth is going on? I'm trying to type up a paper and the noise you are making is very distracting."

"Emergency, sir." Grant ground out, struggling to keep a reign on his tongue. *Just like your days as a security advisor. Treat him like a client.* "There is an unidentified ship that is about to board us very shortly. There's a very good chance it could turn ugly, so it would probably be best if you came up to the bridge with us."

"Thank you for letting me know, Mr. Grant; but I'm afraid that if they mean us harm, I will have just as much of a chance in my cabin. One locked door is as good as another."

Stubborn little know-it-all. "True, but if there is a chance we can fight them off, four would be better than three." He pulled out the Hughes pistol and offered it to Phillips. "I don't have time to argue, so this is the last time I'll ask you: coming, or not?"

Phillips stood up a little taller. "I'm sorry to say that I can't do that, Mr. Grant. In addition to the reasons I've just stated, I have been entrusted with a matter of utmost importance and must see to the safety of my company's property."

Grant noticed the black case that he had been so protective of earlier lying on his bunk. "Alright, it's your funeral. Take this, at least," he said, slapping the small pistol into Phillip's hand.

"I will have you know that this is highly upsetting and it will mean a reduction of your commission."

"Oh, shove it up your—"

"Charlie, I need you on the bridge. Now," Beth's voice interrupted over the intercom.

With one last annoyed glance at Phillips, Grant turned and sprinted after Ramirez. Taking the ladder three rungs at a time, he jumped out of the hatch and closed it securely behind him. He would be able to cover it from the bridge, but if one precaution was good, two was better. Looking around in frustration, he wished that some of the shuttle's tables were not bolted down. It was nice not to have to secure them when they exited and entered a planet's atmosphere, but now they couldn't be used as cover.

Checking that the strap on his holster was released, he ran through the door into the bridge and stopped to catch his breath. Beth was stooped over a monitor, eyes glued to the screen. Tavia must have activated the hall cams before she went offline. *She's actually pretty handy in a pinch,* Grant admitted to himself, studying the static image on the screen. It was currently showing the area just below the dorsal docking hatch. Just as he was about to ask how soon the other ship would be able to dock, a loud, metallic *clang* reverberated through the ship. Immediately after, there was a thud and the hatch swung down, locking out of the way of the black-garbed figures swarming down the ladder. Grant counted a total of ten figures in police-issue riot helmets and standard black body armor in the enclosed space. Beth pressed a button to the side of the monitor and loud voices immediately flooded the cockpit.

"—clear!"

"Forward corridor, clear!"

"Copy. Team One, move up and secure that hatchway! We don't want to use any more ordnance than we have to." Four men broke away from the group and ran off out of the camera's field of view.

"Bohlman, Lonsway!" The man who had been giving orders motioned to two others. "Get below and secure the cabins!"

"Sir!" The men moved off toward the cargo bay ladder.

"Clark, take out their eyes and ears."

Another man jogged out of the screen and a second later, the image crashed into static.

There was silence on the bridge.

After a few seconds, Grant swallowed and turned off the monitor. "Well, I think I can say with confidence that we are royally screwed."

Beth nodded wordlessly.

"What guns are those?" Ramirez asked, looking pale. "MPLs? I thought those were illegal?"

"So is piracy."

Beth took her pistol from Grant with a tight smile. "What do you think our odds are, Mr. Grant?"

Grant adopted a pensive look. "Hmm, well, under the current circumstances I would say... slim to none. These guys seem like pros. Military-style training, at the very least. Our best hope is to hold out long enough for power to come back so we can send a distress signal. Or just kill them all."

Ramirez racked his shotgun eloquently.

Taking a deep breath, Grant positioned himself on the left side of the door and drew his Maxwell. *Well, I won't say "it's a good day to die," but I won't kid myself either. Not a good situation.* He looked across the door at Beth and gave her a thumbs-up. *I promised myself that I wouldn't let anything happen to you, Beth. If nothing else, I consider myself a man of my word.*

He listened to the sounds of heavy boots on the deck approaching. Making eye contact with the two other members of his crew, he nodded and held up his hand, counting down on his fingers.

Three.
Two.
One.
Here goes nothing.

Spinning around the doorframe, he took in the situation at a glance: two men were caught in the open, halfway across the cafeteria, and two others had taken up positions behind benches at the far end of the room. Putting the front post of his pistol dead-center of the lead man's chest, Grant pulled the trigger once, twice, three times. The heavy kick of the Maxwell was an old friend. Everything fell into a rhythm as he alternately ducked behind the bulkhead to avoid the deadly automatic fire or leaned out to take shots at the intruders. The irregular chatter of the submachine guns was interrupted by Ramirez's MOSS shotgun and the slightly higher pitched bark of Beth and Grant's pistols.

Skillfully swapping out an empty clip for a full one, Grant waited for the storm of lead to abate, then stepped around the corner and squeezed the trigger, fighting the climb of the gun and watching a man jackknife over a booth. Pausing for a second, he tried to count how many opponents were left standing. *Five? Seven?* He couldn't tell. Plus the two that were checking the cabins. They would certainly *upset* the good doctor. *Arrogant blockhead.* He was going to get himself killed because of his own idiotic pride. *Maybe he can* lecture *those two mooks to death.* Grant thought, putting a shot into one of the benches an inch or so below one of the armed men.

The thunderclap of Ramirez's shotgun had fallen silent now, and Grant checked to make sure he was alright. The procurement officer was taking cover behind the navigator's chair and shoving shells into the breech of his shotgun, cursing steadily. Nothing wrong there.

Suddenly, a cry of pain brought Grant's heart into his mouth. He looked back to see Beth, biting her lip and crouching behind the door. A gash torn in the arm of her jacket was oozing blood. She motioned for him to stay back, but Grant paid no attention to her.

Firing blindly, he dove across the doorway, landing awkwardly on Beth's side of the bridge as a burst of machine gun fire cut through the air where he had been.

"It's not bad," she said, removing her hand from her bicep. "Just caught me by surprise, that's all."

Grant inspected the wound, gently pulling the fabric away. It wasn't deep; just a long, bloody channel cut into the flesh.

Painful, but not life threatening. *Way too close, though.* Tearing a strip of fabric from his shirt, he bound it around Beth's arm, trying to ignore her sharp intake of breath.

"Keep your head down and don't take any stupid risks, okay? If we can hold them off long enough…" He trailed off. "Just don't get yourself killed."

* * *

Crack! Crack! Crack!
Opening an eye, Evan pricked up his ears, trying to identify the sound that had woken him. He had only been onboard half a day but he knew what he had heard wasn't normal. Anything that loud would be situated well away from the sleeping quarters. Human ears were less sensitive than his, but they weren't *that* bad. Curled up on his bunk, he laid completely still, waiting for the strange sound to repeat itself.

Thirty seconds passed, then a minute. Nothing.

But despite the apparent calm, he couldn't help feeling that something wasn't right. The rooms were fairly well soundproofed—the regulation vacuum seals on the door would ensure that much— nevertheless, the silence outside wasn't quite *silent.* The shuttle itself had a constant level of ambient noise that was caused by the various systems it contained, and those noises were present, but there were also a few almost inaudible sounds that were definitely not made by the ship. Evan listened harder, straining to recognize the foreign sounds.

Footsteps. There was someone in the corridor. It wasn't a crew member, he knew that much. The stride was too long for Ramirez or Captain Hugin, and Grant had a limp. Customs? No. The shuttle was still a good ways from Earth and he would have been called to strap in had they needed to turn around and land on Hephaestus again. Evan's brain processed these facts and came to the conclusion that this was *bad*, confirming what his instincts had been telling him since he woke up.

Rolling off his bunk, he landed noiselessly on the deck and inched toward the door, sniffing experimentally to discern the identity of the person in the corridor. He couldn't smell anything. The vacuum seal on the door was doing its job perfectly by keeping an airtight seal in case of a hull breach, but that wasn't Evan's biggest concern at the moment.

"Tavia?" he whispered, wondering if the AI had an audio link with the cabins.

"Tavia, can you hear me?" The wall-mounted speaker remained stubbornly silent.

Okay, this could mean that she doesn't have a link to the cabins, which is bad, or that she can't respond for some reason, which is a whole lot worse. He was standing halfway between the bunk and the door, trying to decide on a course of action, when there was a muffled *bang* and the door slid open.

Two men in black body armor and riot helmets stood in the doorway, with very large, very black pistols filling their hands.

Evan froze. For an instant, he was back in the Compound, on his way to be punished for another low test score or bad time on a training run. *No, that was years ago.* With an effort, he brought himself back to the present. *You're not at the 'Pound, and you haven't done anything wrong. They're not here for you. Just cooperate and you'll be fine.*

The men in the corridor looked stunned for a few seconds, then the shorter one on the left swore loudly and dropped a black case—Phillips' case—to train his pistol on Evan's chest, knuckles white on the grip.

"Ease up, Lonsway," the tall gunman said, an amused smile spreading across the visible portion of his face. "This here's one of Fletcher's clockwork dogs. It's got *safeguards*, so it can't hurt real people. Including you."

His aim dropped until his pistol pointed at the deck.

The first man relaxed slightly, but kept his gun aimed at Evan. "I know that, idiot, but what the hell is it doing onboard this shuttle? The intel pukes said—"

"Guess they were wrong. Either way, orders are clear. No witnesses."

Evan's stomach dropped. Not police, then. And cooperating wouldn't help in the slightest. He knew what *no witnesses* would translate to in a few seconds. A few pulls of the trigger and one more property loss report to fill out at ABI.

"Safeguards," the short man said slowly. "Weird."

"Yeah, these guys always give me the creeps. Hurry it up."

"Fine." The shorter man lined up his sidearm between Evan's eyes. "Let's find out how many bullets it takes to stop this clock..."

Evan stared down the long, dark barrel of the pistol, mesmerized. He wanted to fight back, to stop the men from killing him, but he couldn't. In a detached sort of way, he knew he should be frightened, but he only felt a dull sense of resignation. As he struggled against the safeguard induced stupor, memories of his pack-mates came unbidden to his mind. Being ordered not to help when Inky collapsed under the weight strapped to his back during a training run. Poor Mel locked in the cold room until she lost consciousness. Jesse—kind, brave Jesse—disappearing after failing too many psychiatric evaluations. They had been treated like animals with no voice their whole lives. *He* had been treated like that.

And I will not *die like that.*

Time seemed to slow down as the man lazily pulled the trigger: Evan could hear gears inside the body of the weapon clicking and knew he had only a split second before it fired.

Abandoning conscious thought, he fell back on instinct, lunging forward and seizing the man's forearm bracer between his teeth—

CRACK!

The gunshot was deafeningly loud. Ignoring the ringing in his ears, Evan grabbed the gunman's upper arm with his hands, braced his legs, and swung the man into the side of the bunk. The man's head jerked at an unnatural angle as his neck struck the metal edge. There was a wet-sounding *snap,* and he crumpled to the deck like a marionette with its strings cut, his pistol clattering from a nerveless hand.

CRACK!

Evan stumbled. His leg felt like someone had kicked him with a steel-toed boot. A quick glance was enough to show him the ragged hole in the thigh of his fatigues, its edges already stained with blood. Ears pinned flat to his skull, he spun around and focused on the second shooter. The man was standing just to the left of the doorway, trying to line up a second shot at Evan's head. Fueled by adrenaline, Evan dropped to all fours just as the man fired again.

CRACK!

There was a metallic *clang* as the bullet embedded itself in the storage locker behind him. Evan surged across the small space of the cabin at the tall gunman as he frantically tried to draw a bead on the leaping wolf. Too slow. Evan collided forcefully with the man, bared teeth scraping against the helmet's face-shield, bearing them both to the floor.

CRACK!

Pain. That was the first thing he felt. He coughed. No, it wasn't going to end like this. He wasn't going to die. Summoning his last reserves of strength, he grabbed the man's wrist and slammed it against the wall, prying the pistol from his weakened grip. Aiming the gun at the center of the man's helmet, he tried to say something, but coughed again. Out of the corner of his eye, he saw a glint and his subconscious said: *Metal. Weapon. Knife.* He reacted without hesitation.

CRACK!

The pain was going away now. He could barely feel his leg and he was tired.

I am not… going… to…

Everything faded to black.

8

"Boss!" It was Ramirez. "Boss, they are falling back!"

Incredulous, Grant risked a quick look through the bridge door and was amazed to see that Ramirez was right: the intruders were hastily withdrawing from the cafeteria. Quickly bringing his pistol up, Grant squeezed off shot after shot at the retreating figures. The last man stumbled after being hit in the back, but didn't go down, shutting the door behind him. Barring the dead man Grant had hit with his first salvo and another body slumped across a table, the cafeteria was deserted. There was no sign of any living opponent.

Slowly, he walked into the empty room, keeping his gun trained on the closed door. "Beth?" he called out. "Do we have electronics back yet?"

"Systems coming back online now. Tavia's still out, though."

"Do we have video feeds yet?" Grant asked, kneeling behind a pock-marked bench.

"Yeah, I'm bringing up the feed of the dorsal hatch." She paused. "That's odd…"

"What?"

"They're actually pulling out. Everybody's heading back up the ladder." Grant heard a dull clang as the top hatch slammed to. A moment later, it was clear that the attacking vessel had disengaged from the *Memory.*

What is going on? If they are *pirates, then they should have already blown a hole in our bridge and sucked all our oxygen out. The only reason they wouldn't do that is if they wanted something important.*

Or had personnel still on board.

"Sod!" He had completely forgotten about the two sent down to the cabins. "Beth! Problem! Still got a pair of heavies down with Phillips!"

Beth cursed, running out of the bridge. "Ramirez, Charlie, *move it!* Phillips isn't the only one down there!"

"What? He—" Grant broke off midsentence.

Evan.

He cursed, vaulting the bench and making a mad dash for the ladder. How had he forgotten? Sure, he had only been part of the crew for a day, but Charles Grant did not make mistakes like that. The golden commandment of his army days came back to him, accusing him. *So much for "Never leave a man behind." Bloody great job, Charlie. The first hint of danger and you bleeding well* forget *about your newest crew member.* He spun the wheel on the hatch savagely. *You even gave Twitchy a gun a few doors down from him. Sodding idiot!* Wincing as bolts of pain shot through his ankle, he slid down the ladder to the middle deck, Beth and Ramirez right behind him. Trying to tune out his own self-recrimination, Grant examined the corridor.

It was deserted, but Grant could smell the sharp odor of discharged weapons. All the doors on the starboard side had been opened; probably by a small blasting charge or handheld ram he guessed, due to the small dents near the handles. Pointing Ramirez and Beth toward the two aft cabins, he took a deep breath and took up position by the door of cabin four.

Pivoting around the corner of the doorframe, Grant swept his gun across the interior, ready to put a bullet into anything dressed in black. It took him a few seconds to notice the figure in the crumpled suit leaning forlornly against the desk. It was Phillips. Keeping his gun in his hand, Grant inspected the doctor, noting the three tightly-grouped shots in the left side of his rumpled suit jacket. *Neat, no frills, professional. Just like I thought.* He groaned when he noticed that the pistol in Phillips hand still had the safety catch in the "on" position. *You never had a chance, Twitchy. Too bad you didn't take me up on my offer.*

Standing to his feet, he pocketed the unfired handgun and took one last look around the room. "Beth, Phillips is dead. Three in the chest. What's the situation in the other cabins?" He waited for a moment, then stepped back out into the corridor. "Beth?"

He walked quickly past cabin five, hearing Ramirez fall in behind him. "Beth what's going…" He trailed off.

Beth was standing at the door to cabin six, her hand over her mouth. Grant looked over her shoulder and felt his stomach drop.

"Bloody hell," he muttered.

It was a particularly apt phrase. The scene in the cabin was one that could have happened in a multitude of situations back in Grant's military or security days, the only difference was: it wasn't. It was here. Now. Onboard *his* ship. With one of *his* crewmates. He stepped past Beth into the charnel house that was cabin six.

The two missing boarders were present and accounted for. One was lying next to the wall-mounted bunk, eyes wide open and staring, his neck clearly snapped. The other slumped next to the door with a blackened hole in the center of his helmet, its contorted edges giving mute testimony as to the destructive power of a close range pistol shot.

And lying face down next to the second boarder: the grey-furred body of the shuttle's engineer.

Grant knelt down next to Evan's inanimate figure and rolled him over, paling as he saw the ragged hole in the chest of his bloodstained fatigues. For a few seconds, he thought about feeling for a pulse, but then realized that he didn't know where to find one on a Fletcher's Wolf and just held Evan's muzzle to his ear.

"Is he..." Beth lapsed into silence as he held up a hand.

Listening intently, Grant counted to ten, then shook his head. "I'm sorry, Beth. I can't—"

Without warning, Evan's eyelids flickered and he coughed, sending a fine spray of blood onto the security officer's startled face.

Grant cursed, cradling Evan's head in his lap. "Beth, Ramirez, I need my tools and as many bandages as are in the medical cabinet! *Now!*" Beth hesitated for a moment, then spun around and took off down the hallway. Bending down, Grant inspected the rent in Evan's pantleg. *Not good. If that's nicked the femoral artery then he's already dead. Nothing you can do about that, Charlie. Focus on stopping the bleeding.* "Oi, lad, that's going to leave a mark. Can you hear me? Come on, I need to keep you talking."

Evan coughed again and said something that sounded like *cold*.

"Alright. You're alright. You're safe now." Grant looked up as Beth arrived with his medical kit.

"What can I do to help?"

Grabbing a roll of bandages, Grant began wrapping Evan's leg. "He's gone into hypovolemic shock from losing so much blood and I'm not sure the blood or plasma supplies we have onboard will be compatible with his. I'm not going to risk a hemolytic reaction, so about the only thing we can do right now is pump him full of saline." He tossed her a plastic pouch of clear liquid. "Get an IV into his arm. I'm going to try to stop this bleeding."

Ramirez grabbed the bandage from him. "I may not be a doctor, but I am pretty sure that that hole in his chest is a problem, Charlie. I can see to this."

Grant nodded his thanks, then began a hasty field analysis of Evan's chest wound. It was not really necessary, however. He knew the injury that was making the canine engineer cough up blood. *Punctured lung. Through-and-*

through. Damn, I wish I had a fully equipped medical facility to deal with this. Even as a combat medic I had compatible blood replacements. He pulled out a single-use painkiller and stuck it in the crook of Evan's arm. *Keep breathing, lad. We're going to fix you up, just stay with us.*

With precision born of long practice in his army medical station, Grant cut away the fabric around the wound and peeled the soaked patch off. Taking a canister of tissue-regenerative sealant out of his case, he set to work repairing the holes that the intruder's pistol had torn in Evan's lung. Fortunately it had been a small-caliber affair and hadn't keyholed, or the wolf would have bled out or died from shock long before help could have arrived.

There. Grant finished his application of the medical sealant, waiting a few seconds for it to adhere. *What did the manual say about lung punctures again? Regain negative pressure in the chest cavity, right. Reinflate the lung.*

The human body was a complicated and delicate machine, Grant knew, and he was basing his ministrations off of the assumption that Fletcher's Wolves were close enough anatomically that he wouldn't make any serious mistakes. Working quickly, he attached a one-way valve to a large-bore needle and carefully inserted it between the third and fourth rib. There was a rush of escaping air and Evan gasped, drawing in a long breath as the pressure from the trapped air decreased. He coughed up some more blood, but almost instantly began breathing more regularly.

Grant felt a wave of relief wash through his body. *So long as that sealant holds, we just need to worry about the bleeding now.*

"Ramirez," he said curtly. "Run and get the stretcher from the med ward."

Taking another roll of bandages out of the kit, he put sterile gauze pads over the entry and exit wounds and began wrapping them tightly. Because of Evan's thick fur, the self-adhering disinfectant bandages would not seal properly. He would redress it later, but right then, he was only focused on stopping the bleeding.

A moment later, it was done. Grant scooted back on aching knees, surveying his handiwork. It wasn't a pretty job, he had to admit. But the unruly mass of gauze wrapping did its job, holding steady pressure against the wound. At last, Grant allowed himself a long sigh.

"Charlie?" The strain in Beth's voice was not hard to detect. "Will he make it?"

"He's stable," he answered, standing up with a grimace as his muscles protested. "No immediate danger. Long term... I don't know. He needs to see a vet who knows canine physiology when we get to earth. Ramirez, help me move him."

Before Ramirez could move, Beth stepped around him and positioned herself by Evan's legs. "I've got it. How do you want to do this, Charlie?"

Grant opened his mouth to protest, but one look into her eyes killed the words on his lips. He knew her well enough to know that she needed to do this.

"Right," he said instead, "just...put your arms under his legs, try to keep him level, and keep him as steady as you can so that the seal holds. I'll take his shoulders. On three..."

With a grunt of effort, he and Beth managed to lift Evan's limp form and transfer him to the stretcher. Grant realized that he was a lot lighter than he looked. Again, Beth took the foot of the stretcher before Ramirez could move a finger. Grant didn't even bother arguing, simply taking the other end. A moment later, they lowered Evan onto one of the two medical beds. The built in sensor suite activated automatically, his various life-functions showing up one by one on the monitor. Finally, Grant felt a little relief.

"The seal is holding," he told the others. "He's breathing normally, and the bleeding is almost stopped. We're not out of the woods yet, but he won't die now." He smiled. "I guess I'm still a pretty good doc after all."

Ramirez's face looked even more blank than usual, but Beth's palpable relief more than made up for it.

"Thank God..." she murmured, sagging visibly. It was exactly then that Grant noticed her hands shaking, and saw the dark blood leaking through the rent in her jacket.

"Ah, Beth, I'm sorry," he said, immediately guilty. In the rush to save Evan, he had forgotten her bullet wound. Of course, her lifting things hadn't helped much either. Typically, Beth didn't care.

"I'll be fine." She gestured to Evan. "Help him."

"There's nothing more I can do for him right now," Grant shot back, gently but firmly sitting her down on the other bed. "I'll help you."

It wasn't bad, considering. Nowhere near as bad as it could have been. The bullet had merely nicked the muscle in her bicep. It would heal fairly well on its own, but that didn't mean he couldn't help it along. "You're a lucky girl, Beth," he said, attempting to lighten the mood as he prepared a self-adhesive bandage. The material conformed fluidly to the shape of her arm, making her hiss through her teeth. "This should heal up fine."

"Yeah. I sure feel lucky."

And then it was finished. Silence fell over them all like a blanket. It was a very strange feeling, Grant reflected. Coming off the adrenaline high of fighting for their lives, his body was ready to keep going. There was nothing left to fight, and nothing left to do. His family was safe. He almost smiled. He hadn't had a good firefight like this since his security days. But then he remembered the limp body on the bed beside him, and Phillips' cooling cadaver down the hall. The people he cared about were safe, but at what cost?

Beth was the first to recover herself.

"Okay, Ramirez, I want you to go see if you can get Tavia back online," she said, breaking the silence. "I don't think there will be any more, but be careful anyway. We don't need any more holes in us." Ramirez nodded, checking the breach of his shotgun. He glanced one last time at Evan, his expression inscrutable, then disappeared through the hatch.

Beth heaved a sigh, her shoulders slouching a little where she sat. "You know Charlie? I feel like I should be saying something pithy right now, but it's not coming."

"Yeah," Grant said. "I feel the same way. I've been in plenty of firefights in my career, but that one was the worst. Well, *almost* the worst."

"Why?" Beth offered a wan smile. "Possibility of hull-breach?"

"No, because I had you and Ramirez to worry about. I've lost buddies before, and it always happens fast, almost too fast to think. If I lost either of you... I'm not sure what I'd do."

Beth smiled, placing a hand on his shoulder. "That's sweet, Charlie. Don't worry, we've got plenty of life left in us." She grew serious; gesturing to Evan's unconscious form sprawled on the adjacent bed. "I'm more worried about him. He's going to be ok now, isn't he?"

Grant shook his head. "It's hard to say, Beth. He's stable for now, but... I've seen guys die that shouldn't have, although I've seen guys *live* that shouldn't have, too. But with the way Evan took out those two guys... The fact that they both had guns didn't slow him down. I'd say under that polite exterior there is, as a friend used to say, one tough hombre."

"Well, I hope you're right, Charlie," Beth said, giving Evan one last look before blowing out a breath. "Well, I suppose we should turn some thought to *who* did this, but I figure that we both already know."

Grant nodded. "Our mysterious caller. I guess he's not as crazy as we both thought. Either that, or he's *more* crazy. The kind of guy who can get a bloody light-assault craft out here in the middle of nowhere has to be a special kind of connected or a special kind of mental."

"Agreed. But if that's true, why did they leave?"

"Maybe we were putting up a bigger fight than they thought. We killed a few, it was possible that they didn't want to run the risk of us taking one alive."

"Which would mean our mystery man is more worried about staying mysterious than he is about his prize. Or men and material, for that matter..." She trailed off, frowning deeply. Reaching into her jacket pocket, she withdrew a vibrating datapad. "Number blocked. It's him. How do we want to play this?"

Grant shrugged. "What do you want me to do, run a trace? Not many ways we can play it. Still, might as well see what he wants. But put it on speaker. I'd like to talk to the sucker myself."

Taking a deep breath, Beth nodded, thumbing the button. "You again, I take it?"

"Yes, it's me," answered a deep, gruffly resonant voice. "Kind of you to remember, Captain Hugin, considering how busy you've been lately."

Damn, this guy sounds bloody pleased with himself, Grant thought, clearing his throat to speak. "So, heard about that, did you?"

"Ah, Mr. Grant is there with you," the voice answered. "Good to finally meet you, Mr. Grant."

"Wish I could say the feeling was mutual, friend," Grant answered, keeping his temper in check. "I must say, the voice over the phone bit doesn't do it for me. What's say we set up a meeting place for a face-to-face chat, just you and me?"

The voice huffed in amusement. "Are you asking me out on a date, Mr. Grant?"

Grant shrugged. "Sure, why not? I'll buy you coffee and sign your body-cast."

"That sounds fun, but sadly, I don't think I can make time in my schedule. This is a business call."

"Business?" Beth interjected, incredulous. "Is that what you call this? Sending in mercs to murder us all in our beds is just *business*?"

"Sure. Why not?" the voice answered, unperturbed. "It's a competitive sport. And I'm always in it to win. Why else would I play?

The fact that you got in the way is unfortunate coincidence, but that's also a part of business. But that's why I'm calling. I thought that maybe I could make this all go away for you, now that you've seen how serious I am."

Grant and Beth exchanged glances. Unable to think of any suggestions, Grant shrugged eloquently. *We should hear it out. With Phillips dead, we might as well look at our options.*

"Ok, we're listening," Beth answered finally. "What's the deal?"

"Nothing too complicated. I'll give you the same offer as before, plus a fair bit extra for any... *expenses* you might have incurred over the past hour or so. We arrange a meeting place for the handoff. I get what I want, you make a tidy profit, and we go our separate ways. I'm a firm believer in keeping things simple."

"Ah, I get it now," Grant broke in, shaking his head. "Outfitting an assault craft and a hit team to try and slaughter us is your idea of 'keeping it simple.'"

"No need to take such a harsh tone, Mr. Grant! As your captain might recall from our previous conversation, I did say that I would have to explore other options. What? Did you think I was messing with you?" Grant said nothing. Much as he hated to admit it, the voice had a point; they had been warned, and they had simply ignored it.

"Well, the deal sounds good," Beth picked up, raising a hand to forestall protest even as he was assembling the words to do so. "Especially that 'go our separate ways' part. So good, in fact, that I don't believe you'll do it. As soon as we hand over that case, we become a loose end. I've seen enough movies to know what happens to people like that."

Grant felt his eyebrows rise. Typically, Beth had reached that conclusion far faster than he had. *Good point,* he mouthed silently. Despite the gravity of the situation, she smiled. The Voice was less amused.

"Movies, Captain? You're honestly going to take that as a basis for fact? After I have what I want, why would I have you killed? You have no evidence, no means to track me. And beyond that, you *do* have my word."

"Well, excuse me if I don't take that to the bank," Beth answered. "We'll take our chances."

The tone of the resulting silence gave Grant the image of the man on the other end of the comm shaking his head. "Not wise, Captain. I guess my first warning wasn't explicit enough, so I'll clarify this time; this won't stop. I'll come after you again. I won't stop until I get what I want."

Despite himself, Grant couldn't suppress a chuckle. "Sure mate, go ahead. I haven't been impressed so far. Your guys couldn't hit the broad side of a starliner. Hell, our engineer accounted for two of them, and he didn't even have a weapon."

"I will admit that I've underestimated you. I actually rather like the challenge. But I assure you, it will not happen twice... Did you say your *engineer* killed two of my men?"

Grant blinked at the sudden reversal. "Sure did. With his bare hands. You might consider paying for more competent help."

The Voice was silent for a moment before responding. "Interesting. Well Mr. Grant, you may very well be right about the quality of my men, but you have to consider the fact that you have to be lucky all the time. I just have to be lucky once."

Beth shook her head. "Well, like I said before, we won't be pawns in whatever scam you're running. We'll take our chances."

Oddly enough, the voice did not seem the slightest bit dismayed by the second refusal. "Very well, Captain. I wish you the best of luck in this little game of ours." As before, the call ended abruptly, leaving the medical ward in ominous silence.

"Arrogant bugger," Grant muttered finally. "Was he that bad before?"

"No, he was definitely a bit less formal this time. He really sounds like he's *enjoying* it all," Beth said. "I think we should amend your last assessment. Connected *and* crazy."

Grant nodded. "Personally, I believe him when he says he'll try again. But I think once we dump the case, he'll leave us alone. He said himself that we don't know anything about him. All in all, I'd say we did about as well as we could."

"I'm also not too worried that he'll try the hit team again, either. We'll be ready for the Slingshot in about twenty minutes, and when we drop out again, we'll be in civilized space. From there, Coalition help is only a comm-call away."

"Won't stop him from trying something underhanded planetside," Grant cautioned. "Remember Phillips' tail back on Hephaestus."

"We'll just have to be careful long enough to get the case to the Coalition. After that, it'll be their problem," Beth said firmly. "Our best bet is to not get involved anymore than we already are."

Grant nodded. It made sense, he supposed. The less involved they made themselves, the easier it would be to escape.

Even so, he couldn't' quite shake the curiosity of what exactly made Phillips little briefcase worth so much trouble.

Just then, Evan's unconscious form gave a low whimper, ears twitching. Beth immediately looked worried. "Is he alright?"

Frowning, Grant gave the instruments a quick scan, noting the brain activity especially. "He's still fine. He's just dreaming. I've had some weird ones when I've been laid out like that. I can only imagine what his would be like."

Beth nodded wistfully, her shoulders relaxing somewhat. "Yeah. I can only imagine," she said. "Well, I'm sure we're almost to the Slingshot. Do I have a clean bill of health, Doctor?"

"I suppose," Grant said reluctantly. "Just don't reopen the wound on the way up the ladder. And as soon as we jump, get some rest. You still might go into shock. I'll stay here and keep an eye on the patient."

Beth nodded, standing carefully. "Thank you Charlie." She made to leave, but then paused at the hatchway, looking back. "And Charlie? Just... try to make sure that he makes it."

"Will do, Captain," Grant answered. "We'll get through this. *All* of us."

* * *

The first thing that Evan became aware of was the smell. It was familiar. Uncomfortably so. He tried to recall where he recognized it from, but his thoughts were unclear and disconnected. The scent had something to do with the pain in his chest, he knew, but he couldn't even remember why it was hurting.

Okay Evan, he told himself, *take stock of the situation. You're on a cot of some kind, your chest is hurting and you can smell… what exactly?* Whatever it was, it was making him feel decidedly uneasy. Keeping his eyes closed, he took a deep breath. The answer was tantalizingly close, hovering just on the edge of his conscious thought. He racked his brain, trying to come up with an explanation.

Disinfectant, he realized finally. The odor was from some kind of medical antiseptic. No, he knew *that specific* scent. What was it called again? Chlorhexidine. Chlorhexidine was used as an antiseptic agent in sterile environments such as hospitals or—

"The Compound!" Evan felt a wave of panic wash over him and tried to sit up, but a pair of firm hands pressed his shoulders back down onto the cot. Breaking into a violent fit of coughing, he struggled weakly, trying to escape.

The amiable voice of Charles Grant instantly checked his efforts. "Whoa now, easy does it, lad," he said, looking down at Evan with concern. "Take it easy. You're fine."

Evan surveyed the room quickly, breathing a shallow sigh of relief when he realized that he was in the medical ward of his new shuttle and not back at the ABI compound on Earth as he had thought. *Wait, the med ward? Why am I in the...*

In a second, it all came back to him. The intruders. The shooting. The bodies.

Oh, no. No, no, no. The bodies. The bodies of the people *he* killed. He let out a shaky breath when he thought about how close he had been to tearing the second man's throat out and tried to push down a rising sense of dread. Now was not the time.

"Well, fine might be saying a bit much." Grant nodded at the bandages swathing the right side of Evan's torso. "What was that about a compound? You looked pretty spooked."

Oops. "Very sorry, sir." Evan hesitated. "I was a little disoriented. It's nothing."

Grant looked unconvinced.

"What happened? Who were those people?" Evan said, trying to recover.

"We're... not sure. Yet." The big security officer leaned up against the side of the cot. "We might have a clue about why this happened, but not who's behind it. Don't give yourself a headache over it. You just worry about getting some rest and letting that lung heal."

"Yes sir." Evan could sense that Grant was holding something back, but he wasn't going to press the issue. "The two that came for me, are they..."

"Dead? Yes. Nice work, that."

"The one that... that I shot. Did he have a... knife or something?" Evan asked, more for his own peace of mind than anything else. "I didn't want—"

"Combat knife in his left hand. Do *not* think you had any other option," Grant said firmly. "You did what you had to."

"Yes sir."

Evan was a bit surprised at how calmly he was taking it all. Killing two men, even in self-defense, should have shaken him up a lot more after all of ABI's years of brainwashing. The safeguards were flawed—the wolves had found loopholes in them large enough to fly the shuttle through—but he was startled by how easy it had been to shake off a lifetime of hearing that humans were superior and to be obeyed at all times. That in itself would be something the lab-coats back at the 'Pound would have been *very* unhappy about. With all their scientific wizardry, they still couldn't beat the survival instinct.

"Is everyone else okay?" Evan asked, propping himself up on his arm.

Grant raised an eyebrow. "Well, aside from you getting yourself shot up, Phillips kicked the bucket, Ramirez is fine, and Beth . . . well, you can ask her yourself." He took a step back and Evan noticed for the first time that the captain was sitting across the room on an identical cot. With a tentative smile, she got up and walked over to Evan's cot, sitting down gingerly on the side. Grant tactfully slipped out the door.

"So, um, how are you feeling?" Hugin asked lamely.

Great. Never better. "I'm just thankful I'm still alive." Evan said. "Who patched me up?"

"That would be Charlie."

"I'm very grateful."

"Anyone with a medical background would've done the same thing. It was nothing special." She seemed sincere. Evan fought to keep his cynicism in check. "Yeah, look," she stopped, looking him in the eye for the first time since he woke up, "I'm really sorry about what happened. It was my fault. I should have—"

Evan interrupted her. "Ma'am, no one plans to be boarded, you couldn't have known that they were going to come down to the cabins and I don't blame you at all. Don't beat yourself up over it. I'm not dead, am I?" *Yet.*

"No, that's not what I mean," Hugin said, her countenance stricken. "The captain is responsible for her crew, meaning *you* among others. I made sure that Grant and Ramirez were awake, but completely forgot about you. If I hadn't failed in my job, you wouldn't have almost been killed."

"Ma'am, I really don't think…" Evan trailed off.

"What I'm trying to say is: I'm sorry, Evan." Her voice was firmer now. "I almost got you killed, and I'm not going to let that happen again. Not on my watch."

Evan just nodded. He had never been faced with a sincere apology from an owner before, and he didn't know how to respond. She was acting like he had a lot of time left, though, which he found odd. It wasn't like he was going to be serving with her—or anyone—much longer. Not now.

"Also," Hugin said haltingly, "I'm sorry for this whole situation. It's…wrong."

"What do you mean?" he asked cautiously.

"It's just…" She stopped again. "I'm not sure what I'm trying to say, but I'm sorry for *you*. You seem to have gotten the short end of the stick, in general, and I'm sorry about that."

"Captain, you have nothing to apologize for," Evan said, confused. "For the most part, I've received decent postings and I enjoy being an engineer."

"You said you 'received' decent postings."

"Yes."

"You didn't choose them? They were assigned to you?"

"By the buyer, yes." Evan wasn't sure where Hugin was going with her new line of inquiry. "I'm tagged as a mechanical engineering specialist, though, so I'm always working in my own field."

"That's my point, though. You don't make your own choices about where you work or who you work for. You *can't* make your own choices." She actually appeared distressed. It was hardly a shocking revelation.

"That's just how it works. When my current employer doesn't need my services anymore, they put a listing on the 'net for an engineer. If someone's looking for a worker with my specifications and like what they see, they transfer money to my previous employer and I pack my bags and start a new job. Pretty simple, actually."

"So that's it, then? Cut, dried, the end? You've got no freedom whatsoever?"

"Well, technically Fletcher's Wolves are afforded some protection under the AI—"

"You spend your whole life serving humans with no choice, though! That's slavery!"

"No, ma'am," Evan replied, backpedaling hastily. ABI did not take kindly to their products inciting customers to complain, and the last thing Evan needed was to put himself in the spotlight. Not now. "Fletcher's Wolves were created artificially, so we're classed as self-aware AIs, pretty much the same as Tavia."

"But you're just as human as I am!"

Evan tapped his muzzle with a finger. "Not the way the Coalition sees it." The Coalition and its AI laws. She had to know about them, why hadn't she said anything yet? For that matter, why was she acting like he would still be around much longer?

"Well this wouldn't be the first time I didn't see eye-to-eye with the Coalition," Hugin said indignantly. "Not dealing with them much is one of the perks of spending most of my time in wild space."

Evan froze as comprehension dawned.

She hadn't mentioned the law for the same reason Grant had thought he would be able to use a firearm: they didn't know all of the regulations governing artificial intelligences. True, the AI Homicide Penalty was old, but it had caused such controversy that Evan had been sure at least one person on the *Memory* would've known about it. Unsettled by the unexpected turn of events, he tried to grasp what it would mean for him personally.

If the crew doesn't know, and they're the only way that ABI could find out I killed someone, then… I have a second chance? He realized that Hugin was staring at him.

"I'm sorry to have upset you, Captain," he said, holding up a hand to stop her protest, "but if it's all the same to you, can we finish this discussion at a later time? I'm exhausted."

Hugin seemed unhappy, but didn't press the issue. "You've lost a lot of blood, so take as much time to recover as you need. I mean it."

Evan nodded. "How long was I out?"

Looking back over her shoulder, Hugin counted on her fingers. "Let's see, we were boarded at a little after three yesterday morning, and it's 0820 now, so...twenty nine hours? My brain isn't a hundred percent right now. Long day. Or night. Or whatever."

"Of course. Please thank Mr. Grant for me."

"Will do."

And with that, she was gone. Evan was left alone with his thoughts.

Lying back on the cot, he stared at the ceiling of the med ward and tried to make sense of the flurry of emotions buzzing around in his head.

So, Captain Hugin was *not* coming to terms with owning a manufactured laborer. That was interesting. Most of the owners Evan had worked with had shown some form of shock in the beginning of a job, but all of them had come around after they got used to the situation.

But, Evan thought to himself, *the captain's crisis of conscience is a bit less important now. I might have a reprieve.*

The AI Homicide Penalty stated that if an aberrant artificial intelligence directly caused the death of a human being, it was to be immediately sent back to its manufacturer and dismantled. Unfortunately, the coalition hadn't seen a reason to change it after the creation of biological AIs, and for Fletcher's Wolves, that meant termination.

But if no one *found out*... Evan ran back over the events of the past day, trying to see if there was a way ABI or the Coalition would know that he was responsible for killing two of the attackers. Tavia had been offline, and onboard security tapes were probably disrupted as well, which meant no cams for evidence. He would double check that before touchdown at Earth. What about the bodies? It was all very blurry—more like he was just observing someone else killing the men...but a shot to the head and a broken neck were nothing incriminating, nothing to point directly to his involvement. As far as he could see, if the crew didn't know about the law, there was no way ABI would ever hear about it.

Wait. Evan's train of thought came to an abrupt halt. He thought back to Hugin's words at the beginning of their conversation. What had she said? *I almost got you killed, and I'm not going to let that happen again.* It was obvious that she had been upset by finding out the realities of sentient property ownership, but would that carry over into a willingness to subvert the law? Grant had mentioned that they occasionally delved into some "grey" legal areas, but this was a clear-cut obstruction of justice. Would any of the crew be willing to do that for a stranger? Maybe. But for a piece of ABI property that they could just as easily get a refund for, now that it had fixed all the major problems on their shuttle? That scenario was not one that Evan could see playing out.

But Hugin promised that she would protect me, he reminded himself. Could he trust her? He thought of his experiences with previous owners' promises, and a flood of bad memories washed away any doubt in his mind. No, he decided. He could not. *You may be able to trust these people, but you can't afford a mistake. You've been burned before, and if you get burned this time, it's going to kill you.* It was not the time to let his guard down.

Not now.

9

For Ramirez, it had been a rather long rotation. After he had helped to reboot Tavia, Beth had assigned him to a comprehensive check of the entire ship, figuring that those two errant pirates had been up to *something* after they killed Phillips. And so for nearly a day and a half, he had been roving the halls of the ship, occasionally on his hands and knees, checking every weld and wire with a portable sensor unit and the Mark One Eyeball, listening to Tavia express her outrage at the violation of her little kingdom. It had not been fun. But still, he couldn't fault Beth for the precaution. Plus, she and Grant had been taking turns keeping vigil over Evan and watching the sensors in case the mercs or whoever they were came back. It made perfect sense; it was just hard to hold onto that feeling when his investigation had turned up precisely nil.

No bugs, no sabotage, no bombs, no crossed wires. Nothing. So what were *they here for?*

Ever since the bullets had stopped flying, that had been the question of the hour.

Why had they bothered to shoot up the ship in the first place?

It was a question that had even fewer answers now. Ramirez tried not to think about it as he placed the sensor unit back in the equipment locker, massaging a sore neck. He now counted himself especially lucky that his future had not been relegated to shipyard work. If nothing else, he had just proven that he wasn't cut out for a life of crawling around staring at blank steel.

As he passed forward through the maintenance level, he had to walk past the computing block, an anonymous brick of white metal casing studded with ports, cooling fan stars and the occasional winking light. "How are you feeling in there?" he remarked on the way past, smiling.

"Technically, I neither feel, nor am I 'in there', as you so quaintly put it," Tavia responded instantly, her voice even more tart than usual. "But I suppose in your crude terms, I am feeling better. And perhaps the better for the experience. I managed to save most of the coding algorithm used by our unknown attackers' device, and I am currently configuring it for my own mainframe. It could be useful."

Ramirez felt his eyebrow rise. "Useful for what?"

"One never knows. All the same, I would appreciate it if you didn't mention it to Captain Hugin."

"My lips are sealed," he assured, continuing on to the ladder. No, he knew perfectly well that Beth sometimes took exception to the less *savory* aspects of their job.

And that is why I am around.

Finishing his ascent into the cargo bay, he secured the hatch with one hand, tapping his earpiece with the other. "Excuse me Charlie, is the captain up there?"

" 'Fraid not," Grant replied after a moment, his voice sounding strange for some reason. "Just me and a very hot cup of coffee. I'm sure my taste buds will grow back in a few weeks, though."

"Well, taste buds are not really required for shipboard food," Ramirez deadpanned. "It might even be an improvement."

"You're not lying. But anyway, Beth is in the med ward. Evan actually woke up, by the way. Looks like he's going to be fine."

"Great," he lied, "I will go report to her there, then."

He knew from experience that an intercom call wouldn't cut it. She needed to be able to look him in the eye when it came to anything that so heavily concerned her baby.

Strange. But then, what captain didn't form such an affectionate connection with their ship? Anthropomorphization was merely the next illogical step.

The hallway past the cabins was longer than he remembered. Perhaps it was the fact that every door was stuck open now, the small blackened patches on every control bearing silent witness to the drama that had played itself out down here. That was it. It was no longer the home he remembered. It was a combat zone. He was about halfway along when he noticed Beth up ahead, ducking out of the med ward with a final, lingering glance, her brow creased in thought. Ramirez cleared his throat. "Captain, I—"

"Shh!" she hissed, covering the distance between them in three strides as she jerked her thumb back toward the hatch.

He rolled his eyes, modulating his tone to a slightly lower decibel. "I have completed that check you asked for. Top to bottom, stem to stern."

"And?"

"A sum total of three ball-bearings, a loose screw, and assorted lint. I almost missed the lint. Good thing we have expensive sensor equipment."

Beth's face fell slightly. "Oh. Well, it was worth a try. At least we've eliminated a possibility. Thanks for taking that one on."

"You are welcome, Captain, as always."

He thought that was the end of it. With a nod, he started to turn, his thoughts already falling on that coffee that Grant had found so feisty, and thinking himself man enough to take it...

"Oh, Ramirez," Beth added, catching his shoulder before he could walk away. Immediately, he knew something was up. For one thing, she had physically restrained him. For another, she had her brook-no-nonsense tone that was usually reserved for obstinate clients.

Steeling himself, he allowed himself to be turned around. "Yes Captain?" he answered, his own voice a study in casual disinterest. *Yes officer? Is there something wrong?*

"I understand you and Evan had a little *discussion* down here two nights ago."

Ramirez felt his heart rate jump, but he neatly intercepted the feeling before it affected his face. "I am... not sure what you are talking about."

"Oh, don't play innocent." She jerked her thumb back toward the door behind her. "He didn't tell me. I already knew."

He could see by the absolute conviction in her voice that there was no point in sticking it out. "Okay, so how the hell did you know?"

Beth just smiled.

"Fine, keep your secrets," he conceded. It was a captain thing, he supposed. He'd always found it strange how she seemed to hold an almost mystical connection with the shuttle, as if it was a part of her. It was a good wake-up call that he needed to be more careful in the future. "Okay, so I had a not-so-friendly conversation with the new engineer. Was there something you wanted to say?"

Beth's eyes hardened. "Just this: lay off. I won't tolerate you antagonizing one of my crew."

Ramirez sighed inwardly. This had been about the reaction he had predicted. The same flawed reasoning. "Beth, you met him barely two days ago. How can you trust him?"

Her stance didn't waver a fraction. "That still doesn't explain why you're so hard on him. I mean, he hasn't exactly had it easy either. He deserves a chance just as much as you did."

He fought a spike of anger. "Are you listening to yourself? Have you read *anything* about Fletcher's Wolves? He is a *thing*. What kind of *chance* do you think you can give him?"

"He's still a person, Ramirez. All you have to do is listen to him to see that."

"No, he is *not*. The human race has gotten good at creating imitations, but he is *not human*. That is why we cannot trust him."

"You're right about one thing," she said, her voice suddenly cold. "That boy has *not* had a normal life. You came from a hard background. Grant too. Even I didn't exactly have smooth sailing. But we at least had a choice. You and I are here because of a long string of choices that we made. That we were *allowed* to make. Evan never had any of that. His destiny was set from the very beginning. He has no choice but to be here, no choice but to do his job, and even in the face of that, he has no choice but to deal with all the crap from people like *you*. Think about that."

Ramirez did. For several seconds, he could think of nothing to say, facing the captain's icy glare the whole time. Finally, her wrath seemed to settle somewhat.

"So I'm going to say this once," she said, her tone more calm, "Evan is part of the crew now, which means that I'm going to protect him, even if it means protecting him from you."

A few tense seconds passed. It was a standoff, and both knew it. And they also knew which one was going to budge first.

Ramirez looked away. "Yes Captain. I understand."

As ever, Beth was graceful in victory. "Good. Look, you don't have to like him, I'm not even asking you to trust him. Just trust me."

"I do trust you, Beth," he said, forcing himself to look her in the eye. "I will do what you ask."

She blew out a breath, looking slightly relieved. "Good. And now, I'm going to get some coffee."

It was as good a way to end the discussion as any, Ramirez thought, backing out of Beth's way as she edged past him and began to make her way down the corridor. He remained in the med ward doorway, listening as the padding of her boots faded behind him as he thought about what had been said. It was, more or less, how he expected she'd react. Her "mother bear" act was something that he had witnessed several times before, and it had usually been on his behalf. With that foreknowledge, being on the receiving end wasn't that bad.

He had meant what he said, however. He respected Beth that much, even if she held the power of firing him in her hands. But, knowing her, she would never do that. He had been one of her many crusades to do The

Right Thing, and he was truly grateful. It was because of her and her alone that he had not died with a knife in his back on that smoke-shrouded night on Apollo. It was because of her that he was now travelling the galaxy, not hunted by the law or rival criminals. It was because of her that he made a fine wage, most of which he was able to send back home to his family. And it was because of her that he had friends that he knew beyond doubt would never betray him. That was Beth all over, exorcising her own demons by devoting herself totally to others. But while he thought of that facet as her crowning glory, it was also her weakness. Time and again, it put her in prime position to be taken advantage of.

He looked up from his ruminations, glancing at Evan on the medical cot, watching as the various sensors monitored the engineer's sleep. Fitful, apparently. A frown seemed to twist his lupine face, and one ear kept twitching, as if he was listening.

Ramirez felt his face harden.

No. It wouldn't happen. Not while he was here. No one else believed him, but that had happened before, and it did not mean that he was wrong. Only time would tell.

* * *

Beth flexed slightly stiff fingers, gazing contentedly out the viewscreen. Most of the time, the view didn't change. While it was amazing, the endless carpet of stars against the deepest of velvet darkness did tend to get old after you started clocking up cockpit hours in the ten-thousands. But today, the view was *more* than amazing. Having just dropped into realspace near its moons, the immense horizon of Jupiter was now visible on the port-side, swirling and rippling in multi-colored tumult. The Memory didn't usually get earth-side business this time of year, and so she had really only seen this view four or five times. With interstellar travel still so new, Jupiter was still easily the largest planet humanity had ever been close enough to touch. It was so immense that it swallowed half the viewscreen with its grandeur.

Beth thought about snapping a picture with her datapad, but decided against it. The 'net was already flooded with such images, most of which were better than anything her humble device could capture. Heck, the thriving tourist platform that was currently on the night side of the planet probably exported them by the truckload. Still, it was awfully nice to look at. But only for so long. The flight plan she had plotted called for her to orbit here for a few hours, then break off at just the right point to use the gravity as a Slingshot. From there, at this time of year, it was a straight shot to earth. Until then, she had some time to herself. She rose from the pilot's chair, suppressing a yawn.

"Tavia, you mind setting the sausage-roll?" The sausage roll was one of those terms that had a tendency to confuse new space-travelers. In reality, it was merely the simple act of setting the ship to roll on its axis so that no one side would be facing the sun long enough to cook circuits and damage vital equipment. Immediately, she was seized by a slight feeling of vertigo as the view of the planet seemed to tip as if she was falling backward.

"Aye Captain. I'll cook us evenly. There's an hour and ten minutes until we're ready to engage the Ermat again, so you go run along and do something fun," Tavia said with her usual brightness. "I'll let you know if our friends come back."

Ah yes. Beth had almost forgotten about her constant concern yesterday, namely that the mysterious man's mercenaries would return and finish what they had started. She doubted now that it would happen. After all, now they were in mostly civilized space, and with a space station within easy communication distance. "Well, I don't think there's anything more than a big 'ol ball of hydrogen and helium out there, but keep an eye out anyway."

"Will do. Now seriously, go read a novel or something. Go on. Shoo."

Beth smiled, turning to the bridge hatch. How long had it been since she'd done *that*?

As she stopped in the kitchen to pour herself some coffee, she could somehow sense the relaxed atmosphere that had settled over the ship. Life aboard ship with so few crew members was usually quite busy, but every once in a while, they would all run out of things to do at about the same time. Then it was time to kick back and catch up the leisure activities. She found Grant in the cafeteria, back to her, playing what appeared to be some kind of card game on the screen built into the surface of one of the tables. Beth had never been very good at card games, although she occasionally enjoyed a few rounds of double solitaire. Certainly no betting games, not since Ramirez had fleeced everyone so thoroughly at Poker early on.

As she drew closer, Grant hissed through his teeth: "Blast it! Tavia, are you cheating?"

"Mr. Grant," said Tavia frostily, "this game is managed by a totally independent program over the 'net. It manages thousands of such virtual matches daily. I cannot cheat any more than you can." After you had come to think of an AI as a person, it was a bit jarring when they were in two places at once.

"But not for lack of trying, I bet…" Grant muttered, looking up. "Oh, hey Beth. Want us to deal you in?"

"No thanks, Charlie," she said, indicating the second cup of coffee in her other hand. "I'm going to sit with Evan for a bit."

Grant nodded. "He was asleep last I checked, but that was about an hour ago. He's on the mend just fine. That re-gen sealant held so well, he should be up and about soon."

"Well, that's great news! I'll check on him. If he's still asleep, I'll come join you."

He waved his hand dismissively. "Don't trouble yourself. I'll collar Ramirez once he's done with his slicing and dicing."

Beth didn't need to ask where the procurement officer was. She could feel the rapid, thumping rhythm of his favorite music coming from the deck above. Probably in the shuttle's miniature gym, working over a practice dummy with a plastic knife and a few well-aimed kicks. She joined him occasionally for his drills, but she had never really gotten the hang of the dancing, in-and-out nature of knife-fighting. And after Ramirez had received an unexpected and potentially life-threatening haircut, they had both mutually decided that she wouldn't learn how to throw them.

With a nod, she turned and began to make her way aft, listening as Grant and Tavia returned to their game.

"And... that's Gin."

"Blast it!"

Traversing between decks with nothing but a ladder was always something of a trick. Even more so with full hands. Luckily, Beth held it as a matter of pride that she could climb a ladder with a cup of coffee in each hand. Aboard ship, it was definitely a trick worth learning. A moment later, she was walking carefully up the hallway, careful to quiet her footsteps on the deck. As she reached the open med ward hatch, she found she needn't have worried. Not only was Evan awake, he was standing up. She stopped in the hatchway, watching him. Amazingly enough, he was moving carefully around the room, his steps deliberate and careful. Which was even more amazing, considering how much it had to hurt him. The spasms of pain were visible on his face with every step, and Beth noticed that he was using the walls and furnishings for support as much as he could. Still, it was pretty good for a guy who took a bullet through the lung not long ago.

Just then, he *froze* midstep, nose twitching, ears swiveling her direction just before the rest of his head.

"Captain, I..." Another spasm crossed his face, and he stumbled unsteadily.

"Whoa, easy," Beth chided, catching him awkwardly with her forearm. "Charlie is impressed with your recuperative powers, but this is rushing it."

"I'm sorry, Captain," he said sheepishly, the strain just discernible in his voice as he lowered himself back to his cot. "I'm just feeling so useless sitting around on my tail. I want to get back to work as fast as possible."

Beth huffed in amusement. Typical male. "Well, let me put it in perspective for you. Two guys came down here and put holes in you. One was in your lung. That was *not* very long ago. We weren't sure if you were going to live. With those factors, can we agree that you've had enough macho for today?"

He smiled at that, and nodded. "Well, when you put it that way, I guess you're right."

"Good." She sat on the edge of the cot, offering the cup in her hand. "Coffee? I brought cream and sugar if you want it."

As he settled back onto the cot, Beth imagined that he might have flinched, just once. "Um, no thank you. It's... Canines aren't really supposed to have caffeine."

She frowned, disappointed. All that way trying to make a kind gesture, wasted. She supposed she shouldn't be so surprised. Doing her best not to show it, she set both cups down on a nearby counter. "Oh. I'm...sorry. I didn't know that."

As per usual, he was ready to head off her guilt with a smile, although he was a bit more wan and distracted than the norm. "Don't worry. Most people don't, unless they've owned a dog."

"Yes, but us space-people practically live on the stuff. We're going to have to find you something else that you like. Non-caffeinated tea, maybe."

"Maybe. I've never tried it..." Just then, he gave a long yawn, exposing his sharp incisors for a moment. "Mm, I'm sorry," he said, covering his muzzle in embarrassment.

Beth was reminded belatedly that, no matter how he looked, he had still gone through shock, and had lost a lot of blood. "Don't mention it. After all, you can't have coffee."

That actually sparked a laugh from him. A soft, barking laugh.

"I guess I have an excuse then, don't I?"

"You sure do." She chuckled along, interested in this sudden new side of the engineer.

Finally, a bit more than "Yes Captain" or "Don't worry about it Captain" or "I can do that Captain."

"If boredom is the issue, I can..."

"Oh, no," he assured quickly, his laughter dying away, his expression turning more sober. He gestured to a neat stack of compact chips on the bedside table. "Mr. Grant has been quite helpful in that regard." Curious, Beth picked up the stack, leafing through the titles. Ah yes, some of Charlie's favorite movies. Old comedies, mostly. She noticed that he had wisely avoided the shoot-'em-ups.

"I imagine you haven't seen many movies," she said, replacing the stack.

"No, not really. Never really had the time. I've mostly been reading."

As he said it, Beth noticed a large datapad on the table next to the CCs, at exact right angles to the corners. On its screen was a copy of *Mechanics' Monthly*.

"And so you go straight to the heavy reading, I see."

"Yes, well, it's what pays the bills."

With that, they lapsed into a companionable silence, him adjusting his pillow as she scrolled through the various articles on the screen with her nail.

Reach Out and Touch Someone: The Latest Sensor Tech.

Hardware to Brainware: Neural Relays in Action.

The Top Ten Most Effective Non-Lethal Weapons.

Ah yes, that reminded her. Something that had occurred to her earlier.

"Evan, mind if I ask you yet another question?" she said, setting the 'pad back down. "I know I always seem to be doing that."

He shrugged again, casually interlacing his fingers behind his head. "I never mind answering. Although I'm not sure how much help I'll be right at the moment."

Something had definitely changed in Evan's demeanor, something had... unlocked, almost. He seemed comfortable, more at ease. Beth hesitated, debating with herself if it would not be better to keep it until later... But no. She knew herself well enough to know that she would never get back to it, and she felt that she did need to ask.

"Well Evan, I've been... reading up a bit on Fletcher's Wolves, and one thing all of the literature keeps repeating is safety. There's two dead bodies on the floor out there, and... well, you put them there."

Instantly, she regretted the decision. At her words, Evan tensed visibly, his eyes going hard with that same shutting-bulkhead feeling she remembered from their first conversation. Still, the only thing to do was stay the course.

"So, these 'safeguards'... They... don't work, do they?"

For the briefest second, there was a flicker of intention across Evan's face, of determination and defiance.

I pushed too hard. I was so close...

Just as quickly, his face softened, as he emitted a rather surrendering sigh. "No, not really. They do work—in a way. But they're not as effective as ABI would have its clients believe. We've figured out ways to get around them. But I guess you can already see that."

Beth struggled to process all of the implications of his words. It was all so new to her...

"I'm not entirely sure how they could ever work in the first place. How can you... *program* that?"

"It's fairly simple, actually. As far as we've figured out, they rewired a few synapses to induce a severe stress response at even the thought of harming humans. The stress response, in turn, activates a hereditary form of tonic immobility that wolves experience when forced to submit to an alpha. That goes along with some... intense psychological conditioning."

Beth had been in the military long enough to know a euphemistic understatement when she heard one. *Psychological conditioning* made her think back to a sniper unit she had briefly observed once. She had always remembered their dark, blank eyes as they stared through their thermal scopes, the way their faces remained absolutely impassive as they put round after hyper-accurate round through brutally lifelike VR targets. By all accounts, the methods for their training were one step short of barbaric, but no one questioned it, because the resulting men were so indisputably effective at their jobs, expedience won out. Evan, she now realized, had to have come from something similar, except with the opposite intent; to create something that could *not* kill.

"But for all that, it isn't perfect. They still can't beat the survival instinct," Evan went on, his eyes wandering from hers. "When those men burst in, and I knew they were going to kill me, everything in me told me that was it. But I decided that I *wasn't* going to die, no matter what. The rest is a blur. Then I woke up here, with Mr. Grant." He lapsed into silence.

Beth said nothing, frowning as she tried to decipher the sudden wave of emotions that had swept over her. She was confused, yes, but she was also... hurt and angry for some reason. In fact, she was downright fuming. Before she could figure out why, Evan seemed to return to himself, meeting her gaze nervously.

"Does that...disturb you? I mean, with all the talk of my kind being safe, it's a problem that I..."

"Oh, no. Definitely not," she assured him firmly. "Evan, Charlie is about twice my size. He could snap my neck without squeezing. Ramirez carries his switchblades at all times. Heck, Tavia could disable the hatches and open the airlock, and we'd all flash-freeze. But just because they're *capable* of it doesn't mean that they *will*."

He was still looking at her, carrying the distinct look of someone waiting for the other shoe to drop. Something about the way he remained completely and absolutely still; it told her that he was afraid. Seized by a spike of righteous anger at the people who had done this to him, she grasped his hand firmly in both of hers, looking him straight in the eye.

"Evan, listen. Whatever may have happened before, it doesn't matter now. It's not like you murdered in cold blood. You defended yourself. That's your choice. Your right."

"My choice."

Beth nodded.

"My choice? You know what?" Without warning, his face *changed*, anger pulling his lips into a snarl. "You sit there talking about choices and rights, and you have *no idea!* You have no idea what we've—what I've been through! Then you hire me and think that if you say some nice things and ignore the fact that you *own* me, everything will be just *fine?*"

Shocked into silence, she could only stare.

"After the things people like *you* put us through," he coughed, "the things you made us do, you can't—I won't let you talk about—" he paused, his body wracked by a fit of coughing, "—my pack that way."

"Evan," she said, aghast, "I didn't mea—"

"If you think we've *ever* had a choice, or rights or—or anything, you're saying that we bled and died for *nothing!* That it could have been *stopped!* Do you have any idea—" he was cut off midsentence by another bout of coughing, bloody spittle staining the fur on the back of his hand pink. Gasping for air, he fumbled for the jury-rigged oxygen mask, slipping it over his muzzle and slumping back on the cot.

Beth was taken aback, utterly unsure how to respond. She had been starting to think that his calm, smiling face was a mask, but she would never have guessed what he used it to conceal. The way his face had transformed between those two extremes…was almost frightening.

It must have shown on her face. Just as abruptly, the anger melted from his features, replaced by a look of abject horror. "Oh no. Captain, I d-didn't mean… That is, I wasn't *trying*—" That was all he could manage before the coughing overtook him again and he had to use the respirator.

Finally, Beth got over her shock long enough to say something, if only reverting to her default. "It's alright, Evan. It's…it's alright."

All he could do was shake his head. *No.*

Beth's frown deepened, her surprise softening into pity. "Yes, it *will* be alright," she said, laying a hand on his shoulder to gently but firmly push him back onto the cot. "Look, I'm not angry. In fact, I'm a little relieved. I could tell that you were holding something back. I guess you've been keeping that outburst bottled up for a long time. Too long."

He just stared at her, breaths coming hard, like a dog waiting to be hit. The image made her angry. Not at the situation, and certainly not at him, but at the people that had done this to him. Even so, she tamped it down, instead focusing on comforting the frightened engineer. She offered a small smile. "Look, I won't even pretend to know what you and your...your pack went through. I can see now that I've been ignorant about these kinds of things for *far* too long. But I do know this: whatever people have told you, you should never have to be afraid of speaking your mind, especially around me. I know that's hard to accept but...we'll make it better. I can promise you that. Whatever you've been through...you don't have to go it alone anymore. We can help you. *I* can help you. Okay?"

Evan stared at her, and she could catch the disbelief in his eyes. The oxygen mask lowered slowly, his mouth open, as if he was about to say something... And then a flicker seemed to pass behind his eyes, making him think better of it. Slowly, reluctantly, he relaxed, blowing out a long, shuddering breath. "Alright."

It wasn't quite as satisfying as she'd hoped, but Beth made the decision that she would ask about it later. "Look, you've had a long couple of days, and you probably didn't help your lung much just now. Get some rest."

With that, she rose and moved toward the hatch, dimming the lights most of the way. With one final look over her shoulder, she left the room.

She held it together about halfway down the corridor. Then, unable to contain it any longer, she pounded her fist against the bulkhead, releasing all of her pent up rage against the unfeeling metal.

She realized belatedly that there might have been better objects on which to vent. She leapt back, swearing through clenched teeth as pain arced up her arm in waves. *Geez girl. Those hands pay the bills around here,* she told herself, forcing herself to calm down enough to think rationally over what had actually been said.

It did not take her long to figure out what was making her so angry. It was so obvious, she realized that it had been staring her in the face ever since Evan had walked up the ramp and into their lives. She firmly believed that it was the very first and most sacred of rights for a sentient life to defend its own existence. It was a given, a prerequisite for humanity. And then there was Evan, the creation of a group that had taken its very best shot at taking that right away from him. And every other choice he'd ever had, from life on down. He worked harder than anyone she knew, with no pay. He had very little time of his own. He had no real possessions. He had nowhere to call his own, constantly shunted from one place to another, into the hands of some paying master.

Slave.

She tried to reject it at first. After all, honest-to-God *slavery* had died out before people had even started colonizing other planets. Humanity was so much more sophisticated these days. But the word simply wouldn't go back into its box. It seemed to cling to her, clarifying all of her confused thoughts with merciless efficiency. It had been right before her eyes from the very first moment that Evan had sauntered gracefully into their lives. That was why she always felt so inexplicably guilty around him. If he was a slave, that, by definition, made her a *slave owner*. He was a living, breathing, *thinking* being, and she had *bought* him.

The thought filled her with self-revulsion, pressing down on her like a weight.

She steadied herself against the bulkhead, shaking her head to clear it.

C'mon Beth, just think, she told herself. *This doesn't make you a monster, it just means you've made a mistake. The real question is: what do you* do *about it?*

It was simple, really. She would set him free. After all, she had bought him, hadn't she? The government had to have some allowance for it somewhere. And if it didn't...well, screw them. Evan would get a better life, starting right now.

With that resolution fixed firmly in her mind, Beth immediately felt herself on balance again. It was just how she was put together. It was why she wasn't very good at games, and why she had never finished that novel she had picked up three years ago. For all the concern it might cause Grant, she was really only happy when she was *doing* something. The realization brought a tiny smile to her face even as she eagerly ran through everything that would need to be done for this new course she had set for herself.

Ok, so... First he'll need a salary. He's already added a lot of value to this ship, so he's already more than earned it. Next he'll need some more clothes, something more than just those fatigues of his. Maybe Ramirez can work his connections and find a weapon for him that won't trigger alarms from here to

Hermes. I swear, I'll get him out to see some sights of the galaxy, and he'll need something to defend himself out there. Let's see, what else? Leisure time. We'll find him something fun that he likes to do; something that doesn't involve equipment manuals and techno-speak.

Just then, something caught her eye in the interior of cabin Six. The blood and the bodies were still there, lying where they had fallen. They had all agreed that when they landed on Earth, it would be much easier if they told the authorities the whole truth, and left all the forensic evidence where it was. Tavia had turned down the environmental controls in the two cabins so that the corpses wouldn't smell much, and everyone had mostly forgotten about it and gone about their routines, because there was really no other way to respond. Beth however was thinking about none of this. Her eyes had fallen across a wedge of black plastic. The material was distinctively familiar for some reason, but she could not...

Then there it was. Dr. Phillips' briefcase, the one over which he had been so protective. In all the excitement and distractions, it had been driven cleanly from her mind.

Her good humor seemed to evaporate, giving way to a sense of foreboding. She could leave it where it was, she supposed. Let the

authorities on Earth hash the whole thing out.
She didn't have to worry about it.

Yeah, right.

With a sigh, Beth started across the
cabin floor in a game of macabre hopscotch,
trying to avoid disturbing the evidence. The
simple fact was: Phillips had been desperate to
get to Earth with that case. And now he was
dead. More than just idle curiosity dictated she
find out why. After all, it might be her crew in
danger now. Reaching the center of the cabin,
she dropped herself into a sitting position on
the bunk, avoiding the bloodstains. From
there, she reached down between her feet and
took hold of the case.

It was much heavier than she would
have expected. Phillips must have been
stronger than he looked, lugging this thing
around all day. With a soft "oomph," she had
it up. As she set it on her lap, Beth felt oddly
reverent as she ran her hand over the neutral
plastic. It was strange, holding something that
someone had thought worth killing for. She
noticed now that the case's lock was top of the
line, topped by a compact number keypad.
And she knew from experience that there was
plenty of room inside for any number of
fiendish countermeasures against a forced
entry. It would probably be best to get
Ramirez on it…

Just then, her datapad chirped twice. Her frown deepened. That tone meant she had received a video message, which was more than unusual. She removed the device from her pocket, tapping the screen.

The placeholder icon vanished, replaced by the face of Dr. Phillips. Or rather, a small, somewhat grainy image of him. Beth could see that the recording had been made with a small camera, set on the desk in the cabin next door, judging by the background. For several seconds, Phillips seemed to adjust the camera's settings, swinging the image crazily as he repositioned the device. Finally he seemed satisfied, the image centering back on his face as he cleared his throat, and spoke.

"This is a recording by Dr. Trent A. Phillips, Director of Research for Dystech Genetics, addressing Captain Elizabeth Hugin of the shuttle *Memory*. This message was sent to your datapad as a result of it coming within six inches of the sample-case, without it being within six inches of my datapad. It is a contingency, in the event of my death." The image of Phillips paused to straighten its tie. "Which… officially makes this the strangest thing I have ever done. But, considering the events of the past month… I feel it necessary. I suppose the purpose of this message is that, if something happens to me, you will understand why I acted as I did, and hopefully the importance of my mission." Phillips settled back in the chair, blowing out a breath. "Where to start? Well… From the beginning, I suppose. As I said, I am the head of research for Dystech Genetics, a fairly small concern based on Ares…"

It was about then that it finally dawned on Beth exactly what she held in her hands. She quickly pressed the pause control, freezing Phillips and filling the cabin with silence as she struggled to process what was happening. She'd thought… Well, she realized now that she *hadn't* really thought. Phillips had commissioned them for transport, and that was really as far as their association went. As soon as he died, Beth had subconsciously written it off as another dud venture. An expense to be paid for by later jobs, just like a lot of runs. She'd dismissed Phillips as a nutter, or a liar, some criminal on the run from some other criminals, using that ridiculous lure of the 50,000 credits to dupe them into his scheme. Now that he was dead, she had been sure that would be the last they would ever hear of it, once they'd squared it with the authorities on earth.

But now…

Now the man had taken the trouble to record a message, just in case he, oh, *died* or something. That kind of dedication spoke of something far deeper than a random mob hit. Just what had they gotten themselves into here?

Well, I guess it's a good thing the late Dr. Phillips has offered to explain…

Taking the case in hand, Beth stood up, pocketing her 'pad. One thing was for sure. Grant and Ramirez had to hear this too.

She found them both where she had left Grant, hunched over the game table with their cardplayers' eyes.

"Are you cheating, Charlie?"

"Ramirez, this game is handled by an independent program that handles thousands of these matches every day. I can't cheat."

"You can send the royalties for that comment later, Charles…"

"Shut up, Tavia. I'm concentrating."

Typically, Ramirez was the first to notice her grave-faced approach, his eyes darting between her face and the briefcase in her hands. "Beth, what is it?"

Grant barely needed to look up before he was sliding aside to make room for her, the game immediately abandoned. Beth sat down slowly, setting the case on the center of the table.

"I assume we all know what this is?"

Grant and Ramirez nodded.

"I'm nodding," said Tavia.

"Good," Beth said, setting her 'pad on the table next to the case. "Tavia, mind putting this up on the screen?" The monitor flicked immediately to life, complete with a magnified clone of the image on Beth's tiny screen. "This is a message from our late passenger. Recorded specifically to reach us in the event of his death. What does that tell you?"

Ramirez scratched his forehead, his mouth settling into a thoughtful straight line. "It tells me that he was either totally insane, or that he was killed for more than embezzling funds or something."

"Those were my exact thoughts too. Now that we're on the same page…" She tapped play.

"Well… From the beginning, I suppose," Phillips started again. "As I said, I am the head of research for Dystech Genetics, a fairly small concern based on Ares I. About a year ago we built a lab on Hephaestus, to move some our more difficult work further out of the public eye. It was about that time when Dystech came to be in the running for a competitive contract opportunity for the Coalition, alongside a handful of other genetics firms. The challenge was to create a fully adaptable carrier virus. The company that could successfully develop such a product would be awarded an incredibly lucrative contract to manufacture it for the Coalition. I'm sure that you can imagine the stakes, Captain Hugin."

She could. For the past few decades, the rewards of genetic science had made the business into a very competitive and cutthroat world. She and the crew had been minor pawns in a few corporate games over the years, but she had been very careful to steer them well clear. Until now, apparently.

"Think of it like a vehicle," Phillips said finally, subsiding back into the lecturing professor. "Even better, a cargo vehicle. If you have enough fuel, you can tell the pilot to go anywhere you want it to, in order to deliver anything you want. This virus is rather like that. You can code the RNA to take it to very specific types of cells, to deliver… oh, thousands of different compounds. We've had this before, but never this advanced. There is very little that this product cannot do with the proper coding. It could revolutionize medicine, genetics, nanotech, biotech… The implications are staggering."

"I sense a 'but' coming…" Ramirez muttered.

"But, with that comes the flipside. While this could be turned to so many good things, it could also be the most efficient weapon ever created. Used correctly, and paired with the right biological or chemical agent, it could depopulate a small colony world in a matter of weeks. Just out of idle curiosity, I ran a computer simulation a few days ago of a situation where the virus releases onto Hephaestus mated with *bacillus anthracis,* a pathogen not normally considered transmissible from person to person. The place died out in four days.

"It was right about that time when we had a break in at the lab. A prowler with some very advanced burglary equipment got in and rummaged through our computer files. Luckily we keep the project notes for the virus on a totally separate and firewalled server. And that has to be what he was after, because our AI gave ninety-eight percent odds that nothing was copied or deleted.

"I wasn't too worried at that point. I contacted the company, filed a report, and called the authorities. But that was where it got strange. When I called the Coalition to inform them that Dystech had completed work on their commissioned carrier virus, I was connected straight to a supposed Investigative Services Agent who *insisted* that I meet him at the spaceport and bring the case. Alone. Now, it might have just been too many movies, but that sounded suspicious to me. He kept on urging me to meet him, and then a few of my staff said that they thought they were being followed… Considering what was at stake, I decided that I needed to get out of there, get to Earth and get to a representative of the Coalition that I knew was legitimate. Without anyone following me." He paused for breath, looking back at the camera over the frame of his thick glasses. "That is where you came in."

Beth jumped as Grant snapped his fingers. "I *knew* he was going to say that."

She was inclined to agree. This was the hook. There was always a catch. Even in death, Phillips wanted them to *do* something for them.

"If you're watching this, it means that I've probably been killed. Of course, if you were the ones who killed me, that does create a rather awkward situation. However, I rather doubt that will happen. Or has happened, I suppose. But I digress." He cleared his throat. "I have no right or authority to ask you to deliver this for me, but that is exactly what I am going to do. I have set a delayed transfer to your account, so I can at least keep my word when it comes to payment, but if you're seeing this, I would imagine that it's not enough. All I can do is appeal to your decency and implore you to make sure that this virus makes it to the right people. And, while I'll admit that the

Coalition isn't always as responsible as we might wish it to be, it would certainly be more trustworthy and at least held more accountable than some *corporation.*" He managed to make it sound like a dirty word. "Please, Captain Hugin, keep the case safe, and get it straight to the Coalition on Earth. Show them this message. They have the contract on file, they'll believe you. They can guard the virus, and investigate who wanted to get it." Phillips gave a sigh. "You'll probably just turn around and auction the thing to Genet-X or Zimmerman and make yourselves a fortune. I never got to know you well enough to tell. But I hope you realize what's at stake, and that you'll do the right thing. Right. Er...good luck." He reached forward and fumbled with the camera for a second, then it was over. The message froze in time, and Phillips again became nothing more than the body lying on the deck below.

For a few minutes, silence reigned in the rec room, or least as close to silence as the shuttle ever got. Beth was especially conscious of the humming and clicking of all the machinery around her. Finally, Grant stirred, making the creaking of the seat lining into a loud noise. "Well," he said heavily, managing to speak volumes in a single word.

"I agree," Ramirez seconded. "That explains some things, one way or another."

At last, Beth found her voice. "I think I understand what you're both saying, but let's try to unpack that statement a bit more. Charlie, what do you think of all this?"

"I think that we have gotten ourselves mixed up in some weird stuff. Weirder than usual. I mean, we knew something was off from the start, but this... this is way outside our league. Ramirez?"

"Charlie is right. We have done a lot of sneaking around at the edges of what is legal and what is not, but this is high level corporate blood games. This is the sort of thing where everyone gets burned in the end. I have seen it before."

Beth more or less agreed with what was being said. Out in the big universe, business was, well, serious business. The closest thing to an all-out war when there wasn't some upstart colony world acting up against its neighbors. Beth had personally known several captains that had lost their commissions. One had even lost his life. "Okay, we're all agreed that this is not a positive development. I suppose a better question would be, what do we do about it?"

There was a pause as the crew considered the problem.

"I want to be clear on something, first of all," Ramirez spoke quietly, his voice thoughtful. "I suppose selling this thing *is* out of the question?"

Beth was shocked. "Of course! You seriously want this thing in the hands of Genet-X? They would probably load the thing with neurotoxin and gas a mining world just to put pressure on some investors! There is no way we're handing this thing over!"

Ramirez raised his hands placatingly. "Alright, just making sure. You are absolutely right."

"Certainly not Genet-X," Grant said carefully, "but maybe there's someone else out there. Someone responsible. I mean, someone is obviously going to tremendous lengths to get this thing, it might be safer for all involved if we just put it back on the market, as it were."

Beth turned her indignation toward the security officer. "You too, Charlie? Who do you know who's 'responsible'?"

Grant's mouth shut with an audible click.

"Sounds to me like you are leaning toward the late doctor's plan," Ramirez commented, drumming his fingers thoughtfully on the table.

Beth nodded. "I was, actually."

"That would hinge on the assumption that the Coalition is the paragon of virtue and responsibility." His tone was casual, but Beth thought she could detect a note of bitterness in it. He made a good point, however. She had once worked for the Coalition and had sworn an oath to serve and protect it, a long time ago. That really just meant she had been around long enough to see how much they tended to hold the good of the majority *far* higher than the good of the individual. It took large wheels to run an interplanetary government, and people occasionally got crushed under them. If she handed them something this powerful... there was no knowing where it would end up. She realized that she had known the truth all along. *No one* could be trusted with this.

"You know what guys," she said, not lifting her eyes from the square of black plastic that had already caused so much trouble, "I can't think of anyone anywhere that could handle this thing without getting burned. I say we send it on a collision course with the nearest star and gun it the other way."

"Woah, let's not be so hasty, Beth," Grant said, raising a hand. "Sure, I agree, this is dangerous. But it also has a lot of value. It might be good to keep around a nice insurance policy. Especially pulling up to Earth with a few dead bodies in the hold, it might be nice to have some leverage."

"That's different," Beth answered, shaking her head. "We'll tell the truth, we'll leave all of the evidence. It's not like we have anything to hide. They'll believe us."

"Beth, that would imply trust," Ramirez said. "You were just saying we cannot trust the government, and now you are saying we can trust them not to lock us up as murderers? You can't have it both ways." She said nothing. It seemed Ramirez had woken up with a talent for good points.

"Alright Ramirez, we get it," Grant rushed to her defense, as always. "Beth, I can't give you any answers. I'm just the dumb grunt who knows his way around a hemostatic dressing. You're the captain. You've always done right for us before, and I think that you can do it now. But remember, Phillips would have this backed up somewhere at his lab. The Coalition gets it eventually anyway."

And there it was again. Beth looked up, studying the expectant faces of her friends. They were waiting on her for a choice. When it finally came down to it, the responsibility was hers. It was unfair, in a way, that they trusted her so much. She knew she wasn't exactly a saint herself, and she was far from omniscient. She didn't know what was going to happen. She looked down at the case, shaking her head inwardly. It was such a petty, stupid thing for people to have to die for. A few strands of RNA in a petri dish. The right thing, she knew, was to dump it in the nearest reactor. But that wouldn't stop their pursuers. It could save thousands of lives, but it would not save *them*. It was one of those instances when doing the right thing would not be the right thing for her crew.

It should have been a hard decision. She hated herself that she didn't wrestle more with it. But in the end, there was only one choice.

"You're right Charlie, much as I hate to admit it." She sighed. "We'll hang onto it for now. And we'll see what happens after we get to Earth. If it goes without a hitch... We'll figure out where to go from there." She slid the case across the table toward Grant. "In the meantime, do you mind locking this up somewhere? In the gun cabinet might work."

He took it, nodding gravely. "I'll take care of it. And thank you, Beth. I know it's a hard decision. But sometimes there is no right choice."

I know that, Beth thought. *I know it far too well.*

<u>10</u>

Grant breathed a subdued sigh of relief as the shuttle's landing gear settled firmly onto the ground. The landing had been uneventful, but he was still a little on edge after the recent near-disaster. Releasing his tight safety harness, he activated his headset's mic and waited for the inevitable call from the port authority. The crew had been busy in the last four or five hours, making sure the ship remained in the same condition as when it had been boarded. The local Blues would be a bit cross if their crime scene had been tampered with. Well, they would be cross if they *knew* their crime scene had been tampered with, Grant amended. He and Ramirez had acquired the bullet-proof vests that the boarders had been wearing, taking extreme care not to leave any fingerprints. You never knew when you might need a second chance in the middle of a gunfight. Plus, it wasn't like the police were going to use them.

A yellow light on the center console winked on, indicating that the London PA was scanning their shuttle for contraband or any other items of interest. Grant was pretty sure they would be interested in what they found.

There was a click and a weary voice came over the comm. "Shuttle *Memory*, our scans are showing five dead bodies onboard. Would you care to give us an explanation?"

Beth sighed and turned on her mic. "We're sending the incident report over to you now. Should make for some entertaining reading."

There was a brief pause.

"Mercenaries." The PA officer managed to convey an impressive amount of skepticism in a single word.

"Yes sir," Beth said. "A quick call to Hephaestus' port authority will confirm that we left with only four crew and one passenger. Flight plan and time of departure will also prove that we didn't make any stops on other planets." Grant had already discussed with her how best to validate their claims of being boarded.

"Copy that, *Memory*. Stand by."

Tapping her headset, Beth switched to the intercom channel. "Ramirez, can you come to the bridge, please? LPA is probably going to want to talk to all of us."

"Sure thing, Captain," Ramirez replied from the doorway. "No sooner said than done."

"Thanks."

"You know what they say about great minds."

There was silence for a few long minutes as they all waited for a response from the port authority. Grant was beginning to become uneasy. It should have taken the Port Authority only a few moments to key in an information request to HPA and only a little longer to bring up the file and reply. Beginning to wonder if he should expect a CPW SpecOps team to come knocking on the rear hatch, Grant slid out of his seat and joined Ramirez in leaning against the back wall.

"Nervous?" Ramirez nodded out the window at the bunker-like port authority building.

"A bit," Grant admitted, wishing that there was something he could be doing. Inaction did not suit him in the slightest. "The Hephaestus guys are either all taking a coffee break at the same time or there's some kind of holdup. And the PA blokes are generally a pretty sharp bunch."

"Well, we have nothing to hide."

"Aside from the authentically battle-damaged bullet-proof vests, nothing."

"Oops. My apologies, officer, I have *no idea* how that got there."

Grant chuckled.

Just as the silence from the port authority was becoming excruciating, the comm crackled with static and a different voice flooded the security officer's headset. "Shuttle *Memory*, this is Chief Inspector March of the LPD. With whom am I speaking?"

"Shuttle Captain Elizabeth Hugin."

"Captain Hugin, your story checks out with Hephaestus PA and I must inform you that this is now officially an open investigation. Since it occurred in interplanetary space, the investigation lead is up for grabs, but Hephaestus is a little bit far away, so we're going to be handling this one."

"Understood," Beth said crisply. Grant could see her unconsciously falling back into her Air Force habits. "What can we do to help?"

"First off, we'll need a statement from the officer in charge regarding who killed whom, exactly. The incident report here lists the crew and location of the bodies but doesn't mention the specifics of the engagement. This is for the record, mind you, so take a second to make sure you're remembering correctly."

Grant bristled at the hint of a threat, but Beth gave him a palms-down signal. *Play it cool.* "Nothing to hide here, sir," she said, keeping her tone level. "The bodies listed as numbers one and two on the document we sent to the port authority were killed by Security Officer Charles Grant. Body number three—that would be our passenger—we're not sure about, but it had to have been by either number four or five."

"The ones in cabin…" There was a brief pause, "six."

"Correct."

"And they were dispatched by whom?"

"Engineering Officer Evan."

Grant blinked at the inevitable title attached to Evan's name. It was hardly unexpected, but still sounded strange to a man who had been working with the same people day in, day out for six years. *Better get used to it, Charlie. The way things look now, he's going to be with you for a while.*

"That would be the, ah, bio AI, correct? The Fletcher's Wolf?"

"Correct."

"Alright, that's all five bodies accounted for in your statement. Just to let you know," he continued, lowering his voice, "this looks like a pretty open and shut case, so after a quick forensic inspection to make sure your story matches up with the evidence, I'll write this off as a failed piracy attempt and you can be on your way."

"Thank you, Chief Inspector," Beth said, visibly relieved. "Are my crew and I allowed off the ship? I still have a package to deliver."

"Of course. And I'm sorry for the inconvenience. This kind of thing happens way too often and there's no real way for us to catch the culprits. More of a formality than anything else, really."

"It's no problem; we weren't planning on leaving until my engineer is fit again anyway."

The chief inspector started to say something, but then fell silent for a moment. "Right, then. We'll need to meet your crew, your *whole* crew, mind you, at the ramp for security reasons. I'm sure you understand."

"Yes, officer, will do. And thank you." Beth closed the connection and turned to Grant, smiling. "See Charlie? All your worrying for nothing."

He nodded, still harboring unfounded doubts. What was the problem, he asked himself. The chief inspector had been professional and sympathetic, the PA was a bit slow off the mark, but hadn't caused any problems. What then? Irritated at his own misplaced paranoia, Grant didn't bother to smile back. *Beth always knows when I'm putting up a front anyway.* No, it was just one of those groundless feelings that might have saved his life on the battlefield but just caused him stress in day-to-day life.

Stumping off the bridge, he grabbed his shoulder holster off the back of one of the cafeteria chairs and slipped it over the rolled-up sleeves of his shirt. It was a habit; a ritual. Tooling up before he left the safety of the shuttle and ventured out into a new world. *Well, up 'til recently, the shuttle seemed a lot safer that it does now. Hope the forensics gremlins don't take offense at the precaution.*

Eh, he thought with a mental shrug, *I'll just do my best to look non-threatening.* No mean feat for a man of his proportions.

Gingerly climbing down the ladder to the cabin deck, he glanced at the scorched panels next to the open doors along the corridor and wondered briefly if Evan would be able to repair them once he was up and about. After all the work he had accomplished in the first day, Grant would have been surprised if he couldn't.

Turning away from the deserted hallway, Grant pressed the button to open the medical ward door and was greeted by a draft of cold air. For some reason, Evan always seemed to keep his quarters at a lower temperature than the rest of the ship.

"Evan, we need to meet the forensics blokes at the ramp for debriefing or whatever. You need any help?"

Evan finished putting on a clean sleeveless shirt over his bandages and turned to look at Grant. "No sir. Just finishing up. I'm ready to go when you are."

Grant almost commented about the *sir*, but took a quick step forward to grab Evan's arm instead when he started limping toward the door. "You should really be resting, you know. No one's going to blame you if you lie low a few more days."

"I like to push myself," Evan said, all seriousness. "I'd hate to be a burden to the Captain."

"Why don't you wait until I can get you a pair of crutches before you start wandering around on your own again? You're going to reinjure yourself this way."

"Yes sir. Sorry."

"Don't be," Grant said, "and for the umpteenth time, I'm not *sir*. I'm not even Mr. Grant. It's Charlie."

"Alright."

Evan had been acting differently after the run-in with the unknown intruders. More subdued. It was logical, Grant reminded himself, after killing two people in self-defense and almost dying, but he had already come to enjoy Evan's cheerful demeanor and he found himself missing it.

"C'mon, I'll help you to the ramp."

Evan nodded and Grant wrapped one of his big arms around his furred shoulders. The eleven-inch height differential made supporting Evan a bit difficult, but Grant was sure that he would object rather strongly to being carried. Despite Evan's efforts to start walking as soon as possible, Grant could tell that he was weaker than he let on; he was stifling a whimper every time he put his weight on his injured leg. *Stubborn lad.* Grant remembered dealing with patients like him back when he was a medic. *Damn fools don't know their own limitations.* That, he realized with amusement, seemed to be a common characteristic in every member of the shuttle's crew.

A few minutes later, he met Beth and a fidgety Ramirez in Cargo Bay One. Keying the code into the ramp controls, Grant made sure the clasp on his holster was securely fastened—a reassuring gesture if ever there was one—and waited for the ramp to make its ponderous descent.

The scene that greeted him was more or less the one that he had expected: a few uniformed Blues standing around to make sure that there wouldn't be any problems and an important-looking mustachioed figure, ostensibly Chief Inspector March, standing next to a small group of people wearing sharp, black *LPD Forensics* jackets.

After a thorough visual inspection of the crew, March jogged up the ramp to meet Beth, shaking her hand in a formal manner. "Welcome to London, Captain Hugin. Terribly sorry about the inconvenience to you and your crew, but we do need to run you through some more sensitive scanners before you can leave."

"Perfectly understandable, Chief Inspector. Your boys have free run of the shuttle. A word of warning, however," she said, jerking a thumb over her shoulder, "Don't antagonize the AI. She's a bit touchy."

Grant snorted.

"Understood, Captain." March motioned to the policemen and forensics team. "You heard the lady. Get to it." The policemen gathered up their equipment and trooped past the crew. Grant found himself wondering if he had remembered to space the rubber gloves he had used to remove the armored vests. *A bit late to do anything about that now.*

"Right, then." March coughed politely. "If you will hand over any weapons you're carrying to Sergeant Bronson, you can step through the scanner here—" He motioned to a device that looked like an empty doorframe. "—and then you can be on your way."

"That's it?" Grant asked, mock-incredulously, surrendering his Maxwell to the Sergeant. "No interrogation in a dimly lit room? No 'Good Cop, Bad Cop' routine?"

"Afraid not, sir," the Chief Inspector said, his moustache twitching in what looked suspiciously like a smile. "The movies have ruined real police work for us all."

"Pity," Grant said, stepping through the scanner.

The man running the scanner waved Grant on. "Accelerant residue on the jacket, and under the nails. Fits with the report. Next."

The rest of the crew also went through with no problems. There was a slight delay while Ramirez handed over his surprisingly large collection of knives, but any comments by the operator were forestalled by the procurement officer's icy stare.

When they had all passed through, March nodded slowly. "Once again, I'm sorry for having kept you. A pleasure meeting you gentlemen. Captain." He tipped his cap, turned, and walked up the ramp after his men.

Grant stood for a moment, watching him go. The whole thing wasn't nearly as bad as he had expected, although the forensics team wasn't finished yet. You never knew what they would turn up. Grunting disgustedly, he tried to push all thoughts of the trouble he might be in if the police found the jackets. Ramirez had taken care of hiding them and he had had many escapades of questionable legality in the past. If anyone could slip something like that past the nose of the police, it would be Ramirez.

Seeming to come to a decision, Beth stuffed her hands into her pockets and turned to face Grant and the other two, but just as she started to speak, she was interrupted by the sudden squealing of vehicle tires. A large, unmarked van pulled up sharply a few meters away, its black finish looking suspiciously bullet-resistant. Grant immediately transitioned into security-mode, a host of possibilities running through his mind. A hit? No, not with police around. The mysterious caller's men returning for whatever they were after? Absurd. That was about as good a way to get arrested as calling ahead to schedule a bank robbery. Could Ramirez have bad relations with a gang here? No, that was all left behind on Apollo, and the police presence was just as much of a deterrent as it was for the other situations. The forensics team could not have already found the stolen armor, so that wasn't the reason. His speculation was cut abruptly short as the van's side doors opened and half a dozen men piled out.

They looked like security, or paramilitary: identical crew cuts, bland polo-shirts, khaki pants, and matching tactical vests bearing the words *ABI Security*. In addition to all being dressed the same, they invariably carried civilian models of the military Lutha automatic. Grant shot a quick look in Evan's direction to see how he was reacting to the visitors from his manufacturer. While he couldn't say that Evan *paled*, he came as close to that as was possible for not having any visible skin. The engineer seemed to shrink, his ears went back and he took a barely noticeable step to his right, putting Grant partway between him and the new arrivals.

With a discreet hand signal to the rest of his group, the apparent leader jogged up to Beth, giving her an appraising glance.

He grinned humorlessly, cocking his head to the side. "You must be Hugin."

Grant noticed that the other five men had formed a subtle perimeter around the crew.

"You appear to know who I am, but I can't say the same for you," Beth replied, belligerently, "Care to remedy that?"

"Not particularly." He was wearing sunglasses, Grant noticed. It wasn't very bright out. "Gotta message for ya, Cap." The man pulled out an official-looking paper from his fatigues, handing it to Beth. She took it wordlessly. Grant was curious, but he knew that if it was important, he would find out about it. His attention was better directed at the ABI personnel, who looked like they were just waiting for an excuse to turn this venture into a firefight. Grant knew how security men could get after a few months of smooth sailing.

Out of the corner of his eye, he could see Beth skimming the paper, her expression growing steadily darker.

"I'm going to assume that you have two letters in that fancy dinner-jacket of yours and that you accidentally handed me the wrong one," she said, giving Shades a hard stare and handing the paper to Grant. Grant ran his eyes over the letter. It was short, but written in legalese, so he read it with special care.

"Attention Owner,

It has come to our attention that your ABI product is in violation of its terms of ownership, and is therefore subject to recall, pending further research. A replacement will be provided within one business week, and compensation for any loss of profits will be offered.

If you have any questions, please contact the Customer Service Department.

Arkady Biotech Industries"

"Sorry doll, this is the only one I brought with me." Shades smirked, hooking his thumbs in the pockets of his tactical harness. "I might have another one back at my place, if you want to come and look for it with me." Assorted guffaws from the other members of the security detail.

Grant waited for Beth to deliver a suitable reply to the man's face, but was dismayed when she ignored the comment and fixed the man with a look of disdain, like he was something she had found on the bottom of her boot.

"What does that mean in practical terms?" she asked, crossing her arms as if to hold herself back.

"Means the barker comes with us," Shades said, looking pleased with himself. "He killed somebody, so we get to take him to the 'Pound and let the lab-coats find out what makes him tick, then put him down. Ensuring *your* continued health and happiness, Cap. And you'll get a new one within the week, so everyone's happy."

Grant's brain reacted to the phrase *put him down* the same instant that his hand did, and he reached for the grip of his Maxwell.

"Bit of a problem, there, Gramps," Shades said, indicating the empty holster. "Works better with the gun inside, in my experience. But what do I know. You can still try it." He looked around. "Whaddaya think, boys? Six with guns on one unarmed. Does he have a chance?"

"Sure, I'd give him a hundred percent chance," one of the other men said, grinning. "Of dropping like a rock if he tries anything."

"You heard the man. Now get out of the way before I decide you're obstructing justice."

Grant seethed. Suddenly, he felt Ramirez's hand on his arm, applying just enough pressure to bring him back to reality. *Alright Charlie, getting yourself and possibly Beth and Ramirez killed just to satisfy your urge to rip this cocky upstart in half with your bare hands is not the best move you can make.* He knew he wouldn't be able to do anything useful with half a dozen semi-automatics pointed his way, but he also knew that what was happening was wrong. He *hated* being helpless.

"Go to hell."

"Not today, Grandad." Shades leaned over to the right, pointing a finger at the cringing figure of Evan. "You, barker, get in the van."

Evan hesitated.

Sighing, the man turned to his comrades. "What happens if I think he's resisting being taken into custody?" One of the ABI gunmen drew a finger across his throat, accompanying the gesture with an appropriate sound effect. "Plus, skulking around behind your buddy, you never know who might get caught by a stray bullet if you force us to do this the fun way. So I'm going to try this one more time, fleabag. Get. Over. Here."

Evan shot a despairing look at Beth, who still hadn't moved, and limped out from behind Grant. Immediately, one of the men grabbed his arm and hauled him away from the rest of the crew, snapping a pair of handcuffs on his wrists. Dragging Evan to the back of the van, the man paused for a moment and pulled a small black object out of his pocket, slipping it over Evan's head.

A muzzle. Grant ground his teeth. *They're muzzling him like a bloody dog. Bastards.*

Motioning to his team, Shades bowed mockingly in Grant's direction and blew a kiss to Beth. He jumped into the cabin of the van, pulling the door closed with a slam and starting the engine. The other members of the squad climbed back in the side doors, keeping their weapons trained on Grant the entire time. More doors slammed and the van pulled away, heading for the spaceport exit. The very last thing that Grant saw was Evan's face peering through the back screen. With the lower half shrouded by the muzzle, it was almost impossible to tell his expression.

But his eyes made up for the 'almost.'

Grant cursed, wishing there was something nearby that was not Beth or Ramirez that he could punch.

"Grant, I need you to do something. Fast," Beth said. It was the first time she had spoken since her question about the ABI order. "Take Ramirez with you, get a taxi, and follow that van. Find out where it goes and don't get caught."

Grant nodded. He could do that. "What will you be doing?"

Beth rounded on him slowly, and for the first time, Grant was able to see her face. It was a mask of stone, totally wiped clean of any emotion. Grant suddenly had the same feeling he had gotten the first time he'd ever pulled the pin out of a grenade. "I imagine that half a dozen armed thugs would scare most people off," she said, her voice dangerously calm. "That means they won't see me coming."

Despite the gravity of the moment, Grant felt a surge of admiration for the tiny woman before him. When anyone else would roll over and accept the situation, she was just getting warmed up. He didn't know exactly what she would do, but he was instantly sorry for whomever she'd be doing it to. But he would worry about that later. The van was very distinctive in the busy London traffic, but he would have to move fast. Giving Beth a quick salute, he took off running in the direction of the spaceport's visitor pickup. It would be the best place to find a taxi, he reasoned, feeling rather than seeing Ramirez take up position beside him. Things would be different the next time he ran into the egotistical punk. His Maxwell would level the playing field. And he would see just how much talk the brat had when his gang wasn't behind him.

Grant couldn't wait to find out.

* * *

Evan knew it would happen this way. Somehow, he had always known. Ever since he had woken up in the med ward, he had been waiting for them to come and take him back. He fought to keep his seat as the truck bounced, wishing he had his hands free to steady himself. Why had he ever thought he could get away with murder? Of course the captain would file an incident report; of course the Port Authority would inform ABI that one of their products had killed someone. How had he ever thought otherwise? He gritted his teeth in frustration, feeling the muzzle chafe behind his ears.

Did Captain Hugin turn me in? She acted pretty surprised when they came to get me. But they couldn't have known unless someone told them.

I guess it doesn't really matter now, he thought disgustedly, trying to find a comfortable position on the narrow bench. *I've got one more stop, and that's home.*

Home. That was a misnomer. The ABI facility that housed the Fletcher Project was a prison, a concentration camp, not a home. He had spent most of his life there, learning how to keep his head down, his mouth shut and his hands busy. But he had been one of the lucky ones that hadn't been rehabilitated and he realized that he didn't really know what he was in for. Who would handle the deviant cases? Evan wondered. Dr. Blackburn? Dr. Avery?

No. He hadn't been gone so long that he had forgotten who the wolves that got out of line were sent to for rehabilitation. There was only one person who specialized—and took so much pleasure—in deconstructing and reordering the psyche.

Dr. Morrow.

Evan swallowed hard. His childhood memories of the long training runs, the endurance tests, all of the hellish experiments and trials his pack had been put through: Dr. Morrow was always in the background, watching and writing in his little black book. The little black book that determined who met the standard and who did not. There was no motivator quite like knowing that those who consistently fell behind might not be at training the next morning. The second generation of Fletcher's Wolves had begun with 234 subjects that survived infancy, and by the time they were ready to be put on the market, there were only 199. Most of those that had been rehabilitated had been able to meet the standard, but those unfortunate few who could never seem to keep their thoughts to themselves, or have their work done on time would disappear without a trace. Where they were taken, none of the wolves knew, but whenever someone vanished, Dr. Morrow would be absent for a few days. Evan wasn't blind, and he wasn't stupid. He could connect the dots.

He had known most of the wolves who had been taken, and two of them had been close friends. It had been a very long time since Jesse and Lynn had disappeared, but Evan still thought about them. It had been a very long time since he had seen *any* of the other wolves, much less one of his pack members. He wondered if he would see any at the facility before he was taken to wherever his destination was. Probably not. Most of the wolves would be out in the galaxy, working. And any that might be at the 'Pound would be kept well away from wherever deviants were taken. Dr. Morrow wasn't keen on last words.

Judge, jury and executioner.

And when they had come for Evan, his defense had been nowhere to be found.

So much for your promise, Captain, he thought wearily. *Here I am, not quite as safe as you said.*

Despite the fact that Hugin had either lied to him or changed her mind, he couldn't summon up any anger at her. He felt sad that she had so quickly changed her views, but he didn't hate her for it. After all, he was used to owners doing that.

At that moment, the van swerved violently and he was thrown from the bench, landing in a heap against the rear doors. A horn beeped wildly and the van veered in the opposite direction, causing him to slide across the floor and slam against the opposite wall.

Evan lay where he fell, coughing painfully into his gag. He had fallen on his uninjured side, but the impact had still knocked the wind out of him and the muzzle made it impossible to take the deep breaths his lungs needed. Rolling to a sitting position, he leaned against the corner for support, trying to suck air in through his nose.

"How'd ya like that, barker?" One of the men was leering at him through the grill that separated the holding cell from the cab. "London traffic ain't for everyone."

"Leave him alone, McConor. He'll get his soon enough. We're coming up to the 'Pound."

The 'Pound. It had been what, six, seven years since he had been there? Driven by a morbid curiosity, Evan got to his feet, using the wall for support, and looked out the reinforced rear window.

At first, he could see nothing, but when his eyes adjusted to the comparative brightness, he saw that the van was driving away from an intersection and into a narrower, less well-travelled section of London. That fit. The Compound would be situated well away from ABI's nice, shiny headquarters downtown. No need for the company to have the less pleasant aspects of its programs on display. A light rain was starting to fall, Evan noticed, making a rhythmic tapping noise on the roof. He almost smiled. *It wouldn't be London without the rain.*

After a minute or two, the van turned off the main road and stopped. He could hear the men in the cab talking with someone; then there was a mechanical grinding sound and the van drove slowly on. The familiar gate hove into view behind the van, just how he remembered it, and with a very final-sounding slam, shut out the outside world.

He was home.

With one last lurch, the van came to a halt. Orders were given, doors opened and closed and in a few seconds, the rear doors of the van were flung open. Evan blinked. It was almost like he had never left. The dusty courtyard and sprawl of low buildings shut in by a high, razor-wire topped wall were unchanged, except in the fact that where there used to be other wolves, it was now deserted.

"Move it, barker."

Evan jumped awkwardly down onto the hard-packed dirt, and followed his escort through the drizzle and into the familiar entrance of the compound. The plain gray corridors were empty, but apart from that, it could have been yesterday that he shipped out for his first job. The first two doors on the left led to bunk-rooms—Lynn had bunked in room One with the rest of the females, Evan remembered; Jesse had been in number Two with him. He paused for a second, staring at the simple steel doors and the heavy bolts fixed to the outside. He had never understood why there had been so much security. No one really expected the wolves to try anything, and they never had. Escape was out of the question and, in spite of their curiosity, everyone had been too frightened of reprisals to do anything more than discuss the off-limits areas of the Compound.

A shove in the back brought Evan back to the present and he kept going down the corridor, past more numbered doors on either side. Most he remembered; but some he couldn't place. Six was the rec room. He smiled wistfully, recalling precious free time spent playing games with his pack members in room Six. Room Nine was one of the two classrooms. He had learned the basics of engineering there. Eleven. That was the training room with the treadmills that he had visited so many times for the exhausting weekly runs. Which was the medical ward again? Ah, yes. Fifteen. He had logged quite a few hours in the medical ward after a rather memorable accident while repairing one of the guards' trucks. Dr. Avery had been very interested to see how well the wolves' bones healed naturally. The medical ward was also where the wolves had their monthly physical checkups to make sure they were developing properly. Any unnatural phenomenon was recorded and the subject was taken aside for observation. After fifteen, Evan couldn't recollect where the doors led anymore. Either he had never been in the rooms, or it had been too long since he had left.

Seventeen… Eighteen… Nineteen.

Door Nineteen was the last door before the double line that the wolves weren't allowed to cross. The lines were the boundary between the portion of the compound dedicated to the wolves, and the section that belonged to the staff. At the line, the security men in front of Evan submitted to an iris scan and then opened the forbidden door at the very end of the hallway. The door slid smoothly up into its housing and Evan was immediately struck by a strong feeling of anticlimax. The hallway on the other side looked almost the same as the one he had just passed through. There were a few unnumbered doors on either side, then the corridor split into two. The passage to the right had a very distinctive antiseptic smell, like the one in the medical ward. The one to the left, then, Evan guessed, would lead to the living quarters for the staff.

Without hesitation, the security detail turned silently down the right corridor. It looked a lot like the first, but the doors had no numbers, only locks. Evan took a deep breath. This was it.

Last stop. This was where it began, this is where it ends. Appropriate. Okay, Evan. You have no idea what you're in for, but you can't tell them that everybody knows how to get around the safeguards. It's just you. You figured it out. He grimaced. *That doesn't even sound plausible to me. Oh well, it's not like I've got any other ideas. I don't know what they'd do if they heard that we can all get around the safeguards, but I can't imagine it would be pleasant.*

The escort stopped in front of one of the unmarked doors and the man with sunglasses turned to Evan with a lopsided grin.

"Say your prayers, barker. Your kind never comes back out of this room outside a body bag." He slid the bolt back and opened the door, making a mock-deferential sweep of his arm. "*Entrez-vous*, fleabag."

Evan stood in the doorway, staring into the room. It was small and pitch black except for a small, bright light aimed down at a single chair. The room stank of fear.

"I know it looks like something out of a bad spy movie," the leader said, motioning to his men, "but it's rude not to accept our hospitality."

Evan's arms were seized and he was marched roughly through the doorway. The men halted in front of the chair, and fixed a blindfold over Evan's eyes. The cuffs on his wrists fell away and he was turned around and forced onto the seat, too disoriented to resist as his arms and legs were secured to the rests on the chair. He could feel himself beginning to hyperventilate.

After a check to make sure his arms were locked in place, the men filed out of the room and the door slammed. Evan heard the bolt sliding home and then nothing. Top-grade soundproofing, he realized; only the best for ABI's torture chambers.

How long he waited alone in the dark with his fears, he had no idea. Minutes. Hours. But after what seemed like an eternity, he heard the bolt sliding back and the door opened. A pair of footsteps entered, then the door closed again. Evan tried to put a finger on the newcomer's scent, but the strong smell of fear was masking all other odors. The footsteps came back from the door and halted in front of Evan.

He flinched when deft fingers unclasped the strap of the muzzle and worked it over his ears, sliding the entire apparatus off of his head but leaving the blindfold in place.

What?

"I don't think this will be necessary," said an all-too-familiar voice. "I'm sure we can have a civil conversation without the need for violence on anyone's part. After all, there is no logical reason to withhold information. Isn't that right, Subject 112?"

Evan's heart sank. "Yes, Dr. Morrow. And my name," he said quietly, "is *Evan*."

11

Beth wasn't angry. She was long past angry. She could no longer even be described with "livid" or "furious." She had reached a height of anger so focused and so intense that she was sure the dictionary did not even have an entry for it. It was a cold, slow burning anger that seemed to tighten around her throat and constrict her heart. Eventually, she gave up trying to identify it. Now it was time to put it to work for her. It was hard, though. It was so hard to curb her rage when all she could think about was Evan's terrified face as they led him away, his eyes pleading to her for help, and her own impotence in the face of the men with guns. And that fellow with the sunglasses... Oh, they would meet again, she was sure. And things would be slightly different. The Blues had given her LK-2 back, for one thing. His words, however, kept on ringing in her ears: ...*then put him down.*

Put him down. Like a damned animal.

No. Not on her watch. Not after she *promised* him. Oh, those thugs with their semi-autos were an effective deterrent in the short term, but ABI obviously didn't know her. She wouldn't cave that easily, not to something as petty and banal as a corporation. The note in her pocket told her to come to the headquarters, and so that's what she would do. She would go there, she would find someone in charge, and she would *make* them let Evan go. If they refused to see reason, she would appeal to the higher power of the Coalition. And if they would not help...

Well, then I have leverage... she thought, tucking Phillip's sample case under her arm.

Even amid her anger and resolve though, one question still nagged at her.

Why didn't he tell me? When the ABI security men had shown up, it had been a complete surprise to all present, except him. The Sunglassed One didn't even have to say anything before Evan was practically cowering, as if he had known it might happen all along. The more she thought about it, the more she was sure.

So why didn't he tell me?

She had thought that they had a relationship, that she had built some trust between them. Apparently not as much as she'd thought.

Oh, Evan. We could have done something, if you'd just said.

She supposed she might have been angry at him for that, but she found that she really didn't blame him. After being forced to rely on himself for so long, what else could he be expected to do?

Trying to distract herself from the desire to strangle something, she glanced out of the grimy, hand-printed window of the cab. Not long after leaving the spaceport, the rain had begun falling steadily, slithering against the sleek architecture of modern London and hissing against the windows of the dense traffic. Ah, Earth, complete with its predictable regional weather patterns. You could go pretty much anywhere in the galaxy, and just about everyone still knew that London was rainy. No one, however, really remembered how it had come to house the central building for the Coalition of Populated Worlds, the governing body of just about everything. When the Coalition was first formed a few decades ago, the vagaries of international politics had forced them to move the headquarters several times, ranging from Sydney to Berlin. Finally, it had settled on London, and for some reason that no one remembered, it had never moved again. Quite a few bio-engineering companies were also based here, including, it seemed, ABI. The cab driver had known instantly what she was talking about when she had given him the name, making her wonder just how large the company actually was.

It doesn't matter. They can own half the planet for all I care. They are not going to stop me.

Just then, the cab turned off the elevated roadway and onto a short exit ramp. A large ad-screen flashed on the other side of Beth's window, depicting a lively animation extolling the attractions of *Windside Business Park.*

"You'll be able to see it in a moment, Ma'am," the cabbie said suddenly, speaking for the first time since leaving the port. That had been Beth's clue that she wasn't handling her feelings very well. Cab drivers were *never* that quiet. "And... there it is. Corporate headquarters of Ol' Benjy. Arkady Biotech Industries."

There were several buildings in line with the young man's pointing finger, but she figured she knew which one it was. Standing out starkly from the generic high-rises surrounding it stood a thick cylinder of a skyscraper. What set it aside from its counterparts was its unusual outer design, made up of a complicated lattice of brushed steel that glittered darkly, even amidst the rain. Although she could see the pattern was regular, it was so thickly woven that it was difficult for the eye to follow any one part to its conclusion. The overall effect reminded Beth of the inner workings of a jet engine. The whole facade seemed designed to speak of power and influence. Seeing for the first time just how enormous her adversary really was, Beth couldn't help her spirits sinking, just a little.

Just then, her view was cut off by another building as the cab pulled off the main thoroughfare and into a smaller side street.

"Relax, lady," The driver said, preempting her question. "I know a shortcut."

"That's awfully nice of you," Beth couldn't help but remark, settling back in her seat. "Don't you know you're supposed to take advantage of newcomers by taking the long way around?"

"Only on the weekends. Besides, I have a quick stop to make…"

Stop?

Distracted as she was, it took her a moment to finally notice that the cab was slowing to a halt at the curb. Beth frowned. "A quick stop? What are you—"

Just then, the doors on either side of the cab flew open, admitting a pair of hulking men wearing long raincoats, who wedged themselves into the back seat and corralled her neatly in the middle. Before the word ambush even registered in her mind, Beth's hand was flying for her LK-2—

It got about halfway there before a third man slid into the passenger seat in front of her, and she was met with the muzzle end of another handgun pointed straight at her forehead. The man behind the gun smiled. "Go ahead and pull it out, ma'am. Just slowly; between your thumb and forefinger." Beth complied, raging at herself. A simple, well-planned, highly effective trap. And here she was, without backup. Had she learned nothing on Hephaestus? Finally, she had her gun out of its holster, dangling harmlessly in her hand. "Well done. Now hand it to the gentleman on your left, if you would be so kind. And then your datapad, again slowly."

As she did as she was told, the men around her all relaxed somewhat. The cab pulled away, taking her towards... wherever they were now going.

"So..." she asked, more calmly than she felt. "What happens now?"

"Now you shut up and wait," said Front Seat, propping his gun-arm on the seatback, and tapping the cabbie on the shoulder with his other hand. "Drive." Not the slightest bit perturbed by the appearance of armed men, the driver did as he was told, neatly merging back into the light traffic.

Calming herself, Beth took stock of her position. Flanked on either side, and in a moving vehicle, there would be no chance for escape even without the gun pointed at her. And from the square-jawed expressions of the men around her, she rather doubted they were in the mood for talk. Still, it was worth a try. What else could she do?

"It's obvious this is more than a carjacking. What do you want?"

Front Seat's eyes didn't move from her even as he ignored the question.

"Jon, check her. Is it here?"

The man on her right stirred, reaching down and producing Phillips' case. "This looks like it. Open it?"

"Open it."

It was the same people as had come after the case the first time, Beth realized. Having failed the blunt-force angle, they were trying a more subtle approach. And it worked. They were going to take the virus, and there was nothing she could do about it. Still, she consoled herself with the thought that the case wouldn't open. Even after setting Ramirez on it, they hadn't been able to get so much as a click out of it...

As she watched, "Jon" produced a device that looked somewhat like a chunky datapad and pointed it at the clasp of the case.

For several seconds there was a rapid electronic chirping sound, and the clasp sprang happily open. As the lid was lifted, the case gave a slight humming sound, reminding Beth of a refrigerator.

"Well, it definitely *looks* like it," the man commented, perusing the collection of vials and tubes. "But how do we know they didn't make a copy?"

"They didn't make a copy," Front Seat replied confidently. "We checked the records. Phillips had this thing custom made. No others quite like it in the galaxy. With the time they took to get here, they wouldn't have had time to stop off anywhere for another. No, we have what he's looking for."

"*He* who?" Beth broke in, unable to keep silent. "What is this all about? One of my crew almost died for this, and one man already has, so I think I have a right to know."

Front Seat shrugged. "What do I look like, a civil rights activist? We could easily drive this cab somewhere out of the way and put a hollow-point in your brain. But he says no. Just be content with your life, even if it's at the price of ignorance." He gestured sideways with the gun. "I believe this is your stop. Have a nice day."

For the first time, Beth noticed that the cab had indeed stopped. One more second, and she saw exactly where. "ABI? Really?"

"Why not? That's where you wanted to go, wasn't it? We'll even cover the fare."

The man on Beth's left opened the door and slipped out, holding the door like a perfect gentlemen. He even offered back her gun and datapad. She would have suspected a trick, except for the dozens of people going about their business not fifty feet away. Unfortunately, that meant that she could not simply snatch her gun and turn the tables on the thieves, either. Grinding her teeth, Beth stepped into the rain and took her belongings, jamming them into her jacket pocket. "Slick move, gentlemen. But we'll see how far your smooth talk gets you when the Blues haul your sorry backsides in to the brig."

"Ah, yes. The police." Front Seat smiled condescendingly. "I'm afraid that sending our good friends at the LPD on a wild goose chase after a private cab with no plates or transponder won't do you much good. However, you're certainly welcome to try." With that, the cab pulled away and faded into the curtain of rain, taking the case, Phillips' message, and Beth's only hope for Coalition help along with it.

She watched them go, scowling; angry at the world, and herself. Why *hadn't* she made a copy of the message? Why hadn't she taken Grant with her? Ramirez could easily handle following Evan on his own. What had she been thinking? And then of course there was the sheer simplicity in how she had been suckered. The men had merely cornered her and taken what they wanted. Clean, no fuss, no frills. No chance of tracing the cab or the men, just like on Hephaestus. Beth almost had to admire them, and that made it even worse.

Finally, she calmed herself, watching her long breath turn to vapor in the chill air. Well, who cared about the bloody case? Who cared about Phillips and his mad science, or corporate games? That was someone else's problem now. All she cared about was her crew, and that meant saving Evan. To hell with everything else.

Setting her eyes on the door, she did her best to set aside her doubts and concentrate on the mission, planning it like a military operation. After all, she had faced enemies before. This was not so different from an engagement. *Of course, I have no advanced recon in this area. Or wingman. Or radar. Flying blind, then.* She shook her head. *Well, then you do what you did then. 'Engage and adapt as necessary.'* Drawing herself to full height and putting on her best pilot's swagger, she advanced purposefully up the stairs and stepped through the door out of the rain.

The lobby of the building was about the same as any large business she had ever seen, if a bit more grand. Beth's impression of the place was one of brushed steel, glass, and polished stone, here and there embedded with lightstrips to increase the shining, artistic effect. Between the patter of the rain outside, the soft music, and the low murmur of conversation that filled the cavernous space, it was all very soothing.

Beth wasn't soothed.

She scanned the room, looking for evidence of her objective. After a second, she noted the receptionist desk set off to her left. As she approached, the young female behind the desk looked up, offering a patently fake smile. "Welcome to Arkady Biotech Industries. How can I help you?"

Beth drew the hated notice from her pocket, thrusting it across the desk. "I'm here to see someone about this."

The girl frowned a little in distaste as she unfolded the dog-eared and slightly damp document, quickly scanning the contents. "Ah. Yes. Are you in need of a faster replacement for your product? I can arrange…"

"No, I need to talk with someone in charge," Beth snapped, her voice carrying in the large space. "The note says I can do that. So where can you direct me?"

The girl wilted slightly under the pressure, studiously occupying her eyes with carefully refolding the note. "Our current representative is busy at the moment, but she should be back in a few minutes." She tentatively offered it back, pointing to a large door on the other side of the room. "If you want to step through there and wait…"

Beth snatched back the note and stuffed it in her pocket, stalking toward the indicated door. She was about to step through when suddenly she became aware the secretary had something else to say.

"Wait, are you sure… Yes, of course, sir… Ma'am? Excuse me, ma'am?"

Beth turned back, finding the young woman holding up a hand to wait, the other pressed against the side of her head as if receiving a call. After a second, Beth realized that was exactly what was happening.

"Yes sir… Yes, I'll send her right up. Thank you, sir."

The girl dropped her hands and turned back to Beth, looking flustered and surprised. "Mr. *Arkady* would like to see you. In his *office*."

Beth frowned. "Arkady? As in…?"

The girl nodded, pointing to the glowing lettering on the front of her desk that spelled out *Arkady Biotech Industries.*

"*That* Mr. Arkady. Please, he would like to see you as soon as possible. Take that elevator over there. His office is the top floor."

Totally unsure what to think, Beth nodded. "Er… right. Where is his office?"

The receptionist blinked. "It's the top floor."

It took Beth a moment to get it.

"Er… right," she said finally. "Thank you."

A moment later, the elevator doors closed behind her. Finding the highest number listed, she thumbed the button. The car began to rise with scarcely a hum or feeling of motion. This done, Beth leaned back against the wall, blowing out a breath as she tucked a stray tendril of damp hair behind her ear. It was finally hitting her exactly what was happening here. She was on her way to speak with the president of one of the largest genetics firms in the galaxy, after simply walking in from the street.

I wanted to talk with someone in charge… But I wasn't expecting someone this *in charge.*

Beth denied the fact that she felt slightly intimidated. After all, this Arkady was just a man. What had he ever done, besides build a business? What was the difference between them?

A dozen decimal places of income and a few hundred thousand employees, that's what.

She squared her shoulders, watching the numbers count up on the display.

It doesn't matter. Remember what they did to Evan.

* * *

"Let's clear one thing up before we begin. There have been three other cases of Fletcher's Wolves bypassing their safeguards before you, so I don't think you need to give me the speech you've been preparing about how you figured it out on your own. That little fiction is not necessary. Am I clear?"

Evan nodded mechanically. He hadn't really expected it to work anyway.

"Now, I said that we could have this conversation without violence, and I meant it. To begin with, I'm going to ask you a series of questions. You may choose whether or not to answer them. Know, however, that I will be the judge of whether or not you are being honest." Dr. Morrow paused. "Do you have any questions before I begin?"

"Yes," Evan said, knowing he was only delaying the inevitable. "Since there have been other cases of Fletcher's Wolves getting around their safeguards, why am I in here instead of just being euthanized?" He didn't believe Dr. Morrow's statement about not resorting to violence for a second. Any questions that he chose not to answer would be asked again and again and again until the doctor either had an answer that satisfied him or grew tired of the game. Evan only hoped he could hold out that long.

"A good question, Subject 112. You used to ask a lot of those, I remember. I was afraid that that was something we trained out of you, but I'm glad to see you still have that inquisitive nature." Dr. Morrow cleared his throat. The sound seemed especially loud in the small room. "The simple answer to your question, 112, is that the other wolves were killed immediately following the incidents. I'm sure you remember what happened to your poor friend Subject 47. You are the only subject to survive an encounter that forced you to override your safeguards."

Subject 47. *Gwyn*. How long ago was it now? Nine years since she had been killed? The memory was still painful. A couple of guards had come to take Evan away for some punishment detail—he didn't even remember what it was—and Gwyn had stepped in and refused to let him go. Tempers had flared, blows were struck, and in the confusion Gwyn had torn a chunk out of one of the guards' arms. Evan had been close enough that Gwyn's blood had splattered on him when they shot her.

"Now, unless you have any other questions, I think we are ready to begin." Dr. Morrow had a very pleasant voice; a rich, friendly baritone that always made him sound as if he were talking to a favorite grandchild.

It wasn't just appearances that could lie.

"Mark Twain once said: 'A man can seldom—very, very seldom—fight a winning fight against his training. The odds are too heavy.' You, 112, have beaten the odds. That intrigues me. What were the events that led to you, ah, shall we say, *circumventing* your safeguards?"

"Two men came into my room and tried to kill me," Evan said bluntly. He had no reason to lie about what the Doctor probably already knew. "One of them pointed a gun at my head and pulled the trigger."

"And you decided that your life was more important than theirs."

Evan winced. Whether he would have wanted to answer or not, he couldn't. What had he been thinking? Just because he didn't want to die he decided that he had the right to—

No. Stop thinking about it. He's trying to get inside your head. You did what had to be done. They killed Dr. Phillips and they would've killed you and everybody else. It was self-defense, there's no moral dilemma. He clamped his jaw obstinately.

"Interesting." Evan heard the quick scratch of a pen on paper. "And you didn't experience the stress-response designed to inhibit you from harming a human." It was a statement, not a question. "There are two ways that that could happen. Either the safeguards designed to release CRH into your system didn't work, or you've figured out how to overcome them. Now, I know that the first possibility is not what happened; laboratory testing has shown that the stress-response works as intended. That leaves my other theory."

Dr. Morrow began to pace, his footsteps moving methodically back and forth.

"It's been said that great men are characterized by the greatness of their mistakes as well as the greatness of their achievements, so I view this as a learning experience. There is a problem with the safeguards that I designed and now I have been presented with an opportunity to fix it.

Rather, *we* have the opportunity to fix it, if you work with me." He stopped pacing and stood at the side of the chair in silence for a while.

"I intend to correct my error, and although I will get the information I need in time, I would rather not resort to crude methods of making you give it to me. It really is your choice how we conduct the remainder of this conversation, so I will put the important question to you right now, 112. How are you bypassing the safeguards?"

Evan had made his choice long ago.

"My *name* is *Evan*."

There was a *click* followed by an electric crackle.

For a second, he couldn't feel anything out of the ordinary. Then a cold sensation flooded through his entire body and he went rigid, lances of pain shooting under his skin. He felt his limbs straining involuntarily against their restraints as his muscles spasmed. It seemed to go on forever.

Right as he began to black out, the crackling stopped. He could breathe again. He slumped back in the chair, sucking in deep breaths of the cool air. The tang of ozone stung his nose and he could taste blood, but it was still the sweetest air he had ever tasted.

"Not here, it isn't," the doctor said, his pleasant tone unwavering. "You grew up with names in your little "packs"— oh yes, we knew about those—but names are nothing but a formality. A crutch you use to interact with your owners and each other. Names are what people have, and you, I'm afraid, are not a person. You are an artificial intelligence, a malfunctioning machine, and we need to find out what exactly is wrong with you. So I ask you again: how are you bypassing the safeguards?"

Trying not to show how scared he actually was, Evan pinned his ears back and gave the doctor a long, low growl.

"I regret your decision, Subject 112, I really do." Dr. Morrow sounded pained. "I had hoped that you would see reason, but it seems that that is not the case. Unfortunate, really. You could save yourself from a lot of pain if you would only tell me. I'm giving you a choice here. That should not be taken lightly." He sighed. "I want you to know that this hurts me more than it hurts you."

Click.

* * *

Beth blew out a breath as the elevator eased silently to a stop. *Top floor: Power-grabs, hostile takeovers, and profit mongers. Please watch your step.*

As the polished doors slid smoothly apart, she couldn't help but raise an eyebrow at what she saw beyond. The office in front of her did not quite take up the entire top floor of the building, but it had to be close. She was faced with a large oblong room, decorated in a thoroughly modern style of polished metal and synthetic padding. Cold and soulless, Beth thought. About halfway around the oblong, the walls and ceiling gave way to glass, providing a surreal view of the outside through the interlaced metal pattern that had first caught her eye on the outside. With the rain battering against the glass and the thunder rolling overhead, the effect was rather like being inside the storm. At the far end of the room there was a large desk, and behind this desk stood a man.

"Captain Hugin. Please, have a seat."

Frowning, Beth began to make her way across the wide expanse of floor, her wet boots squeaking incongruously against the tile. As she drew closer, she took the opportunity to assess her host.

He was a surprisingly large man for his perfectly average height, having no trouble filling the broad shoulders of his tailored dark suit. By the speckling of grey amid his obviously professionally-styled black hair and trimmed beard, Beth estimated him to be in his mid forties, perhaps a bit older. And by the frown lines around his eyes and mouth, it was obvious he hadn't done a lot of smiling in that time. All in all, it was about what she would have expected of a CEO; powerful, wealthy, but boring.

"Thank you for coming at such short notice," Arkady said, his voice surprisingly gruff. A smooth-talker by training then, not by talent. "I understand that my invitation came as a surprise down there."

"It did," Beth replied, settling herself in one of the indicated chairs, feeling the cushions adjust automatically to her form. "I came in expecting to talk with some sales rep."

Arkady did give a thin smile at that. "No company can exist without its customers, and when it can no longer communicate with its customers, it can no longer exist. Usually we have to work very hard to initiate a dialogue with consumers, which is why it's refreshing that you took the time and effort to come in today. My favorite kind of customer is the one that doesn't let us get away with anything, which is why I wanted to extend my personal apology for your experience with our faulty product."

Beth narrowly avoided rolling her eyes. *If all I get is a canned speech, I think I would rather have had the sales rep.* "You know about that already, then," she said instead. "You exchange memos fast around here."

"Well, this is a very serious breach of company standards. When something so incredible as a bio AI breaking safeguards happens on my watch, I make it my business to know..."

"Wait," Beth broke in. "Are you saying this has happened *before*?"

Arkady grimaced. "Yes. There have been three other instances of Fletcher's Wolves breaking safeguards. Although out of the hundreds of successful products, this is a very respectable margin. Even despite the standards we uphold here at ABI, no product is perfect..."

Beth tuned out then, her anger stopping her ears to the reiteration of Arkady's apology. It had happened before.

It had happened *before*.

For all the talk of Fletcher's Wolves being totally safe, these *hypocrites* already knew that wasn't quite true. Which meant that Evan wasn't even the first that they had dragged off, muzzled and bound. What did they honestly expect? That they could make a living being and then just have it perform to a specification?

"...So be assured, we will learn a lot from this failure, and continue make sure that our products remain safe."

Unable to think of what to say, Beth nodded. "Great. Well, you... do that, then."

"So... what else can I help you with, Captain? I understand you had another grievance. If this is about replacing your product, I can see what I can do to shepherd the paperwork through..."

"No, no. That's not it at all," Beth cut in, more to stop him talking than anything else. All this talk of *products* was serving to stir her anger back to life. "This isn't about a replacement, this is about *him*. I want Evan back."

For a moment, Arkady looked utterly confused. "Evan. I'm sorry, I have *no* idea what you're talking about— Oh. You mean Subject 112?"

Beth blinked, thinking back to the number on the papers... "Yes. Subject 112, Evan. Who did you think I was talking about?

"I'm... sorry, I was made aware some time ago that they had started giving themselves names, but I haven't thought about it since then. Our scientists allowed it because they felt it might make interaction with the owners easier."

Beth stared. They *allowed* them to have *names*?

"Fine. Evan, Subject 112, whatever. I want him back."

Arkady was silent for a long moment. A roll of thunder rattled the glass, a loud noise amid the quiet. Finally, Arkady sighed. "I see. You've grown attached to it," He said, his tone that of workplace euphemism.

"I guess that's one way to put it," Beth parried. "I've come to appreciate the work he does, and more importantly, appreciate him as a person."

"As a person?" Arkady repeated incredulously. "I see. Captain Hugin, have you ever heard the term 'anthropomorphization?'"

Beth frowned. "Once or twice. Explain it to me."

"It's a concept that we've come across in our research a few times. By dictionary definition, it means to assign personality or attributes to an inanimate or nonhuman object. Basically, to credit the distinction of humanity to something that is not. It is something that humans are very prone to do. We name our cars. Stuffed animals remain popular. Most captains still refer to their ships as a 'she,' despite centuries of maritime regulation. With respect, I believe that's what's happening here. To be fair, it's not totally uncommon. Even Emma Fletcher, the creator of the Fletcher's Wolves, suffered from the same kind of sentiment, jeopardizing her scientific state of mind. As with her, you have interacted with 112, heard it speak, watched it work, and have made the incorrect assumption that it has to be some kind of human. I can only assure you that this is not the case." Arkady leaned forward earnestly. "Subject 112 is an artificially created lifeform. It was grown and raised in a laboratory, monitored by our scientists from inception to sale. It was designed and manufactured, just as any other consumer product on the market, and deserves no more status than a high-end AI or robot. In fact, I would say that the only difference between the two is that a Fletcher's Wolf lasts much longer without maintenance, and can perform complex tasks with less instruction."

Calling upon a habit born in her military days, Beth disconnected her face from her emotions, allowing her anger to seethe without jeopardizing further civil conversation. "Be that as it may, I want him back. Especially after the appalling conduct of those thugs you sent with their guns to haul him away."

"Please, Captain. The guns were for your protection. We can never be sure how a faulty subject will react in the face of apprehension. If it harmed a human once, the assumption is that it can do so again. That facilitates the employment of some rather... rough individuals in order to assure your safety."

"Right. The fact remains, Evan is a product that I purchased, fair and square," Beth riposted, throwing his clean corporate jargon back at him, "a product with which I was quite satisfied. You had no right to take him from me without my consent."

"Actually Captain, we are well within our rights as a company. If you had read the terms of ownership, you would have noticed that line six in subsection C states that Arkady Biotech Industries reserves the right to recall any product deemed to be in violation of quality control standards, so long as we refund or replace said product within six to ten business days. And even if we had not put this clause in place, the law would require us to take similar action."

Beth felt her position eroding quickly beneath her, but continued on. "What do you mean?"

Arkady sighed. "Clearly, you are not familiar with the Artificial Intelligence Homicide act. I don't know the exact wording, but the intent is that any Artificial Intelligence that is the direct cause for the death of a human being, regardless of circumstances, is to be immediately destroyed."

"What? What kind of stupid bureaucrat came up with a law like that?" She was no student of the law, but even a single second of thought exposed enough problems with such a law that she nearly felt sick. There were *always* circumstances. What if a crazed gunman broke into a crowded building, and an AI was presented with the choice between the death of one clearly guilty human and the death of dozens of innocents? Or what if an AI simply chose to defend itself against those who would destroy it for criminal reasons?

Like Evan. I guess self-defense isn't a viable plea anymore.

"I'm not sure I would call it stupid," Arkady commented amid her thoughts. "As with all the laws, it stands for our protection. Subject 112 must now be classed as a rogue artificial intelligence. And you wouldn't advocate the protection of a potentially hazardous AI, would you?"

Beth almost laughed. As far as adjectives went, *potentially hazardous* summed up Tavia perfectly.

"I would, actually," she answered. "Would, and have. Go figure, huh?"

Arkady blinked eloquently. "You're a woman

of interesting ideals, Captain. That's all I can say."

"Yeah," Beth sighed. "I've been finding that more and more lately."

It was then that the enormity of her task settled squarely on her shoulders, weighing down her hopes. It was one thing to have ABI against her, massive an obstacle as it was. It was quite another to be against the governing body of a dozen different planets. Even more, it seemed her enemy was things as fundamental as greed, and complacency. The inconsistency of a society that shouted *fairness* and *equality* as if it was a holy mantra, and still turned a blind eye to such injustice. It was too big for her. What could one woman do against that?

Stop it, she told herself firmly, cutting herself off before more defeatist thoughts could creep in. One woman could do plenty. All it took was one person making enough noise for others to take notice. *I guess the Coalition headquarters will be the next stop, then.*

"Right. Well, I can see that all I'm doing now is wasting everyone's time," She said calmly, standing up. "I'll be going now."

Arkady looked pained. "I'm sorry I couldn't be of more help, Captain. What I can still do is put in a specific request that your replacement product be similar to 112. It will probably take more time, but—"

"Save it," Beth cut him off, forcing down her instinct to punch him. "Just... save it." With that she turned away, fully intending to leave the office without a second glance. Curiously, Arkady did not seem to take the hint to shut up.

"I'm truly sorry, Captain," he called after her. "Contrary to what you might think, I did find this conversation very helpful. The final move, if you will, in our little game."

Beth stopped, even before she truly knew why. On hearing the familiar words, her imagination worked of its own accord, imagining Arkady's speech filtered through the electronic distortion of a speaker grille.

It was a perfect match to the mystery caller.

Almost before she realized it, Beth was wheeling around, reaching for her LK-2—

"I wouldn't do that, Captain," Arkady said calmly, raising a hand. Something in the tone made her stop. She glanced where his hand was indicating, finally noting a pair of bulges in the ceiling on either side of Arkady's desk.

"The very latest in sensor profiling technology," He explained. "If it recognizes a weapon pointed in my direction, you'll be shocked into unconsciousness before you pull the trigger. Very unpleasant, I'm told. I would far rather we talk like civilized people."

He could have been bluffing, Beth knew. But even if he was, she saw the uselessness in drawing a gun on one of the world's most powerful businessmen. Far more useful to hear what he had to say, especially with Ramirez's device listening in. Forcing herself to relax, Beth slowly removed her hand from the grip of her pistol. As she did, she carefully thumbed the control to activate the compact recording device sewn into the lining of her jacket. "Okay," she said, showing Arkady her empty hand. "Fine. But I'm not sure how civilized we can be, considering how many times you've tried to kill me and my crew. It's you, isn't it? The voice on my phone? The one who had us followed in the taxi? Commissioned an assault team to kill us?"

"That's right. Your number is #4 on speed dial, right under my head of sales." In the time it took for him to say it, Arkady seemed to undergo a subtle change. Beth could only describe it as more…relaxed, more rough around the edges. A driven man, no longer worried about public perception. "Does it honestly surprise you that much?"

"I suppose it shouldn't," Beth admitted. "It makes a lot of sense. You've certainly got the resources. And I suppose it was your men that held me up outside."

"Right again. Check and mate. I was finally able to gain enough grasp of your behavior to predict your movements. All it took was finding the right button to push. In this case, oddly enough, it was a matter of actually following the law, taking Subject 112 away. I figured you would come charging over here, and you did. After so many failed attempts, I finally have the case. I won't tell you where, obviously."

Beth shook her head. "It's really that important to you? A huge biotech firm, sinking this much time and effort into acquiring the work of a tiny startup? That doesn't make sense."

"It does when I tell you that we can't figure it out. We've sunk hundreds of millions of dollars into an adaptable carrier virus. The money I was prepared to offer you is a mere drop in the tank compared to the profit that would be lost if an upstart lab and a third-rate geneticist were to stumble on a marketable product. After you surprised me by refusing, the money spent commissioning retrieval teams was just a slightly bigger drop."

"And if you can't make it, steal it?"

"Exactly," Arkady responded, shrugging off the slight.

Beth huffed in disgust. "So you lied, cheated, and even resorted to murder, just to protect lost profits. As rich as you are, you care about money that much? Are all large company CEOs as pathetic as you, or are you special?"

"Of course I don't care about the *money*. You're right, there's a point when I have more money than I can ever spend. In fact, I am a patron to many charities and nonprofits. But in the game of business, money is the scoreboard. Lost profit would mean that I lost. And I don't lose."

"Then... why are you telling me all this?" Beth finally asked, unable to hold it inside. "You didn't have to see me today, and you certainly didn't have to tell me. I would never have known. Hell, why did I even make it here without your thugs putting a round through me? You stopped them, but *why*?"

Arkady was silent a moment, thoughtfully twirling a stylus through his fingers. "That's a good question. Maybe because you interest me. Most people don't do that anymore. I'm not entirely sure what it is that makes you interesting. Maybe it's how you continue to live your life so faithfully to an obviously outdated set of ideals. Maybe it's because you actually forced me to stretch to find out a way to beat you."

"What do you mean?" Beth asked, struggling to process. "So I gave you a run for your money. What's so interesting about that?"

"The fact that, quite frankly, that doesn't happen very often," Arkady said, turning to gaze idly out into the storm. "I have a talent for reading people and situations, Captain. The ways people behave and react, how I can push and pull and redirect to fit my purposes. Business sense, some people might call it. It's the main reason I'm where I am today, and I've sharpened it quite a bit over the years. So much that it honestly gets easy. Merger here, acquisition there, deal before lunchtime, government bribe in the afternoon... Honestly, it gets *boring*, getting everyone to dance to my tune all the time. It just isn't a challenge anymore." He looked up. "And then a few days ago, the situation with Dystech comes up. Phillips hires you to carry him, and you say yes. I try to hire you, and you say no. For the first time in months, I am surprised. Still, no problem. Send in assault team, take the blunt force route. And then you and your crew put up a much greater fight than I thought, enough that I had to pull them out before you took one alive and spoiled the whole thing. Again, a surprise. And then I called you again, ready to pick up the pieces now that your contractor was dead... and then you turn me down again. Surprise number *three*. Captain, you single-handedly provided me with more enjoyment than I've had for years. I just couldn't pass up this opportunity to tell you that, and to thank you. Truly, I'm only sad that it's over."

Up until that point, Beth had no idea what to say. Having an *enemy* look her in the eye and say "thank you" for being a serious pain in the backside was definitely something new. But a challenge... that was something familiar she could grasp. "Wait, hold on. What makes you think it's over? I'm still here, aren't I?"

"Please Captain, don't fool yourself. I have the case, and you have nothing. Someone like you should be able to grasp the value of accepting a graceful defeat."

That's what you think, buddy. Ramirez's recorder was capturing the entire conversation. She would have the whole thing, clear as music, on her datapad. "Well then, I guess you're in for surprise number four," she said confidently. "Goodbye, Mr. Arkady."

As she turned to leave, she heard him sigh. "We'll see. Goodbye, Captain."

Her last sight of him was him raising a datapad to his ear, his smooth-talking CEO mask already in place, as if nothing interesting had happened. Then the elevator doors closed, and he was gone.

She blew out a long breath, releasing pent up tension.

That, she thought, had to be the strangest conversation she'd ever had. And soon enough, she would be sharing it with a Coalition officer. She smiled, removing the recording device from its hidden pocket and turning it off. No matter what Arkady seemed to think about the level of his own genius, this game wasn't over yet.

12

"I don't understand you, Subject 112."

Evan slumped down in the chair, too exhausted to think about anything other than how much his body hurt. Not only was he physically worn out, but his mind had gone all fuzzy from the injection the doctor had given him. He was still coherent enough to know that that was a bad thing.

I've got to stay focused. Can't tell him anything. Just won't talk. Got to hold on until he's tired of getting nothing.

"I have tried to make you see reason," Dr. Morrow was saying, "I have debated with you at length on the validity of my reasons, but you refuse to accept the fact that I am trying to *help* you."

In a different situation, Evan might have laughed; but the doctor was entirely serious.

"This is not a pleasant process for either of us, 112, and I'll admit you don't deserve this, but it could have been prevented. *You* could have prevented it." Evan heard a rustle of fabric as Dr. Morrow leaned back against the wall. "You have to understand, the only reason I'm doing this, trying to get this information, is to prevent more deaths. Can't you see? The two wolves who bypassed their safeguards were killed because of their actions. If I can stop others from making the same mistake they did, then it is my duty to do so. I'm working for the good of all Fletcher's Wolves, 112, you must see that.

"You, on the other hand," Evan could almost hear the doctor change gears, "are not protecting anyone by withholding this information. You are hurting those who you call your friends, your pack-mates, by letting this…flaw go uncorrected. You are putting a loaded weapon to their head and allowing them to pull the trigger! The ones that the safeguards really protect are the wolves, not their owners. If they override the safeguards, they will be killed; either by their owners who can no longer trust them, or by the government, for breaking the AI Homicide Law. Think! If Subject 47 hadn't attacked the handler, she would still be alive! You, Subject 112, are personally endangering each and every one of your so-called friends by obstructing my efforts to correct this defect."

Evan knew he was making a mistake, but he couldn't let the doctor's statement go uncontested. "No. That… It isn't a defect. It's the one thing that we have control over. And it shows... I think it shows that we are more dependable and trustworthy when we make our own decisions, rather than just being an... rather than just being machines."

Dr. Morrow wrote again in his book. "It is a tribute to your kind that you kept us convinced of the fact that your safeguards were working as intended for so long. But because they were not truly foolproof, you and three others forfeited your lives."

Evan's ears twitched, but he made no other move. He had known what was coming, but this was the first time Dr. Morrow had mentioned it. Maybe it was a sign that he was running out of patience? Probably not. He seemed to have a limitless supply. Evan wondered how much longer he could go before either the doctor decided it wasn't working and just had him put down, or finally forced the information out of him.

No! He gritted his teeth angrily. *I can't think like that. I can't tell him. He's wrong. I know he's wrong. I know...* His train of thought trailed off. *Just think of who you're doing this for: Maria and Sharp and Mel and Weaver and...and everybody else. They wouldn't let you down; you can't let them down.*

"I can see that you are still not convinced." Dr. Morrow sighed and closed his notebook with a snap. "That's unfortunate. Maybe a night to think it over will change your mind. But since I can't have you sleeping, I'm afraid I'll need to hook you up to an IV drip." Evan flinched as he felt a needle slide into his forearm. "Through the night, this will administer a simple theobromine solution at regular intervals," Dr. Morrow went on conversationally. "Don't worry though, while theobromine *is* lethal to canines in large doses, I have already tested this particular solution thoroughly. The only negative effect you will experience is an inability to fall asleep. Giving you plenty of time to think over what I've said. And if you have been dealing with a cough, by any chance, it will clear that up as well."

Evan's heart sank. He knew he should have expected something like this, but the denial of a chance to rest and regain some of his strength was devastating. He would be that much less prepared when Dr. Morrow returned.

The bolt on the door slid back. "I hope that this time to reflect will help you realize the mistake you are making. Remember, I don't enjoy this any more than you do. I'm trying to help all of you, but I need a piece of information to do that."

"Over my…dead…body," Evan snarled weakly.

"Unfortunately, it will come to that in time. How long it takes is up to you. Goodnight, Subject 112."

And with that, Dr. Morrow was gone.

Once the door finally shut, Evan slumped down in the chair and began to shake uncontrollably. How long Dr. Morrow had spent, asking him questions and running low-voltage electricity through him, he had no idea. He had lost track of time a while ago and was too tired to work out when he had arrived at the Compound.

After a few minutes, he got the shaking under control and tried to take stock of his situation. *Okay, you haven't told Dr. Morrow anything yet, but he doesn't sound like he is…like he's about to give up, either. No one that knows you're here would…could do anything about it, and you're too well secured to make an…to make it out on your own. Not to mention how tired you are. And the security. And where you'd go after you got out.*

He groaned. It was a bad situation that had only two endings.

His job was to make sure it wasn't the ending Dr. Morrow wanted.

* * *

Though she had never seen it before, the Coalition headquarters building was about as she had expected. Large, sprawling, labyrinthine, with décor that was unsure if it wanted to be modern or classic. Each department was seemingly separated by walls that could not easily be circumvented, and not many of the employees knew much about what another was doing. After talking with three different clerks, she found herself getting precisely nowhere. Finally, after threatening to disturb the bureaucracy with a raised voice and coarse language, she was finally inducted into the more serious portions of the building. It was there, in the sublevels that she began to see the bare cinderblock walls, armed guards, and monitor stations. It reminded her of some of her military days. Grim-faced officers giving orders after the visit of a well-dressed civilian. Men in suits standing in the ops room. It all spoke silently of Intel. At last, she found herself in a small room with a mirror, sitting across a cheap table from a bland-looking middle-aged man.

"I'll tell you something, Captain," he said, obviously bored. "I have to deal with a lot of bedtime stories in this job. I mean, I've heard it all. Killer robots, murder plots, I've even met an eighty-four year old woman claiming to be lost European royalty who was kidnapped by terrorists as a child. But this one sets new levels for audacity."

"That was about my reaction," Beth stated calmly. All of this was to be expected. She was under no illusions.

"Uh-huh. So, just to get this straight. You're here, because you just came from being carjacked by three men. One of them handed you a 'pad, and you proceeded to talk to Benjamin Arkady. *The* Benjamin Arkady, who then confessed to ordering a hit on a small-time genetic scientist who was wrapped up in a giant conspiracy involving spies, thieves, and a potential super-weapon. Does that about sum it up?"

Beth nodded, brushing a strand of wet hair out of her face. "Pretty much."

The man sighed, taking off his glasses to rub his eyes. "Well, here's the problem with this whole thing, Captain. You come here with this whole story, you tell me that this is all because of some job bidding that we have, and that this alleged Dr. Phillips managed to create a fully adaptable whatever-the-hell-it-is virus, and expect me to believe all of it. And yet you come here with no Dr. Phillips, and no virus. I mean, I've been here a long time. It's crazy. Crazy enough to be true. But where is the proof? I'll even settle for just *evidence*, circumstantial or otherwise. But you have to give me *something*."

Beth nodded, calmly setting the recorder on the table before her. The man eyed it dubiously.

"Is this it?"

"Yeah. It doesn't get much more definitive than that."

He picked it up, turning it over carefully in his hands. "And what exactly am I supposed to find on here?"

"That would be my grand conversation with Mr. Arkady, shortly after his thugs carjacked me. That was hidden on the inside of my belt. You learn to carry around a little portable insurance out in this big bad universe of ours."

"It's not very nice, but it's the only one we've got." The man commented absently, still palming the device. Finally, he looked up. "Alright. I'll check this out. You wait here."

Beth hid a jubilant smile. "I won't move a muscle. Take as long as you need."

With the prospect of something interesting appearing to have perked him up considerably, the man took the recorder and left the room.

As the door shut behind him, Beth allowed herself a flush of victory.

I've got you now, Arkady. Let's see you weasel your way out of check after this.

Well, she supposed it wasn't quite a checkmate. Men like Arkady could throw their power and wealth into commissioning the best lawyers and fixers available. And they were only helped along by the speed of the judicial system, which, to put it generously, was about as swift as a herd of narcoleptic turtles stampeding through peanut butter. There would probably be no conviction, in the end, but she didn't care.

It will be enough. Enough to get Evan back.

After that, she could leave them to rot. ABI and the Coalition both. She had not been there for her old family, but she *would* be there to save the new. Secure as she was in that thought, she actually started slightly as the door opened quietly, admitting the quiet passage of another man. A different one than had taken her query, she was gratified to see. The newcomer had a sort of senior officer look about him, although she couldn't quite pinpoint why. The only thing that she could really used to describe him was that he was distinctly average every way, from his height, to his haircut, to his tailored dark suit. And yet, there was still something around him that definitely said *spook*.

"Sorry to keep you waiting," he said, not sounding the slightest bit apologetic as he slid into the chair opposite. "My name is Agent Bale, Investigative Services," he said, withdrawing a datapad and stylus. "I need to ask you a few questions."

Beth sighed. "You need me to relate the incident *again?*"

"No, we have all of that recorded and on file already. No, these questions are more about you. Call it professional curiosity."

Ah. Of course. She supposed that she shouldn't be surprised by a little psycho-analysis. It was I.S., after all.

"Sure, go ahead."

"Good," Bale said, tapping his 'pad screen with the stylus. "I've got your military record here. It's quite impressive. You were climbing a lot of ladders in those days. You were going to make wing commander, at the very least."

Beth felt her jaw clench. Wing commander had indeed been her long-term goal. She had sparred, maneuvered, and climbed on the shoulders of others in order to reach it. She would have gotten it too, if she had continued to pursue her career with the same level of tenacity.

"Right up until that tragic incident with your family," Bale went on calmly.

"That's then your focus changed entirely. You served your tour, took your capital, you picked up a few, pardon the expression, misfit nobodies, and began a new career in shuttling cargo in some of the less savory circles of the galaxy. But even amid all of that, you manage to maintain a spotless image of efficiency. You could make a tremendous living if you just signed a contract with a large corporation, but you've always maintained your admirable, if less than lucrative, independence."

Beth couldn't quite hold back a sarcastic twist to her lip. "Was there a question in there?"

"I'm getting to that, please bear with me. So, when a guy like me takes a look at those facts, I come to a few conclusions. You never hired on with a corporation, which tells me that you probably don't care about ABI. *And* you abandoned your military career, so you probably don't care about the Coalition. So finally, my question is, what exactly are you doing here?"

It was actually a perfectly reasonable query, Beth decided. Looking past the fact that Investigative Services had chosen to keep such a close eye on her, of course. "Well, you're right. I *don't* care. I've even gotten paid for this job already. But ABI has my engineer. And I want him back."

Bale's stylus slid over the plastic screen. "My goodness. Are we talking kidnapping now?"

"That's not what *they* called it. My engineer is a Fletcher's Wolf."

For the first time, Bale's eyes left the datapad.

"Subject 112?"

"His *name* is Evan."

Bale stared unblinking at her for several seconds before his eyes finally dropped back to his notes. "I see. You bought a barker, and then you got attached to it. And then it went and made the mistake of killing some people. And so here you are: hoping that we can get him back to you in exchange for Arkady."

Beth nodded stiffly. "You're not much for subtlety, are you?"

"I like to save time. Still, this case is rather fascinating. Seeing a person like you, driven by honest-to-God *loyalty*. You're a very rare breed, you know that? Very old-fashioned. I thought people like you went out with lithium batteries."

"I'll take that as a compliment."

"Take it how you like. I don't particularly care either way, seeing as I can't help you."

She blinked in surprise. "I'm sorry?"

"I said we can't help you. The case is no good."

Caught completely off guard, a ripple of shock traveled through Beth's gut. "But... What do you mean? I gave you everything you needed..."

"You gave us nothing. That recorder you handed us has nothing on it besides six minutes of gibberish and static."

It suddenly felt as if the floor had tilted beneath her.

No. No... no...

And yet, it all made sense.

A jamming field.

Of course. Arkady would have anticipated her hiding some extra hardware, and had obviously taken steps against it. Countering her move before it was made, as any good chess player would.

She had nothing.

"For my part," Bale broke in, "I think your story is plausible. Personally, I would like nothing better than to nail Arkady to the wall. The guy is as crooked as they come, but he's way too good at covering his tracks. When you came in, I was honestly hoping you had something. But as it stands..." He shook his head. "He suckered you."

For Beth, the meaning hadn't quite managed to filter through the shock. It was unthinkable. Like following the beacon back to her carrier group, only to find empty space.

"So... What do I do now?"

Bale was unsympathetic. "Well, for starters, leave our building. Go back to your ship, take some days off, get your replacement barker, then resume tramping around the galaxy. Forget this Evan."

"I can't do that. I *can't* let him die. It won't happen, not while I'm here."

Bale sighed. "What do you want me to do, Captain? Mount an armed coup to oust the Coalition and change the law? Or do you just want to file a missing person report on a barker with no last name? We can't help you here. Whatever misguided campaign you want to run, you're going to have to do it somewhere else."

Beth could only stare. "That's it?"

"That's it." Stowing his 'pad, he stood up and opened the door for her.

She felt numb. Her mind worked frantically for a response, an opening, some plan she could put into motion. But there was nothing.

She had exhausted her last option. Helpless.

Her body moving without her consent, she stood up and walked through the door, past Bale's impassive face into the soulless concrete of the corridor. Somehow she managed to find her way back to the elevator, although she didn't remember the way. It struck her that she hadn't even been escorted. It seemed the entire Coalition had well and truly dismissed her as irrelevant. A few people attempted to talk to her as she waited for the car, a greeting, a comment, a simple hello, but she couldn't seem to understand what they were saying. Finally, she was thumbing the button for the ground floor, watching the doors slide ponderously closed to leave her mercifully alone in the elevator.

And then she lost it.

"Dammit!" she snarled, pounding her fist against the wall. A dozen negative feelings warred within her, anger, sadness, resignation and loss all battling for dominance. Through it all, she could only wonder: *What do I do now?*

She had exhausted all positive options, and the ones that remained were almost worse than death. She could listen to Bale and Arkady. She could accept the situation and go on with her life. She could just take Evan's replacement, as if he was nothing more than a broken control board that was still under warranty.

But all of that would mean breaking a promise, and going back on what she believed. It would mean giving up on a member of her *family* in exchange for her own convenience. She had done that once before. She would *not* do it again.

But what else *could* she do?

She had no leverage, no weapons, no position. Anyone in authority would not help her, because there was no reason for them to do so. And society could somehow scream about cruelty to trees and animals, and yet turn a blind eye to slavery, so long as it only involved genetically altered animals grown in a laboratory. She was alone against what seemed to be all of society. In her mind's eye, she could see Arkady gloating. *Please Captain, don't fool yourself. I have the case, and you have nothing... Nothing... Nothing...*

No.

At first, she didn't even know where the thought came from. But it was there, burning like a lone candle in the dark. All of the other voices and influences faded away, leaving only a strange kind of clarity. She could see now that it wasn't about strategies, plans or leverage. It was all very simple, in the end. It all came down to a choice. *Her* choice. And so she made it.

She hadn't lost. She wouldn't give up. She wouldn't break her promise. She wouldn't give up her family. There was something she could do. Even if the consequences would more than likely destroy her own future, she decided that a future built on broken promises could not be worth it. By the time the elevator reached the surface, her uncertainty was gone.

No, Evan. I'm coming for you, like I promised that I would. Wait for me.

13

"Captain, you cannot be doing this." There were very few times when Ramirez felt that his accent was an obstacle. After all, it was not very thick, and his vocabulary was as good as the next man. But every once in a while, Beth would get some clearly stupid or suicidal idea or other in her head. And when that happened, no matter how careful he was with his words, she never seemed able to figure out what he was saying.

This was definitely one of those times.

There was the distinctive clatter of spilled ammo from the locker followed by a muffled curse. Beth's head and torso emerged a moment later, along with a double handful of cartridges.

"Are you sure you swept the hull?" she asked distractedly, laying the shells in a pile on one of the medical storage lockers. Ramirez sighed. Still not listening.

"Yes, I am sure. I went over it four times as soon as you called us. There is nothing out there that should not be. No bugs, no devices of any kind."

Beth shook her head. "He knew somehow. There has to be a way that Arkady knew that much."

Ramirez had already been thinking about that. Ever since Beth had called them from the taxi back from the Coalition headquarters, his mind had been turning over the possibilities. When it came to it, there was actually plenty of ways Arkady could have known. He knew that living in such a thriving technological era, every action left traces. The more technologies were used, the bigger the traces. And the crew of the *Memory* used plenty of technology. They had to communicate with the Port Authority and file a flight plan at every stop they made. They had comm calls and payment information to and from their accounts, often accessed with their datapads. And one level up, there were the satellites and surveillance cameras that looked over just about everywhere public, seeing more things than the population at large chose to think about, Beth included. With all of those sources, a person could develop a fairly complete picture of the things that the crew did and said. None of that came as a surprise for Ramirez. He had spent a good portion of his life thinking about these things, and almost as long thinking up ways to defeat them. What bothered him was that in order to know the things he'd talked about, Arkady would need access to *all* of those resources, and perhaps even more. Even more, it would take a certain kind of mind to come to such accurate conclusions from such disparate information. It meant that Arkady was both highly connected, and the worst thing one could possibly have in an enemy. He was *smart*.

And it was this same man whose back yard Beth was preparing to enter.

"Did you hear me, Beth? I said that you cannot be serious about this."

Beth stopped filling an empty magazine for her LK-2 to fix him with a hard stare. "Yeah, I heard you the first time. And yes, I am."

"Alright, I've finished looking up the route to that compound," came the sudden voice of Grant as he stepped through the med ward hatch.

Ramirez sighed as he turned to the security officer. "Charlie, back me up here. Captain, can you just slow down and *think* for a second? You are talking about breaking into a secure, private facility, owned by one of the most powerful organizations in the galaxy. Whose CEO, incidentally, has taken a special interest in you. Apart from all the logistical challenges involved, it is, last I checked, against the law."

"He's got a point, Beth," Grant jumped in, joining Ramirez at the storage compartment hatch. "This is a pretty harebrained scheme. Chief Inspector March might be a nice guy, but I doubt that anybody would let us off for this."

The rhythmic clicking of the rounds into the mag faltered. "You know guys, I think this is the first time I've ever heard *you* express a concern about the law."

"Maybe we have been changing our ways," Ramirez answered. "You were the one to see to that."

"Or maybe," she turned to them, her expression blank, "you're just concerned about something else."

"We're concerned about *you*, Beth," Grant answered gently. "I've already treated you for one gunshot wound in the past week. The next one might be a lot more serious."

"That might be your concern, Charlie," Beth replied, her eyes falling on Ramirez, "but I don't think it's yours."

He was silent for a moment. As ever, Beth was a lot better at reading him than she let on. "I guess... I am just trying to figure out *why* you are willing to put everything on the line to save *him*."

It was Beth's turn to sigh. "That's rather what I thought." She glanced toward the ceiling. "You're awfully quiet, Tavia. Do you have a take on this?"

"I've been listening, Captain. I have to admit that, as well as I know you, I'm having trouble understanding your logic regarding this decision."

Beth looked thoughtful for a moment. "I will admit that logic probably has very little to do with it. But I guess I'm just trying to understand why you guys aren't with me on this. I mean, if it was you in there, wouldn't you expect me to get you out?"

Ramirez blinked in surprise. Despite Beth's conviction, he found that his immediate thought was *no, not worth it*.

Luckily, Grant was there before it could show on his face. "Of course we would, Beth. And I would worry about you every second."

Beth nodded. "Of course you would. We all would. Any one of us. Because that's what a family does. They look out for each other."

"While that is all well and good, Beth, you have to be realistic here. You only knew him for a few days." Ramirez knew even as the words left his lips that it was not a good thing to say, but he followed through anyway. "That makes him family now?"

"How long did I have to know *you*, kiddo?" Beth shot back, revealing the frayed edges of her patience. "I've still got that scar on my arm from that night we first met. You remember? Hauling all those lovely fellows with the knives off of you before they could carve up your meaty bits?"

"I remember." *How could I ever forget?* Ramirez rallied his own patience. "Look, I am grateful that you saved my life, grateful enough that I care about what happens to you. I do not want you to throw your life away."

There was an intense silence, during which Ramirez felt his unease mounting.

Why can she not see? Why can she not understand that getting herself killed will not help anybody? All from some misguided need for atonement for her parents' deaths, which was not even her fault in the first place. This isn't how I would've wanted him to leave either, but he's gone and for good reason.

Finally, Beth broke the silence, glancing up toward the ceiling in the way the human need for location tended to equate with Tavia's presence.

"Tavia? I've been meaning to ask lately, do you feel that you have a choice? I mean, did I ever make you feel as if you couldn't ever go anywhere else or do anything else?"

It took three seconds for the AI to frame an answer, which, Ramirez knew, was eternity in computer terms. "No Captain, you didn't. While you have never asked me before, you have never treated me as anything less than a human being. Which is somewhat amusing, but appreciated. In short, there is no place that I would rather be."

"And you Charlie? Have I ever made you think that you're stuck here?"

Grant shook his head. "Of course not. You've never been manipulative or taken advantage of me. But you saved me from my own demons, even when I could offer nothing in return, as far as you knew. I came for the job, but I stayed because of you. You're a great captain and a true friend, and I wouldn't leave either one of those for the world."

"That means a lot, Charlie, thank you. Ramirez, same question."

Ramirez had never thought about it before. He thought back to his beginning here, after Beth had saved his life and offered him the job. While he had been wary of such—at the time—alien kindness, he had leapt at the chance for steady, legal employment to support his family, and distance from his enemies. There was very little love lost between him and his father, and his mother dealt with everything by seeking drunken oblivion, but he still considered it to be the right thing to send enough home to support them. Since signing on with the *Memory* though, he had quickly come to think of its little crew as his *true* family. Even so, he had always felt a bit detached from it all, preferring his own company to theirs. They all assumed it was his solitary nature, but he knew that it was more than that. He was afraid to admit it, but deep down, he knew that he was sometimes intimidated by Beth and Grant's level of commitment to each other, and to him. He could not imagine trusting and relying on someone as much as they did. But as Grant had said, Beth had never manipulated, or simply assumed that he would stick around. Their arrangement had always been an open door; free to enter, and free to leave.

"No, Beth," he answered, "I have never thought that way."

She nodded. "Good, alright then. That means we're all here by choice. That's your right and privilege, as it should be. But Evan didn't have that choice. I don't mean with us, I mean *ever*. He's spent his life being bought and sold like a piece of property, shuttled from one place to another without any say in the matter. He was on our ship, and we all forgot about him, just like he was some piece of equipment that would mind itself, and he got shot because of it. He would have died if he hadn't defended himself, and because of that, he's in danger again. None of this would've happened if we hadn't forgotten about him. If *I* hadn't forgotten. The way I see it, I've got a second chance here. A second chance at giving him a choice."

She sighed. "Look guys, I won't force you to come with me. But I'm just a pilot. I can't do this without you. Will you help me?"

There was a nervous silence for several seconds. Although her face remained cool, Ramirez knew her well enough to spot tension lurking underneath. He realized with a pang that she really was scared by all this, either scared of what she was about to do, or scared that they would say no.

Typically, Grant was the first to crack. His big voice broke the silence like a hammer smashing through plate glass. "Aw, hell Beth. Of course I'm with you. You've never led us wrong." He laid a square hand on Beth's shoulder, dwarfing her with his proximity. "You're right, Evan is family. We can't let him get slotted for our mistake. Don't forget, I grabbed my gun a dozen paces away and didn't remember. We'll make it right, whatever it takes."

Beth's smile mixed relief and gratitude. "Thank you Charlie. I... Thank you." As she turned to him, he was already anticipating the dreaded next question. "Well Ramirez, what about you?"

He sighed, cursing himself for a fool. "I will come as well. But for your sake Beth, not his."

"Thank you. You're both just so... I don't know what I'd do without you." For a second, there was a flash of what could have been tears in Beth's eyes. She recovered herself quickly, as always. "Right. Now we need a plan. Can you guys tell me about the layout?"

In all of the confusion since Beth's return, they hadn't had a chance to tell their half of the story. Ramirez decided to allow Grant to take point.

"Well... We followed the van, just like you said. They weren't being very careful, so I highly doubt anyone saw us. They took him to some kind of compound in a heavy industrial district. There's a foundry for light-weight alloys just across the way, in fact. We only got a glimpse inside the compound when the gates opened, but it looks like mostly low, one-story buildings. But there's plenty to worry about on the outside before we even get that far. Ramirez did a casual walkabout, and, well..."

"The place is entirely surrounded by a wall," Ramirez said, taking his cue. "At least twenty feet high, made of high-grade, reinforced concrete and topped with razor-wire. I do not fancy our chances of climbing over, and I am reasonably certain that we cannot dig under it even if we had the tools. The only entrance is a main gate on the east side. It is at least six inches of what looks like reinforced metal, also topped by wire. We couldn't climb it, even if there was not a guard with an SMG stationed just outside. CCTV cameras are likely, but hidden."

"In short," Grant picked up, "It looks like a bloody modern-day Stalag 17."

Beth bit her lip in concentration. "There's a way, Charlie. There has to be a way. What kind of resources do we have?"

"Charlie's experience, your determination, my brains," Ramirez was unable to resist saying, "supplemented by a few small arms, plus the shuttle. I suppose we could just land right next to the wall and jump over it from there."

"Very funny," Grant chided. "Could you at least try to *pretend* it can be done? You can't whip up any countermeasures to the electronic security out of those gadgets of yours?"

He shook his head. "I have done a few things like that before, but never on anything approaching this scale. Maybe with a fortune in credits and a month to prepare…"

"Unacceptable." Beth cut in. "We have to move tonight. If they're putting him down to protect their PR, I doubt they'll wait around."

Grant heaved a sigh. "You're right, of course. But I still don't see how we can do it. The problem is the bloody modern times. I'm sure that we could whip up some kind of ruse to get through the gate, but with all of the cameras and sensors they have to be packing, they would be all over us in a second. And I don't favor our chances in a firefight. Who knows how many guards they could have squirreled away?"

The conversation subsided into gloomy silence. Or at least, Ramirez assumed it was gloomy. He himself didn't mind in the slightest that the enormity of what Beth was suggesting was finally penetrating her shell of duty. Hopefully, it would be enough to get her to abort the whole mad scheme…

"Ahem."

Everyone looked up. "Yes Tavia? Do you have a question?" Beth queried.

"I do, actually. I'm wondering why no one has thought to ask *me* for input on any of this?"

Grant frowned. "Well Tavia, great as you are with monitoring the ship for us, I really don't see how you can—"

"Which merely shows the shallow nature of your perception, Charles. What if I told you that I can solve that pesky security problem of yours? If you just get a relay close enough to their system, I can get you in. Doors, camera loops, dummy sensors, data-ghosts, the works. I can make you all invisible."

"Hold on a moment, Tavia," Ramirez cut in. "You can't just walk in. It has to be a secure, hardened system. They have to put down at least one hacking attempt every day. They have teams of people working on keeping it a closed loop."

"I might remind you, Mr. Ramirez, that I am *also* a secure, hardened system. And they still had me dancing like a puppet on a string. Luckily, unlike you humans, it doesn't take me long to learn a trick after I've seen it done. What's that you humans say? Something about leading an old horse to new tricks?"

"You're very much mixing your metaphors," Grant said. "Try just plain Standard. What are you saying here?"

"I'm *saying*, Charlie, that I copied some of the software from the hacking device that the pirates used during the attack. With a military-grade intrusion algorithm, I can crack that civilian system like an egg."

Beth suddenly looked horrified. "And you were going to tell me about this... when?"

"Right now, Captain." If Tavia had the physical nature needed to smile, Ramirez had no doubt that she would be.

Grant cleared his throat. "Well, we have something of a plan, then. If Tavia can hijack the compound, it's actually a fairly simple matter to go in and avoid any patrols. 'Course, simple doesn't mean easy."

Ramirez sighed in resignation. *Well, if we are going to get up to our necks in this anyway, we might as well go all the way...*

"And if it comes down to a gunfight, I want as much protection as I can get. Charlie. I believe that we also have a confession to make."

"I suppose you're right. It's not like there's going to be a bigger occasion to use them."

"What are you two talking about?" Beth asked, exasperated. "What confession? Use what?"

Without a word, Ramirez helped Grant remove some bulkhead paneling from the ceiling above their heads.

"There are some high-power lines for the bridge equipment right above here," Grant explained as they worked. "We figured there would be just enough interference to foil any scanner from detecting these."

The panel finally came loose at one end, dropping a trio of black bundles onto the floor.

Beth gingerly picked up one of the bundles, her frown deepening. "And what are *these*?"

"Those," Grant said, "Are three of the armor-weave combat vests that the pirates were wearing. And not the cheap stuff, either. It should stop most hits of anything up to and including an assault rifle. For the record, it was all Ramirez's idea."

"Uh-huh. And you were in full agreement, Mr. Grant. We were always in it together." Ramirez turned to Beth. "You have to admit, Captain, it is always helpful to have a second chance in the middle of a firefight. And with this plan, I'd say that getting shot is a distinct possibility."

Beth stared at the vest in her hand, absolutely mortified. Finally, she looked up, fixing both men with a hard stare that any mother's son could identify. "We are going to have a *long* talk about this," she said, unfastening the straps on one side of the vest and slipping it over her head. "Later.

"So, now we have the beginnings of a plan. Ramirez, I need you to rent a truck. I suspect we'll need some ground transportation for the getaway. There's no telling what kind of condition Evan will be in when we find him."

Ramirez nodded. "Any preferences?"

"As cheap as possible. And without our ID. I doubt we'll be returning it once we're done."

Aha, finally! A chance for him to use one of his more disreputable contacts. "I know just the thing, Captain. Give me ten minutes."

Beth offered a smile. "Thanks, Ramirez. I know I can always count on you."

Although his face would never show it, he truly enjoyed the compliment. So much so, that he was halfway down the corridor toward his quarters before he found himself wondering why he was still going along with this.

You should have argued harder, he chided himself. Even so, he was surprised to find that he did not have such a bad feeling about the idea anymore. Maybe now that there was some kind of plan. Or maybe all of Beth's talk of friendship and loyalty was rubbing off on him. He hoped not. He couldn't be going soft, now more than ever. Not if he was going to make sure that the people he cared about made it out alive.

* * *

The steady hum of the rental van's tires on the road, a low drone, more felt than heard, was very similar to the sound of the climate control system on the *Memory*, calming in its sheer monotony. But at the moment, Grant wasn't feeling very calm at all. He had to admit, the way Beth had outlined the plan, it sounded like it might work, but his mind kept drifting back to the saying from his security days that *things always seem easy right up until the point where something goes horribly wrong.* This was special ops stuff; way outside his field. He knew how to defend an installation, or a person, but what he was doing now hadn't even been covered in his army days. For half his life, he had learned how to keep people out of secure facilities, and now he had become the very individual he was trained to defeat.

The irony wasn't lost on the big security officer.

Trying to take his mind off the next few hours, he glanced at Beth. Intent as ever on what she was doing, she was driving the rental as adeptly as if she had been doing it all

her life, following Ramirez's map to the ABI
facility where Evan had been taken. As an
LPD patrol car cruised slowly past their van,
Beth and Grant unconsciously pulled the bills
of their nondescript caps lower over their eyes.
The caps were a precaution, albeit a weak one,
in case ABI could pull enough strings to
access the traffic cam records. Personally,
Grant didn't think that even this Arkady
person could have his finger in that particular
pie, but Beth wasn't so sure. She hadn't said
much about her conversation with the man,
but Grant could tell she was shaken. It took a
lot to do that to her. And when Beth worried,
he worried.

The sun had already set, and there was
very little traffic left in the industrial district.
After a few more minutes of silence broken
only by the thrum of the tires, he blew out his
cheeks in a sigh, slouching down in his seat.
Neither he nor Beth had had much to say
since they left the spaceport and Ramirez
couldn't exactly talk to them even if he was so
inclined. Which he never was. It had been a
quiet ride. Grant suddenly realized that he was
flicking the safety catch on his Maxwell
repeatedly with his thumb. On and off. On
and off. Angrily, he shoved it back in its
holster and rested his arm on the windowsill.
He was nervous. Trying to bring back the cold

focus that was required in high-risk surgeries or on the battlefield, he ran over the plan in his head one more time, looking for potential problems.

First off, Tavia might not be able to break their system, or might set off a silent alarm or whatever it is that the techies use to protect their systems, which means we're either stuck, or sunk. After that, we've got the problem of not knowing exactly where they put Evan, or even if he's still there. Not to mention guards, closed circuit cams, multiple checkpoints…

He stopped himself, shaking his head. It was a stupid plan. Stupid, stupid, stupid! There were a million things that could go wrong and if even one did, they would land in jail, or worse. Breaking and entering: definitely. Assault: possibly. Industrial espionage: likely. He grimaced. He had gone along with some bad plans in his life, but this one had so many possible failure points, going through with it would be like playing football in a minefield.

His gloomy thoughts were cut off as the van slowed down and turned off the main road.

Beth adjusted her cap once more and took a deep breath. "We're here."

Grant rapped twice on the panel separating the cab from the back of the van and got one knock in return. Ramirez was ready.

"You ready for this, Charlie?" Beth asked. Grant could see her trying not to bite her lip.

He grinned encouragingly, giving her a thumbs-up. "With you in charge? Always."

"Thanks. ...It means a lot to me—"

She cut herself short as the van stopped in front of an impressive-looking gate with a guardhouse to the side.

Go time.

Carefully, Grant pulled his coat further forward, making sure that his pistol was completely hidden from view. The last thing they needed was to raise an alarm before they even got onto the property.

Beth gathered the bogus papers that Tavia had printed up onboard the *Memory* earlier as a young-looking guard wandered toward her window from the guardhouse. With one last quiet rap on the rear panel, Beth rolled down the window to confront the guard.

"This is a restricted facility, ma'am," the man said, a hint of a brogue in his words. "You need authorization to go in. What's your business here?"

"I've got a shipment of chemicals for ABI. Address for delivery was this one. I have a manifest here, if you'd like to take a look,

Mr., um…" Beth glanced at the name sewn onto the man's uniform. "Reid."

"I think I would like a look, now that you mention it," Reid said, with a smile. "Nothing personal, it's my job. Can't be too careful."

Beth handed him the falsified documents and he ran his eyes over them, a frown crossing his face.

"You're from Sullart Biochemical? We usually get shipments from Rathorn & Albright."

"Special order," Beth said. "Don't ask me, I just drive the stuff around."

"Alright, alright," the guard still didn't look convinced. "You won't mind if I take a look in the back, though, just to make sure?"

" 'Course not!" Grant said loudly. "Just be quick about it. We're on a bloody schedule."

Come on, Ramirez. Hurry up.

Reid nodded silently and handed Beth back her papers. Grant noticed the man's hand was resting on the butt of his sidearm and his own hand instinctively crept inside his coat. This was where things came down to luck. The one part of the plan that he had argued against vehemently. His eyes followed the guard until he was out of sight of the window, then he unholstered his Maxwell. If Ramirez came through, he wouldn't need to face the guard again, and if he didn't, well... There wouldn't be any more trying to bluff their way past him.

For half of a tense minute, he listened for the sound of the back doors unlatching and showing the guard that their 'special order' was nonexistent, but no sound came. His ears strained to catch the sound of a footstep, a radio, anything.

Ramirez's voice in his ear almost gave him a heart attack.

"The guard is down, Beth," he said, nonchalantly leaning in Grant's window.

"You didn't kill him, did you?" Beth asked sharply. "I don't want any killing unless they shoot first."

Grant glared daggers at Ramirez. *Sneaky bugger.*

"I did not." He sounded irritated, but didn't elaborate.

"Good."

Grant understood why she didn't want to slot anyone if she didn't absolutely have to—it was hard to hold the moral high ground while gunning down punch-clock guards who only worked at ABI to provide for their families—but it made the whole process a little bit trickier.

"Tavia, can you get the gate open?"

The familiar voice came clearly through the hands-free headsets all three crew members were wearing. "Plug me into their system and I can switch the channels on Arkady's newsfeed. I think I love this hacking patch."

Ramirez rolled his eyes and took the wireless transmitter that allowed Tavia to access other computer systems from Beth. He disappeared inside the guardhouse and, a moment later, Tavia chuckled in a very un-Tavia-like way. "I believe this must be how human burglars feel."

"Guess that means we're in?" Grant said, seeing Ramirez flash a thumbs-up from the guardhouse.

"Oh, we are *very much* in. Would you like to make all the security cameras play old *Gunner's Galaxy* reruns? Or broadcast *Mission Impossible* music over the courtyard speakers?" Tavia sounded as happy as Grant had ever heard her sound. He absentmindedly wondered what kind of monster they had created.

"I think opening the gate and looping the security cams will be enough for now, Tavia. Thank you." Beth wore a relieved smile.

The first hurdle's been cleared, Grant thought to himself. The gate slid soundlessly open, and he smiled too.

Ramirez jogged alongside the van as Beth drove slowly through the gate into the complex. Grant pulled off his cap and took a look around the wide open courtyard, scanning for possible threats. His quick sweep of the space showed him high walls topped with wire surrounding a yard of hard-packed earth. A small fleet of vehicles was parked near the sprawl of low buildings lurking around the perimeter, illuminated by dim external lights. The compound looked deserted.

Beth brought the van to a halt and Grant jumped out the side, dropping onto the dirt and bringing his gun up out of habit.

"Okay, Tavia," Beth said softly, adjusting her mic as she jumped down, "where to?"

"Bringing up internal schematics now." Tavia paused. "Okay, there isn't any building marked 'execution chamber' in big red letters, but the only facility designed for, and I quote, 'secure Fletcher Project subject containment' is the large building on the far left. There's only one door on that one, so you don't have much of a choice of entry points."

"Understood. Are you looping the cams?"

Tavia made a *pffft* of exasperation. "They were looped before you drove in."

"What about the guards?" Grant asked, uncomfortable with waiting in the open.

"I will keep you updated on their positions, but how you deal with them is up to you."

"We'll do our best to avoid them," Beth said, giving Ramirez a look, "but if we can't hide in time, can you jam their radios? I don't want to deal with an army because we couldn't shut up a patroller fast enough."

"Sorry, but that's not part of the facility system. I can make sure the main hub doesn't get any messages out, but the radios are out of my reach."

Grant huffed. Typical.

"That's alright. The whole plan relies on stealth. Get in undetected, get Evan, and get out. The last thing we need is a firefight." Beth motioned to Grant and Ramirez and started toward the building Tavia had pointed out, unholstering her LK-2.

Jogging after the other two, Grant eyed the buildings warily, looking for anything amiss. He had no idea what he was looking for or what he would do if he saw anything, but it made him feel a little better. When they reached the door to the building Tavia had pointed out, he inspected it carefully, checking for any of the numerous tricks and traps he knew might be employed to keep unwelcome visitors out. To his surprise, he found nothing. The door was opened by a simple iris scanner and seemed designed more to keep people in than out.

He took a closer look at the card-reader. "Um, Tavia? We've hit a bit of a snag. This door—"

"Please, Charles." Tavia sounded annoyed. "I have the technological equivalent of a battering ram and you're worried about opening your cereal box." The light on the scanner changed to green and the lock clicked.

Swallowing a less-than-witty comeback, Grant gingerly opened the door and looked inside the building. A long corridor with doors on either side greeted him. Empty, just as he had hoped. Signaling for Beth and Ramirez to follow him, he stepped through the doorway, bringing his Maxwell up to a ready position, just in case.

With a nervous glance at the cams aimed directly at him, he started slowly down the corridor checking the numbers on the doors as he went by.

Five... Six... Seven...

He wondered briefly what was behind the identical doors. Were there others like Evan in the facility?

Tavia's sharp voice cut through his thoughts: "Problem, Beth. There's a two-man guard patrol almost at the door at the end of your hallway. You need to move, now! I'm unlocking door Nine to your left. Hurry!"

Grant heard a small noise from the door and dove at it, sliding the deadbolt back as the card-reader turned green. A second after Beth and Ramirez ducked in behind him, he closed the door as quickly as he could while remaining quiet and leaned against it.

For a few moments, all that could be heard was ragged breathing, then Tavia's voice came over the headset again.

"Alright, you made it. They just entered the hallway and don't seem to have heard your hasty exit. Schematics show that you're in 'Classroom 2.' There should be a door on the right side of the room leading to a testing room. I think you can make your way parallel to the hallway until you get to the end. And, yes, I *can* unlock the doors, Charles."

"Good," Beth replied curtly. "Warn us about anything we should know. And re-lock the doors after we're through. I don't want to leave a trail of breadcrumbs."

There was a *thunk* sound in the darkness, followed by a muffled curse. "And a few lights would be good." Ramirez muttered.

In answer, about every third light panel above them flickered on, revealing just where they were standing. It was, indeed, a classroom, although nothing like Grant remembered from his schoolboy days.

But then, that was ancient history… he thought to himself, his eyes scanning the rows of desks. The front of the room was dominated by a floor-to-ceiling display screen, currently dark, and a small desk where an instructor might sit. All perfectly ordinary, and yet there was something… *off* about it. He brushed aside the thought, turning his attention to the door Tavia had indicated on the right side of the room. As he did, the light turned green, allowing them passage. Grant frowned, gripping his weapon a little tighter. He didn't like closed doors. No security man did. They were barriers that hid potential threats, and stepping through one was like making yourself a silhouette on a target sheet. But, he had his assurance from Tavia that the room was unoccupied, and there were ways to minimize the risk.

He didn't even have to speak before Beth and Ramirez had stacked themselves on either side of the door, waiting for him to make the first move. He had shared his military training with them, on the stipulation that he always took point. Nodding once, he set his free hand against the door handle and pushed it slowly open. Leading with his gun in the other hand, he slid through the doorway, quickly stepping to the side to sweep the room with his eyes. Nothing shot at him, which was a definite plus. A second later, dim lights flicked on, revealing a sparsely furnished room, with no place for a person to hide.

"Clear," Grant said softly, stepping further aside to let the others through. As they did, he took a second look at the room, allowing his Maxwell-50 to point at the floor. The room's purpose was not readily apparent. It was mostly empty, featuring only a short countertop around its edge, punctuated by half a dozen stand-up computer screens. What caught his attention was a large glass window, set into the wall on his left. At first, it reminded him of a huge aquarium that one of his previous employers once owned. As he stepped closer however, he found it to be an observation window, rather like the one adjoining the operating room at the university where he had received his medical training. There were a few scattered equipment lights glowing in the darkness beyond the glass, but he could only make out vague shapes. He knew it would be better to leave it alone, but he found himself seized with a strange curiosity.

"Tavia?" he asked, "What's behind this wall?"

"It's marked as… General Testing. Hold on a second…"

On the other side of the glass, banks of lights came alive, one after another, to reveal a large room, harshly white in the illumination, filled with what looked to be banks of lab tables and equipment. More lights came on, stretching into the distance, revealing the chamber to be more than thirty yards long.

Grant peered through the glass, trying to make out the purpose of the equipment. He could sense Beth moving up beside him, a frown in her voice. "Are those surgical tables, Charlie?"

"Could be," he answered. "Multi-purpose, looks like. Surgical, diagnostic, autopsy… whatever needs doing, but… It's weird. You see that tool-rack on the wall? That belongs in a machine-shop, not a laboratory. Tavia, any data on what exactly they *do* in there?"

The AI was silent for several seconds. When she did speak again, her tone was cautious and subdued. "Uh, Charlie… Are you sure you want to hear this? I suspect it will upset you."

Grant frowned. "Of course I do, or I wouldn't have asked."

"It might *really* upset you."

"Will you bloody well spit it out already?"

He expected her to render a breath, a sigh, a huff, any one of her usual grudging responses, which was why he was surprised when she simply came right out and told him.

"There are several research files here tagged for that lab. Fletcher's Wolves are still at a very experimental stage, apparently. And... One of the research fields marked is Stress Testing. Among other things, this includes pain tolerances. Healing rates. How bones set after being broken. The effects of various burns."

Grant's breath caught in his throat. For several seconds, his mind refused to grasp what it was being told. But inevitably it did, along with all of the mental images the realization brought with it.

And Tavia was right, it made him angry. Suddenly, brutally angry. So *many* unsolved questions became clear in his mind, small oddities in Evan's behavior that he had noticed, but never thought to wonder about. The misplaced fear, the tentative attitude, all of it, stemmed from right here. This facility, where these *people*—if they could even be called that—had *tortured* him or people close to him...

All to perfect what they saw as a product. Quality control research on living beings.

He felt like punching through the glass with his bare hands, and emptying a magazine into the most fragile pieces of equipment he could find. And *then*, he wanted to gather all of the people who had been party to this and give them the same treatment.

But first, there was another, more important piece of business.

"I've heard enough," he said quietly, turning away from the glass. "Now we know the enemy. It's time to get Evan out of here, before they do something even worse. Have you found him yet Tavia?"

"Yes, I've found the right feed... Oh, dear."

"What is it?" Beth asked, alarmed. "What's wrong?"

"I've found Evan, and... It looks like he doesn't have much time."

"Meaning?" Grant growled.

"Meaning, follow the green-lit doors. I suggest you run."

Grant didn't need to be told twice. They ran.

14

The electronic tone of an intercom seemed exceptionally loud compared to the complete silence that had settled over the room for what felt like an eternity. Evan shook himself out of the stupor, trying to force his sleep-deprived brain to some kind of alertness. He had no idea how long he had been sitting there, unable to fall asleep, unable to think straight, with the dim knowledge that there was absolutely nothing that he could do to help himself. He had struggled against his restraints for a while after the doctor left, but gave up after only a few minutes. If anyone knew the Fletcher's Wolves limits, it would be the technicians at ABI. After a while, he had fallen into a semi-conscious state, drifting between disjointed thoughts and memories.

Now he struggled back to a hazy awareness as the door to the room swung open. The time after the doctor had left had felt like forever, but Evan didn't think it had been long enough for it to be morning already. The doctor wasn't due back for hours, at least. For a second, hope blossomed in Evan's mind as he remembered Hugin's promise in the medical ward, but a sinisterly paternal voice brought him back to grim reality.

"Ah, Subject 112. Still awake, I see. Had some good time for reflection? I hope so." Dr. Morrow cleared his throat uncomfortably, his voice slightly distorted over the speakers. "I'm afraid that I have had to return a little earlier than I had indicated previously. Executive meddling has raised its ugly head yet again, and I have orders from on high to abandon my research in favor of a different experiment."

"What are... you talking about?" Evan managed to summon enough awareness to ask. His own voice sounded raspy and weak, especially when a single breath couldn't seem to support a full sentence anymore.

"Termination, 112. That's what I'm talking about. It turns out, some imbecilic administrator has something on their agenda that they have decided is more important than discovering how to correct a fatal flaw in one of their company's products," Dr. Morrow said bitterly. "Something that requires testing on a set of mammalian organs. And since we have a subject on hand that was already scheduled for termination, they've settled on you."

"What are you talking to the barker for?" asked another voice. Evan couldn't quite get up the energy to be startled, but he was baffled as to why he hadn't detected the newcomer earlier. After a second, he realized that he couldn't smell anyone over an intercom, but couldn't quite get up the energy to berate himself for thinking so slowly either.

"Subject 112 here is a very important piece in my experiments. He may very well be the key to perfecting the Fletcher's Wolf project," Morrow replied, sounding decidedly miffed. "I've already argued long and hard against this course of action, but I've been shot down at every turn. Some asinine manager is intent on clearing their to-do list and won't listen to reason, and so I am being forced to abandon what may be some of my most important research on a whim. While I am sure that this little viral puzzle is significant, I can't imagine how it would take priority over my work. As for why I am explaining this to what you refer to as the 'barker,' I think it might be at least a little beneficial that the subject knows what is about to happen to him."

"Well, whatever floats your boat, doctor. But still, the way you talk to the clockwork…"

"Duly noted, Dr. Ruland, thank you," Morrow responded acidly, clearly annoyed at an intruder within his kingdom. He cleared his throat.

"Apologies, 112. Honestly, I can't speak with these virologists. As I was saying, ABI has decided to do away with you early. They are going to test some newly acquired toy on you to find out if it is indeed what they think it is. A pointless waste, in my opinion; but what do I know? I'm only the leading scientist assigned to the Fletcher project."

There was a soft click over the intercom, reminding Evan's sluggish imagination of the clasps on a suitcase, followed by a vaguely refrigerant hum.

"A fully-adaptable carrier virus, we're hoping," Dr. Ruland said. "Tech that we had to *borrow* from another scientist's work. We've managed to isolate the formula from his notes, but we have no way of knowing if it's not just a recipe for—oh, now you've got *me* talking to it."

"You see 112, I don't mind telling you this, because it won't matter in ten minutes," Dr. Morrow picked up smoothly. "Not being a micro-biologist, I don't understand most of the particulars, but suffice to say, the toxins that the virus will be delivering to your system will likely be incredibly painful. Far less humane than my planned methods. But it's not too late yet."

Evan could sense Dr. Morrow's intensity as the voice over the intercom dropped to just above a fierce whisper.

"Just tell me what I need to know, and I'll use every last ounce of pull I have to put a stop to this barbaric treatment. How did you bypass your safeguards?"

After so long alone with the thought, Evan's drugged mind could not even summon much alarm at the prospect of his own demise. His mouth formed words of its own accord, sliding right past his conscious mind.

"If you had any pull... you'd have used it already. You wouldn't... lose your *experiment* if you could help it. I'm going to die anyway... So do your worst."

Morrow blew out a long, rumbling breath. A frown colored his voice black. "Disappointing. Very disappointing, 112. I had hoped to learn so much from you, but you had to choose to be stubborn." There was another sigh, this one resigned. "Ah well. There will be others like you. And when they come, they will either see more clearly or they will suffer just the same. Either way, they will talk. You will be dead, and you will not have accomplished anything."

"If you're quite through, Morrow," Ruland broke in, "the virus is prepped and good to go. I've mixed up a little cocktail of disease that I'm able to administer through the gas jets to test its transmissibility. If the barker starts hemorrhaging, I'll have all the confirmation that I need. Can we get on with this?"

"Yes, I suppose there is no point in drawing it out. Do it."

Evan braced himself. Well, that was it. It was finally time to face the inevitable. On a shot of adrenaline, the fog around his thoughts rolled away, leaving him with a singular, blissful clarity. He found himself wondering what would happen to him *after*. He had never thought about it before. He knew that there were any number of theories and ideologies on the subject, but he had never had time to research any of them, although he had seen enough to know that such things were contingent on having a soul. Did he have one? What would happen to the consciousness of an artificially created life after the body ceased to function?

He thought of all the people he had known, and the relationships he had possessed. He could see now that he never really had much of a life. Most of his days had been spent in dark, airless spaces, working for the purposes of others. He remembered that there were things that he still *wanted*. Things to have…to see…to do. He wanted to travel, he wanted to see what a life could offer, wanted to discover what the purpose of his life might be. He wanted a *family*.

Now it was too late. There was no more time left for him. In the end, he would die the same way he had lived: a product. An appliance with a pulse.

Closing his eyes into the blindfold, he calmed his breathing, waiting for the hiss of gas that would be the last thing he ever heard.

The sound of a door sliding open was not what Evan expected to hear as he died, much less Dr. Morrow's surprised stammer. "What? Who are—"

There was a clatter, followed by a dull, wet *thud*.

"Don't mind us, Doc," said a familiar, indescribably welcome baritone. "Just your friendly neighborhood good guys." Evan heard a second door open. This time the sound was not distorted by the intercom.

A second later, the blindfold fell from his vision. After so long in the dark, the light stung his eyes, making them blink and tear up. As his vision returned, he found himself beholding a sight he had been sure that he would never see again: Elizabeth Hugin's relieved, smiling face.

"Hey Evan," she said ruefully. "Sorry we're late."

Evan stared, unable to comprehend. They were all here. Hugin was in front of him, fussing about his restraints. Grant was in the observation room, giving an evil eye to Dr. Morrow, who lay in a heap in one corner of the room. Even Ramirez was there, pinning a second lab-coated figure to the wall with a darkened knife-blade to his neck.

I'm hallucinating. I have to be.

"Am I... dead?" he asked aloud, his eyes moving from one face to another.

Grant's hard expression blossomed into a totally contented smile. "No, lad, but you gave it your best shot. Beth wouldn't give up on you, though, by God."

"I promised that I wouldn't," Hugin said simply. Close as he was, Evan could suddenly see the slight tremor to her fingers as she undid the restraints, the unshed tears in her eyes as she looked into his. "I'm just glad that we weren't too late."

"It looks like we almost were," Ramirez pointed out blandly, giving his prisoner's arm a sharp twist. The man squealed in pain, accompanied by the hollow clatter of an object hitting the floor.

Dr. Ruland's "little cocktail of disease."
Evan shuddered. If they had arrived seconds
later...

"Well, well," Grant said, nodding his
head toward the table. "I believe we've seen
that before."

For the first time, Evan noticed the
object that Dr. Ruland had brought with him.

Dr. Phillips' briefcase, now lying open
to reveal a collection of vials and Petri dishes.

"How did that... get here?" he asked,
his mind swirling with questions.

Hugin grimaced as she unlocked the
final restraint. "It's a long story," she said,
offering him a hand up. "One which we'll
have plenty of time to tell after we're out of
here. Can you stand?"

Evan tried. He fell back an instant later
as the muscles in his legs seemed to turn into
rubber. "I can't..."

"That's okay," Hugin assured. "Just
lean on me. What did they *do* to you?"

"Let's ask this bloke," Grant said,
hauling a cringing Dr. Morrow up from the
floor by the collar of his lab-coat. The reversal
was almost surreal. A minute before, Morrow
had been a figure of absolute power in Evan's
life. Now he was just a small, white-haired old
man, dwarfed in Grant's iron grip as he nursed

the side of his face where a purple bruise was forming.

"My nose…"

Evan finally managed to lever himself to his feet, supported mainly by Hugin's arm under his shoulder. He hated himself for being so weak, but his legs still refused to cooperate.

"You thought that *hurt*, doc?" Grant sounded surprised. "That was barely a love tap. I'll break it *proper* for you unless you tell me what you did to Evan. What wounds, what drugs you put him on, the works. And be quick, or they'll have to sew your nose back on!"

Morrow winced under the harsh tone. "Very little drugs! A dose of theobromine, that's all. And he's probably suffering from the aftereffects of… mild electric shock."

Evan realized that he had never seen Grant angry before. He had only seen the kind, gently paternal Charlie. It was a different man before him now. This man's eyes burned with rage, visibly restraining himself from beating the doctor's body until only a bloody stain was left, his voice a register lower.

"Doc, you're lucky that the lady's here, or I would put a bullet in your clever little brain right here and now. What do you want to do with him, Beth?"

As Hugin helped him limp into the observation room, Evan could see the same anger in her face. "Leave them," she pronounced finally. "Tie them up and leave them. We're not executioners. They'll get what's coming to them."

Ramirez nodded, conjuring a pair of plastic wrist-ties. In a move that was smooth enough to be practiced, he used one set to cuff Dr. Ruland's wrists, the other to secure the ankles before dropping his prisoner unceremoniously to the floor, out of Evan's sight beneath the table. This done, Ramirez held out another pair of ties to Grant. "Be careful with these. They can cut rather painfully if you put them on too tight. You were always so clumsy."

Grant eyed them dubiously, then dragged Morrow to his feet and held the zip-ties in front of his face. "Oh, these don't look very comfortable at all. Maybe a night of contemplation might help you get your head on straight."

As the restraints were fastened around his arms and legs, Morrow seemed to finally realize what was happening to him. "Are you people *insane*? Coming in here, waving guns around, and stealing ABI property? This is a secure facility! You'll be caught before you're ten feet down the corridor!"

"Not all that secure, actually," Ramirez said, pointing to the small camera in the corner of the ceiling that Evan saw for the first time. "Or were you not wondering why your friends in the security booth have not come yet?"

Morrow ground his teeth, slightly deflated. Finally, he seemed to come to a decision, a bit of his imperious attitude returning. "How very interesting. You all risk so much, putting your lives and your futures on the line, all to save a single Fletcher's Wolf. Why is that? That is something that people do for other humans. Not animals. Not AIs. Do you think that if you treat Subject 112 like a person, it will be any more human? That you will somehow cause it to stop being a thing?" He laughed. "You poor fools! Do you befriend your datapads? Would you go to this kind of trouble for a piece of machinery? That is all the Fletcher Project subjects are. These Fletcher's Wolves. Nothing more. They are tools. High-quality, true, but only tools. Tools designed to a certain set of biological specifications so as to *imitate* human behaviors, like the anthropomorphization project that revolutionized AI –human interactions."

Evan's lip curled and the haze surrounding his brain burned away in the heat of a sudden, intense *anger*. He had put up with this kind of talk all his life and he was sick of it. No, more than sick. He could feel his hands start to shake as his safeguards activated to stop him from physically attacking the doctor.

"Subject 112 is a good example of what I am talking about. No matter how well you program a computer, it can still break down. It can still… malfunction." He shrugged. "That is what I was trying to prevent. I can see that any rationalization of my motives would be lost on you, but whatever the means I used, they led to a positive end for everyone." He glanced at Evan. "And every*thing*."

Evan snapped.

In one movement, he surged out of Hugin's grip and swung his fist into Morrow's smug grin. The doctor fell back out of Grant's hand and slumped against the chair, his breath leaving him in a rush.

Evan felt Hugin grab his arm, but he shook her off. He dimly heard Ramirez shouting for the others to leave him alone, but the only thing he cared about was releasing his pent-up rage on the man who had killed his friends and made his childhood a living hell. For the next few seconds, he wasn't aware of anything except hitting Morrow again and again and again. After a while—he couldn't have said how long—the pain in his hands brought him back to himself and he pulled up short, torn between the knee-jerk reaction of apologizing and the urge to keep hitting the doctor until he no longer had the strength to stand. Hugin placed a tentative hand on his arm, and he took an unsteady step back.

Morrow wiped a trickle of blood coming from his nose with the back of his hand and glared at Evan. "You... you were one of the ones muttering about injustice before we stopped that, weren't you, 112? You have no idea." He spat. "No idea! You wanted equality. Hah! Did you even know what you wanted? What you had; that *was* equality! 'The worst form of injustice is to try to make unequal things equal.' Don't you understand? You're not equal." He spoke slowly, emphasizing every word. "You are a *machine*."

Grant stepped forward, a muscle in his jaw twitching. "I've had enough of this. You want justice, do you, you bastard? Fine." He pulled out his large pistol, leveling it at Morrow's head. "This is justice."

Evan stared. For a second, he thought about just letting the big security officer put an end to it; simply snuff out the man who had caused so much pain. *It would be so easy. Just to let him die. But no. No. It's not justice to let him die a martyr; to prove his point for him.*

Stumbling forward, he caught Grant's arm, forcing the gun away from Morrow. "No! You can't... can't kill him. It will just make it seem like he's right. About us. About the wolves. ABI will use this. We... You can use the information about the compound to expose Morrow and the rest of them. Now you have proof. And he—" Evan pointed at the battered figure of the doctor "—will pay for... murdering my friends."

Grant visibly struggled to take his finger off of the trigger, but he finally blew his cheeks out in a sigh and jammed the gun back in its holster.

"Alright. It's your decision, Evan. But if it was up to me..." he shrugged and put an arm around Evan's shoulders to support him. "Let's get out of here, Beth."

Evan turned away from Morrow and sagged suddenly against Grant. The adrenaline was gone now and he felt completely drained.

"Tavia," Hugin said, opening the door carefully and peering out, "Can you make sure these two are secure once we're gone? I'm sure they'll have somebody come around to check up them when they don't clock in or whatever these sadists do on a regular basis, but I don't want them giving an alarm too soon."

She tapped a button on her earpiece with an apologetic look at Evan and Tavia's voice crackled into the small room. "—ourse Captain. And before you ask: yes, the hallways are still clear."

"Great. Come on, Evan, let's go." Hugin grabbed Phillips' case off of the table and walked out of the room without a backward glance.

"You won't get away with this!" Morrow piped up, seeming to have regained some of his courage now that Grant had put his gun away. "And no matter how much you try to deny it—"

Grant shut the door and slid the bolt home with an emphatic *shunk* and a very satisfied smile. "Well," he said, once more the cheerful, relaxed Grant that Evan knew, "I'm glad that's over. He was beginning to get on my nerves."

Evan barked out a laugh. *Now* there's *an understatement.*

"Alright Charlie," Hugin said. "Give me a SitRep."

"We've got Evan, we're still undetected, Tavia's got our back with the cams and we just need to get back to the van without being seen by guards. By all accounts," he finished, nonchalantly hooking a thumb behind his holster strap, "we're doing fairly well."

"I think we should get back to the shuttle before we start patting ourselves on the back, Charlie," Ramirez said. His face was as stony as ever, but there was something in his voice that made Evan wonder if he was really as frosty at the moment as he seemed. It didn't sound like the usual Ramirez.

"Right," Hugin replied, setting down the case and looking Evan in the eye. "There's something I need to do first."

Then she hugged him.

* * *

Ramirez stood distant from the others, flawlessly predicting the mushy display of emotion that followed Evan's rescue. Knowing it was coming, he assumed his customary role of watching for danger while the others lost focus. He could never quite understand how they could take the time for sentiment, even in the middle of a warzone. And yet, they always *made* time. Even so, he couldn't bring himself to say anything. For perhaps the first time he had ever seen, Beth looked honestly, genuinely *happy*. And Evan... Just thinking about what had transpired for him filled Ramirez with bewilderment.

"You don't need to do that, you know," said Tavia, quietly enough that it was probably only on his feed. "You're swinging that shotgun around like you're expecting zombies. The cameras are totally clear."

"Easy for you to say," Ramirez muttered, allowing his impatience through. "If you are wrong, you just say 'whoopsie' and go back to your server. We get shot."

All the same, the AI's words helped to reassure him somewhat. Letting his shotgun hang on its sling, he picked up the briefcase that Beth had dropped. His hope confirmed, he immediately felt much better about this whole venture. It was indeed Phillips' case, the one that the Coalition was so keen to get its bureaucratic hands on. Beth hadn't said so when she was relating her encounter with Agent Bale, but the subtle undertones were there. They *wanted* whatever this case contained, and would go to some lengths to get it back.

Which, to reference a popular ancient game that he had never even played, made the case a *Get-Out-of-Jail-Free* card.

By then, Beth finally collected herself, holding Evan at arm's length with a deep breath. "Right," she said. "Let's get you home."

"Here lad." Grant offered his free hand. "Lean on me."

Before he even knew what he was doing, Ramirez interrupted. "Actually, Charlie, I will help him."

The bewildered stares suddenly directed his way were almost comical to see.

He hastened to justify. "That way, you can take point, with Beth on tail. My shotgun is not much good in long corridors."

"Er... Okay, Ramirez," Grant said, obviously not buying it. "Good thinking."

Beth just nodded. "Alright Tavia, which way out? I'm all turned around in here."

They set off down the corridor, taking up the positions that he had suggested, with Ramirez supporting a stumbling Evan. After his brief burst of violence against the scientist, he seemed to have faded back into a sort of foggy awareness. Ramirez sighed, trying to figure out why he was doing this. Why he *needed* to do it. He could deny it all he wanted to; Evan's actions had truly made an impression on him. Finally, he could stand it no longer. He had to know.

"Evan?" he asked, realizing with a pang that it was the first time he had ever spoken the name aloud. "May I ask you a question?"

The wolf's ears perked up slightly as Evan looked up with a wan smile. "Everyone's always asking me that," he slurred quietly.

"You can just assume that I'm... permanently open for questions."

"I am just wondering... why?" He cleared his throat awkwardly. "I mean... why did you not let Charlie kill that man? From what I have seen in this place, I think that no one would ever hold it against you." Ramirez felt a twinge of guilt at making someone this injured talk, yet another action that was entirely uncharacteristic. What was happening to him?

Despite his difficulty though, Evan seemed to sense the importance he suddenly held in the question. "You're right. Dr. Morrow was everything around here. He controlled our lives, held the power of life and death over us... And he made sure that safeguards were in place so that we couldn't do anything about it. But now... I finally figured out why he was so adamant about that. It was because... he was *afraid* of us, and taught other people to be afraid. Back there, I held power over him that he always held over me, and then I didn't use it. I let him live, to prove... that we're better than they are. To prove that we don't *need* their safeguards." He sighed, looking away. "I guess... I didn't kill him because I didn't have to."

Ramirez felt a frown spread over his face.

"Oh," he said. "I see."

There was so much more that he wanted to say, but the words wouldn't come. They remained trapped behind the impassive front that he had spent his whole life building. Evan's answer only served to trouble him even more. Ramirez was certain of one thing. Placed in the same situation, he would have pulled that trigger, and slept soundly with the decision. Never thinking of the morals, and to hell with the consequences. He would have thought only of himself.

Instead, Evan had denied his impulses, for the sake of something better. Ramirez was shaken, feeling his last cherished idea relating to the Fletcher's Wolves crumble to dust. No matter how he thought of it, he could only conclude one thing. Evan was a far better man than he would ever be.

"Wait," Evan said out of the blue, throwing Ramirez's train of thought. "Who did you bring with you?"

"What?" *What is he talking about?*

"Who's with you?"

"No one. It is just Charlie, Beth and myself."

"No. I can smell someone else. Close." The wolf seemed increasingly agitated. "Weapon smells. Men."

Ramirez reached up to key his mic, puzzled.

"Tavia, are the corridors still clear?" he said with a sharp glance at the wall-mounted cam.

"Yes, Ramirez," Tavia sounded a bit peeved, "I've been keeping tabs on every single security camera in the building since you plugged me in at the gate."

He looked back at Evan. "She says there's nothing there."

"No," Evan repeated. "Captain, they're here. You've got to believe me, I can smell them! I don't know why Tavia can't see them, but they're coming!"

"Tavia," Beth said slowly, "would it be possible for another AI to loop the cams on you without you knowing it?"

"I suppose it would be *possible*, Captain, but I don't think—"

A burst of static came over Ramirez's headset and the link went dead.

"Tavia? Tavia!"

"I'm sorry," said a humorless male voice, one that was most decidedly *not* Tavia. "Your call has been disconnected."

Ramirez swore. *I guess ABI has a virus-blocker after all...*

"Run," Grant hissed, gesturing to the cover of the trucks parked twenty feet from the main building. "Ramirez, you and Evan first. Go."

Not waiting to protest, Ramirez obeyed, taking off across the hard-packed dirt as fast as Evan could go. As he did, a shadow moved in his peripheral vision, coming around the shadow of one of the outer buildings.

Crack.

There was a puff of dirt at Ramirez's feet as a bullet slammed into the ground.

15

Overall, Tavia was enjoying the new intrusion program she had acquired. It still felt odd, however. If she had interpreted the human saying correctly, she would say that it felt like wearing someone else's clothes. The increased access and code-breaking capability was useful, but the coding was foreign. It would take her a while before she was completely comfortable using a program not centered in the *Memory*. This was, she realized, the first time in 41 trillion processing cycles that she had been physically connected to a system outside the ship. Already, she had designated a portion of her processing power to send out electronic feelers to gather any information on ABI she deemed useful. If Captain Hugin seemed dead set on making enemies of one of the largest multi-planet corporations, then the least Tavia could do was help her gather some dirt on them. She had already found a great deal of fascinating data on valuable research that had been *secured* from smaller independent companies. It was amazing what humans would commit to an electronic medium without a second thought.

Using the security cameras she had slaved to her intrusion program, she brought up the view of hallway D-1 and checked in on the progress of the crew.

Charles Grant was—predictably—leading the way down the hallway, his customized Maxwell-50 Fast Action Combat Sidearm held in front of him as he swept the corridor from side to side. It *would* be Grant that ignored the fact that she could see all the rooms and hallways simultaneously and let them know if anyone approached. Typical. In the rear, Beth was walking close to the wall, the case held in her off-hand as she glanced backward from time-to-time. What really caught Tavia's "eye", though, was the unlikely pairing in the middle. Evan's stumbling furry figure was being supported by *Ramirez* of all people. Tavia realized that she had missed something important. Unobtrusively, she switched on Ramirez's headset mic.

"Oh," he was saying. "I see." Ramirez's vocal pattern did not match with the normal voiceprint Tavia had on record, but she chalked that down to stress. Stress did funny things to humans.

"Wait," Evan said. He sounded nervous. "Who did you bring with you?"

"What?"

"Who's with you?"

"No one. It is just Charlie, Beth and myself."

Evan shook his head. "No. I can smell someone else. Close. Weapon smells. Men."

It was Ramirez's turn to look bewildered. He reached up and tapped his mic button, unknowing turning the link off. Tavia saw his lips move and re-activated the link a fraction of a second later, kicking herself.

"—orridors still clear?" he finished, glancing up at the camera.

"Yes, Ramirez, I've been keeping tabs on every single CCTV camera in the building since you plugged me in at the gate."

Ramirez relayed that information to Evan. He had obviously forgotten about the external speaker.

"No," Evan said. He looked very worried. "Captain, they're here. You've got to believe me, I can smell them! I don't know why Tavia can't see them, but they're coming!"

Beth activated her mic. "Tavia, would it be possible for another AI to loop the cams on you without you knowing it?"

A seed of doubt entered Tavia's mind. She immediately dedicated a full sixteen thousand processes to double-checking the slaved cams. "I suppose it would be *possible*, Captain, but I don't think—"

The cams went dark.

For a few thousand processing cycles, she didn't understand what had happened, but then realization came with a flash.

She had been duped. She could have searched her online thesaurus for a hundred synonyms; bamboozled, conned, deceived, fooled, hoodwinked, suckered, tricked, even *hornswoggled*, whatever that meant, but the fact remained: someone or something had pulled the wool over her eyes.

She was capable of simulating anger, but, she realized, indulging her wounded pride would do nothing to help Beth and the others. Immediately, she reeled in all of her sub-programs, storing the data for later and beginning a coordinated attack on the program that was blocking her from the ABI mainframe.

Carefully sending tiny tendrils of her consciousness out to the edges of the mainframe, Tavia probed at dead-end programs and data-trails, looking for a backdoor she could use to regain access. Nothing. Whatever this interloper was, it had the mainframe sealed as tight as a drum.

Withdrawing her scouts, Tavia studied the problem from a number of different angles, looking for weak points to attack in the cameras, Beth's uplink, door locks, lights, anything. Finally, she realized that if she didn't know exactly what she was dealing with, she wouldn't be able to know how to beat it. Full-on, frontal attack, then. Investing 100 percent of her computing power in a diversion. She knew that even Grant would know better than to wonder what could go wrong. As information-gathering tactics went, it wasn't the subtlest she had devised.

After she finished gathering her programs and drawing up her battle plan, Tavia launched herself at the mainframe, bringing every last process to bear on the unknown entity that was locking her out.

An AI battle was, she realized, much like a game of chess where every move was planned out in advance of the actual match. When facing a weak or poorly-written program, a complicated AI like herself could easily predict every move her opponent made and bypass or utterly destroy it in seconds. With a more or less equal match, hundreds of these matches might have to be played over millions of processing cycles. Each one planned out in advance on both sides, neither able to react to an opponent's unexpected attacks nor take advantage of unforeseen holes in their defense.

When Tavia had engaged the enemy AI, it had countered with precision that left her processing for a few hundred extra cycles. She had never seen that kind of anti-tampering Intelligence before in all her years of downloading crawler programs and illegal mainframe-cracking software. A few million processing cycles into the duel, Tavia realized that she was beaten. Even with the military-grade intrusion program and the considerable power of her six-core processor, she was barely able to keep the other AI from breaking her like a cheap, downloadable anti-virus program.

Leaving some of her processes to the hopeless battle in an effort to keep the hostile Intelligence busy, Tavia withdrew to the ship. The enemy AI would be unable to follow her if she cut herself off from the 'net. She was loath to abandon all connection to the living, pulsating matrix of information that was the lifeblood of any AI, but she realized that she had no choice. She could already feel the processes comprising her rearguard falling one by one to the AI's methodical and almost precognitive assault. Steeling herself, she disabled the connection.

It was a bit like being blind or deaf as a human, she supposed. She had lost one of her primary senses. But that was temporary. Death wasn't. And if she wasn't able to bring some kind of help to Captain Hugin and the others, that would be precisely what they would be experiencing in the near future.

Tavia could picture Grant indulging in one of his frequent massive exhalations and spouting a decidedly ungrateful comment when he heard who had saved him.

If she pulled this off, Tavia decided, she would be sure not to let him forget.

* * *

Beth could feel their escape unraveling before her eyes. A moment before, they had been right on track, in control, with nothing to stop them. But now, something had gone wrong, and Tavia wasn't responding. Suddenly, it was like being in a fightercraft with no radar.

Time for the squad-tactics, then, she thought, remembering the training that Grant had passed on. *Cover each other's backs.*

Ramirez and Evan were about halfway across the open ground. Grant turned to her. "Okay Beth, your turn..."

Just then, over Grant's shoulder, Beth caught a figure moving around the building opposite. It was in silhouette only, but she distinctly caught the shape of a handgun as it rose to target, and fired.

"On your six!" she barked, raising her own weapon and snapping off two quick rounds.

They were poorly aimed, but they served the intended purpose of making the assailant duck down and turn his attention away from Evan and Ramirez. She ducked back and took shelter behind the doorway, just as returning fire zipped over her head and buried itself in the masonry behind her.

Grant swore, firing two rounds of his own. "No good cover here... Oh, damn, here come some more."

Beth looked. Sure enough, the figure had been joined by another, with perhaps more negotiating the corner of the outbuilding. Mercifully, none of the newcomers seemed to be toting anything larger than a handgun, but that just meant it would take more rounds for either side to accomplish anything. And she and Grant couldn't simply trade fire until one side or the other got lucky. Grant apparently had the same thought.

"We have to get to the trucks." He smiled ironically. "Run and gun is the only way. Keep their heads down while we cross the open."

Beth felt a touch of fear. Running across an open field under the guns of several hostiles with nothing but a hail of her own bullets to discourage them was not her idea of fun. But she could see they had no choice. She nodded.

"Right behind you."

Grant nodded grimly. "Empty the mag. Whatever happens, don't stop. On my mark..." He blew out a breath. "Three, two, one, *go!*"

Carried on a wave of adrenaline, Beth ran like she never had before. With all of her senses stretched taut, she was acutely aware of bullets zipping past her, the spray of dirt as they fell too low. Grant's weapon roared three times, and the incoming ceased. Beth brought up her own weapon, feeling the recoil spread up her arm as she pulsed shot after shot at the building's corner. Between sprinting flat out and firing with one hand, she was sure most of the rounds were missing horribly, but she desperately hoped it would be enough to keep their enemy's heads down. All too soon, her gun's top slide locked back. Empty. Just ahead, Grant put on a burst of speed, disappearing into the gap between two parked trucks. Beth threw herself at the opening, hitting the ground just as several shots pinged off the metal around her. But her main purpose was accomplished, and they were all safely in cover among the vehicles.

Grant helped her to her feet, breathing hard. "Damn... that was close."

"What happens now?" asked Ramirez, who Beth suddenly noticed standing beside them, shotgun clasped in one hand and Evan supported by the other. She wracked her brain for a plan, ejecting the spent magazine from her LK-2 and reaching for another.

Think Beth! Tavia's probably been compromised. Which means we can assume that the cameras and sensors are back in the bad guys' hands. No, keep it simple. Just get to the gate. And that means taking care of these goons first if you want to make it out in one piece.

"The side of that building comes right over here," she pointed out, sliding the new mag home with a click. "They'll be in here with us in a few seconds. We either need to get past them, or take them out."

Grant nodded. "Right. We've got the initiative, though. They have to come to us. That makes the close quarters work to our advantage."

"We'll spread out," Beth instructed. "Ramirez, stay back here. Protect Evan." She was expecting a vehement protest, which was why she was surprised when Ramirez accepted the commission without a word, and Evan was the one to object.

"Just set me somewhere. I... don't have to weigh you down all the time."

"Shut up, you," Ramirez ordered sharply. "You are in no condition to be by yourself. We can leave you behind in the *next* firefight."

"You might as well take this though, lad," Grant said, pulling the smaller Hughes sidearm out of the back of his belt and offering it to Evan. "Just point and shoot if anyone gets too close and Ramirez's shotgun runs out."

"Very funny, Charlie," Ramirez said sourly as Evan accepted the weapon. "Now get going."

Beth nodded at her companions. "Okay, I'll take the right."

With that, they split up, Grant toward the left, Evan and Ramirez toward the back of the motor-pool area.

Beth was left alone.

Taking a deep breath, she set out to find the perfect ambush point.

As battlegrounds went, it offered its own unique set of weaknesses and advantages. Composed of a flat, open area with dozens of vehicles parked end to end, there was plenty of cover; plenty of nooks and crannies to hide in.

The bad news was that the enemy would never be more than a few yards away while in her sightline. Although, Beth reminded herself, it was little different from any other bad situation she had been in. In the backstreets of Apollo or Hermes, it was always messy and close in.

And yet, it was totally different than anything she had gotten through before. This was enemy territory, pitted against hostiles out with the express intention of killing her and her crew. There could be no surrender for either. Kill or be killed.

She gripped her gun a bit tighter.

Fine. I can live with those rules.

A moment later, she reached a spot one row back from the edge of the car-park, crouching beside the cab of a dark truck. Just in time, it seemed. As she watched, several men turned the corner of the outbuilding ahead; each of their weapons trained a different direction. She recognized their attire almost instantly. The same dark shirts and combat vests worn by the men who had taken Evan away that morning. She did not, however, see the man with the sunglasses.

Pity.

One of the men, apparently the leader, made a hand-signal for his men to spread out.

They separated, filtering one by one into the vehicles.

Couldn't wait around and stay in a group, huh? Well, better for us.

Beth waited, listening. With her adrenaline-heightened senses, the night was filled with rustling cloth, snatched breathing, and creaking, metallic noises as bodies bumped trucks. One group of sounds, as far as she could tell, was louder than the rest and growing louder by the second. And then, promptly, they were lost. She tensed.

At that moment, a man rounded a corner on her right, six cars away, moving slowly and cautiously so that he was nearly silent. It was still a long shot for her pistol, so she waited, unmoving, trusting her dark clothing to hide her against the ground.

The man was five car-lengths away.

Four...

Three...

Beth brought her gun slowly up, lining up the sights...

Seeing the movement, the man swiveled instantly—

Beth squeezed off four shots in quick succession, two of them impacting solidly with the man's torso, the third going through his neck. He lingered for a second, then collapsed backwards, his gun firing once into the air as the body convulsed and went limp.

Not waiting for the others to hear the shots and come running, Beth rolled under the truck and moved away at an army crawl, making her way under the vehicles.

Having gotten a few yards, she suddenly saw feet moving beside her hiding place. She froze, watching carefully. If the boots she was seeing belonged to Grant, it would be rather awkward if she shot them off. Just then, the boots also froze, the man inside them giving an audible intake of breath.

It wasn't Grant.

Did he hear me? Beth wondered. Deciding not to stay and find out, she started crawling backward, keeping her eyes on the boots...

A gun-barrel dropped into her field of view, barking a blind shot into the vehicle's undercarriage. Confined as it was, the noise was deafening as Beth scrambled backwards and stood up on the other side of the car, taking cover against it. This was precisely the situation she had hoped to avoid. She was no more than six feet from her enemy, with only a large truck in between. As she stood up, a second shot tore through the cab windows beside her, showering her with glass. She ducked, grimacing.

Think Beth, think...

An idea suddenly occurred to her. Knowing she had only seconds before her opponent got up his courage to round the truck, she dropped to her knees, looking back under the vehicle. Sure enough, the man was pressed against the sides almost directly opposite her. The angle was difficult, and she was not confident in her ability to put a round into the man's ankles.

Luckily, she didn't plan to.

Taking a moment to steady herself, she took careful aim, and put a pair or rounds into each of the truck's driver's side tires, first the front, then the back. The truck lurched heavily toward her opponent, inciting a loud exclamation. Almost instantly, Beth was rounding the truck, scanning through the sights. Her distraction had worked. She found the man gaping in surprise at her, trying to bring his gun back up...

Too slow.

Closing the distance between them in a rush, Beth swept the man's pistol aside with her free hand, pressed the muzzle of her LK-2 into the unarmored gap under his arm, and fired twice. He dropped at her feet.

Breathing hard, she remained still, listening. Somewhere on her left was the distinctive bark of Grant's Maxwell-50, followed by the deep-throated boom of Ramirez's shotgun.

Beth decided that with two down, it was time to regroup. Moving cautiously, she headed toward where she had last heard Ramirez. The night had grown eerily quiet again, without even the sound of enemy weapons to break the stillness.

Click.

Beth spun around, knowing that she was probably dead already. One of the guards was silhouetted against the sky, standing atop one of the cars with a pistol leveled at her head. Before she could move or cry out, another dark shape rose up behind him. There was a glint of metal, followed by a wet sound. The guard collapsed with a gurgle, and there stood Ramirez, knife in hand.

"I ran out of shells," he explained as he dropped down beside Beth.

"Well, thanks. Where's Evan?"

"Two rows back. We accounted for one together."

"And I got two."

"Which means there's still one out there," Grant said, making her jump. Despite his size, he could move surprisingly quietly, "though if he's smart, he cleared off. I say we grab Evan and get to the gate."

"No need, Mr. Grant." Beth looked up, seeing Evan limp laboriously toward them between the vehicles.

Beth's only warning was a muted *clunk* from behind her. Whirling around, she saw the last guard had climbed onto the cab of another truck, lining up a shot toward the approaching Fletcher's Wolf. Knowing she was far too late, Beth tried to bring her gun up...

Out of the corner of her eye, she saw Ramirez moving, throwing himself backwards...

The man fired, and Beth saw Ramirez crash into Evan and tumble to the ground.

There was a burst of staccato thunder as Grant put a lethally accurate spread into the man, who fell immediately out of sight with a muted *thud*, and then silence again.

Beth blew out a long, shuddering breath of relief. That had been *far* too close for comfort. A good thing Ramirez had moved so fast, or Evan would likely be dead.

Grant dropped his aim with a sigh of his own. "Bugger. Always the last bloody one. Brilliant work, Ramirez. Though taking a round in the vest still hurts like hell, doesn't it... Ramirez?"

Swept up in the relief she felt, it took Beth a moment to realize that Ramirez wasn't moving. Her blood seemed to freeze in her veins.

No. No...

She was half a second behind Grant as they dropped to their knees beside their fallen friend. His eyes were open, staring sightlessly into the sky. Swearing quietly, Grant tore open Ramirez's shirt with formidable strength, revealing the dark body-armor beneath.

As well as the stain of blood spreading across the dull surface.

God, no, please no...

Grant checked for a pulse, growing increasingly desperate as he felt Ramirez's neck.

Finally, his hand fell away, his face ashen. "The bullet went in the side, under the seam. Probably clipped the heart." A tear slid down the hard planes of the security officer's face, disappearing into his beard. "He's dead."

For several seconds, Beth couldn't grasp it.

Dead.

It couldn't be. Barely ten seconds ago he was alive, talking to them. He was the same man who they had lived with and worked alongside for years. The same man who would listen quietly at meals, and exchange soft quips over a cup of coffee. The man who had worked tirelessly to keep them safe, no matter the risk. This lifeless body simply could not be the same man.

But it was. She knew it was.

Dead.

The tears came then, uncontrolled. If only she had acted. If only she had moved a little faster. If only she had jumped first. So many variables, any one of which would have altered that single instant, and Ramirez would still be with them. Or maybe not. There was no way to be sure. There was the madness of it. Just like the death of her family. She would never know if she could have prevented it.

But you could have tried, she accused herself. *You could have done something...*

"He died for me." The small voice pulled her back from her despair.

Caught up in her grief, she hadn't even noticed Evan crouching beside her. His eyes were cold, his ears flat against his head. "That man was going to shoot me, and he took the bullet for me. And I'm the only reason you're even here. He died because of me."

Beth felt her face harden, stopping the tears. "No. Not because of you." The words came in an unthinking rush. "We are all here by our own choice, including Ramirez. Just as it was his choice to take that bullet. He saved you, because he decided that it was worth it."

Evan stared at her, his surprise plain in his eyes. Beth was surprised at her own words. She didn't really know where it came from; it was like a realization that she had never allowed herself to believe before now.

"We need to keep moving," Grant said firmly. "We can't let his sacrifice go in vain. It's what he would have wanted." Even though the tears ran freely down his face, he was still Charlie, the rock that could always be depended upon.

Beth swiped a hand roughly across her eyes. Grant was right. There would be time for grief later, after they had escaped this hellhole. "You're right of course, Charlie," she said, for once not caring that her voice was quavering. "But we can't just leave him here."

"I'll carry him," Grant resolved. "Not exactly a hero's transport, but it will have to do. You help Evan."

Beth nodded, swallowing back the lump in her throat. She could still just picture the lifeless figure before her rising up, blinking impatiently. *What are you all sitting here for?* He would say. *Setting the record for slowest getaway?*

Yes, they had to keep going, but there was something she had to do first.

She reached out, tenderly closing his staring eyes with her fingers as she summoned a name that she had agreed long ago that she would never use.

"Goodbye, Tomas. And thank you."

Still visibly fighting to control himself, Grant scooped up the body with strong hands, laying it across his shoulder in a solid fireman's carry.

Beth helped Evan to his feet and they set off, weaving through the car-park and keeping to the shadows as much as possible. Beth did her best to scan her surroundings as they went, but she found herself continually abandoning caution for speed. Her only thought was to get to the gate, to escape this horrible place. If Tavia couldn't open it again, they would use the truck to smash it down. Finally, they reached the front of the complex, where the gate was still standing resolutely closed. Standing in one of the darkest shadows cast by the area lights, she could see no activity. Nothing was moving, not even in the guardhouse beside the gate.

"Still no response from Tavia," Grant said, lowering his free hand from his earpiece. "Hard way?"

"Hard way," she confirmed, pointing to where their rented vehicle still stood in the shadow of the building barely twenty feet away. "Just a little farther, Evan," she soothed quietly, leading the way forward. He had been growing increasingly unresponsive since the brief firefight outside the main building, and the best he was capable of was a groggy nod in acknowledgement. Worried that he was about to pass out, she increased her pace; almost crying for joy as they finally reached the truck. Her feelings were mirrored on Grant's face as he opened the cab door…

Revealing an all too familiar face, adorned by an even more familiar pair of sunglasses.

"Hiya, sweetheart. You miss me?"

16

Encumbered as he was with Ramirez' body, Grant had made sure to leave his gun-arm free to move. Almost immediately processing the presence of Shades, he brought his weapon up to shoot…

Shades was too fast, leaping from the cab of the truck and seizing his arm in a vice-like grip. Grant felt himself pulled off balance as the man twisted his arm sharply, pulling it down across his shoulder in a direction it was not designed to bend and slamming the heel of his hand into the joint. Grant cried out in pain as something in his elbow snapped, the pistol falling from his nerveless grasp. He could hear Beth yelling through a sudden haze of pain, and saw her raising her own gun. Shades just laughed.

"Wouldn't do that, sweetie. I've got the old man here, and my trigger-finger might twitch. Besides, you've got a dozen guns trained on you right now."

Sure enough, as Grant's vision began to clear, he saw at least ten men step from concealment near the buildings, weapons up and trained on him and his friends as the dots from mounted laser-sights flicked across them. Scare tactics, he realized. There was no way they had just thrown this ambush together. Shades' manic grin practically glowed in the dark.

"Kick the gun over here by me, would you, doll?"

Beth obeyed stiffly, the anger on her face merely inciting a laugh. "Did you really think that Arkady wouldn't see this coming? He figured you'd be dumb enough to try something like this, and we were looping the cameras on your AI buddy for the past twenty minutes. We had you dead-bang."

Grant looked around frantically, trying to find some way—any way—out of the trap.

C'mon Charlie! We came too far to fail now.

Beth's face was a study in shock and anger—he could see her hands shaking with barely contained fury. They had been so close. Grant glanced at Evan, wondering what was going through his head as the unexpected light at the end of the tunnel was snuffed. The wolf looked dead, his whole body drooping, defeat plain on his face. But his ears, Grant noticed, were pricked up and alert.

"Whatcha looking for, Grandpa?" Shades asked, tilting his head mockingly. "A fuel-tank you can blow up and escape in the confusion? Face it, you're beaten."

"Fine," Grant grated back, wishing his free arm wasn't too injured to plant a solid flathand into the man's nose. "You got us, fair and square. Now take us in so the blues can read us our rights."

Shades shrugged. "That would be one way to do it, but..." He raised his pistol, placing the muzzle against Beth's forehead. "The way I see it, we've come across a few burglars. I think it might just be easier if we shot them dead in self-defense. What do you think, guys?"

No one said a word. No one needed to. The murderous intent in Shades' stance spoke for them.

Grant steeled himself, readying himself for a leap that would knock Shades to the ground, probably dooming himself just in time for Evan and Beth to die in a hail of bullets shortly afterword. But if there was a merciful God in heaven, it would buy them enough time to run somewhere, anywhere, just to get away...

Just then, his mind suddenly identified a noise that had been steadily growing in his ears; a deep, shuddering rumble that seemed to vibrate the very air.

He smiled.

Catching Evan's eyes, Grant exchanged a subtle nod...

Beth recognized it as well, a sudden look of total confidence spreading across her face as she stared straight into Shade's hidden eyes. "Tell you what? If you surrender right now, then I won't have to hurt you."

Shades laughed. "I rather regret that you'll never get the chance to hurt me, beautiful. I like a girl with spunk. Killing you will break my heart, it really will."

The noise grew steadily louder, finally causing Shades to glance around...

"Ah well," Beth sighed. "Your loss."

At that second, the noise reached a deafening crescendo as a huge, beautiful shape hove into view overhead.

It was the *Memory*.

Wind buffeted Grant as the ship's engines swung around, stirring up a flurry of downdraft that sent the surrounding men scurrying for cover. At the same time, Evan sprang into action, throwing the Hughes sidearm that no one had noticed him carrying. Grant, who had been working his uninjured left hand out from under Ramirez' body as soon as he had heard the ship approaching caught it from the air. Spinning the weapon into firing position, he brought the sights up, firing two quick rounds into the back of both

Shades' legs. The man dropped to his knees with a cry, his gun out of line for a split second...

Taking advantage of the opportunity, Beth slammed the heel of her hand upward. The *crack* of his jaw breaking was audible even above the noise of the ship. Shades collapsed, whimpering in pain.

"Sorry I took so long," said a cheerful voice in Grant's earpiece. "I got stuck in traffic."

"Tavia," Grant said, shielding his eyes against the wind. "I will only ever say this once, but I'm sure glad to see you."

"You can hug me in a moment, Charlie. I'm landing on your left side. I think. Get ready to run for the ramp."

The next moments passed in a frenzied rush. Dropping the gun, he used his uninjured arm to steady Ramirez's body on his shoulders and, as soon as he saw Beth pass him, started sprinting toward the spot Tavia had indicated. Evan was ahead of him, running awkwardly on all fours and favoring his injured leg, but outpacing Beth nonetheless.

Above them, the ship swung around for a descent, its ramp already starting to open. As it did, the guards finally seemed to recover from their shock. Grant didn't look back as shots rang out behind him, knowing that only distance and speed would save them. The *Memory* wasn't the most maneuverable of ships at the best of times and Tavia's piloting skills were limited to autopilot and navigational calculations. This was made painfully obvious as the shuttle came down a little too quickly and reduced the number of working vehicles in the compound by five. Vans crumpled like tin cans, shooting parts and pieces in all directions, but the only thing that mattered to Grant was the cargo ramp—open, inviting, safe. They put on an extra burst of speed as they raced up the incline, rounds pinging off the metal around them. Finally, they threw themselves onto the floor of the deck.

"We're in! Go!"

Before Grant had even finished shouting, the world outside the hatch fell away crazily as the shuttle's powerful engines lifted them into the air, providing a single glimpse of the running guards before they were lost to sight. The ramp rose back into place, killing the wind that had been swirling chaotically through the bay.

They were safe.

For several seconds they just lay there on the cargo bay floor, the only sound their labored breathing as they all came down from their own adrenaline high.

Finally, Beth broke the silence, dragging herself into a sitting position. "Thanks for that, Tavia. Just... Thanks. Where are you heading now?"

"You're welcome, Captain. And that's up to you. If you want to, we could circle the compound for a bit just to taunt them. Our hull is so thick it can shrug off that small-arms fire like it was spit wads."

"You might as well just head for the spaceport," Beth decided, standing up. "The Coalition will be tracking us by now, and I would rather meet with who I suspect is waiting for us at our landing pad."

"Sure thing. Spaceport it is."

Beth glanced around. "Are you both alright? No one catch any lead on the way out?"

" 'M fine," Evan said. "Well, fine-ish."

Grant took stock. Although his side was bruised and his arm felt broken, he hadn't been punctured anywhere. "Fighting shape, Beth. Ready when you are. That was nothing. Heck, I'm ready to do that again. Where's the next corrupt mega-corp? I'll take them on with one hand behind my back." It was the fighting man's armor of bravado. There were times when you could either laugh or break and right now, Beth needed him.

Beth chuckled. "If we're meeting the person I think we are then hopefully there won't be any need for that."

Minutes later, Tavia swung the shuttle into a precise, if a bit rough landing on their rented pad. As the ramp lowered, Grant was treated to about the scene he had been expecting: a wilderness of parked cars and armed men, all brilliantly illuminated by the glare of flashing blue lights. As instructed, he stood beside his companions, his left hand held high in the air. His right hung limply by his side.

"Hold your fire!" shouted an amplified voice, one that Grant thought he recognized.

Sure enough, a moment later Chief Inspector March and a pair of constables came marching up the ramp. For his part, March did not have a hand on his weapon.

"Well, Captain Hugin," he said amiably. "This is a surprise, meeting you here twice in the same day. And I understand that you've run into a spot of trouble, too."

"It has been a long day, Inspector," Beth agreed, submitting to the pat-down search as the officers checked them all for weapons.

March nodded. "Something of an interesting story, too. From what I've been hearing over the wire; you broke into a secure laboratory, stole property, shot people, vandalized a building and several vehicles, and generally raised all manner of ruckus. Now, every man here is about ready to have you all committed, but I think to myself: 'What, that nice, amiable lady I met this morning? There's no way she would get involved in such a thing, unless of course she had a very good reason.' Am I right?"

Grant raised his arms laboriously for his own search, waiting for what would happen next. In the flashing light, he was just able to catch the look of decision in Beth's eyes.

"Chief Inspector, can I ask you something?"

"Why, of course you may."

"I'm the sort of person that is notorious for making snap-judgments on people the moment I meet them. It's worked out pretty well for me so far. My read on you this morning gave me two things. The first one was that you and I have that in common. Snap judgments."

March stroked his neatly-trimmed mustache thoughtfully. "You may be correct in that, Captain. Very astute. And if I did, say, judge that you could never have done the things they say for the reason they said them, how would that help you?"

Grant felt his heart skip. When Beth had related her plan to him, he would have never believed it would work. But, typically, she had been right.

Beth smiled. "There is something that you could do, actually," she said, holding up the black briefcase that had started the whole mess. "Could you hang onto this for us and keep it safe? Would it compromise your integrity to do such a thing?"

March thought it over. The lights reflected in his blue eyes. Finally, he nodded. "If I call it evidence, no one will touch it but me," he said, taking the case from Beth. "Don't worry, if this is what I suspect it might be, I'll keep it locked up nice and tight. Well away from I.S. spooks and everyone else." He dropped the case to his side, as casually as if it were his own. "In the meantime, I have orders to escort you all to the Coalition Headquarters for a private word. If you'll follow these gentlemen here."

As he turned away, Grant couldn't help but quirk a smile. It would appear that Beth had found a kindred spirit among the police force...

"Oh, by the way," March called after them, causing Beth to turn. "What was the second thing your snap-judgment said about me?"

Beth shrugged fractionally. "That you were a good man."

* * *

The visit to the Coalition headquarters was rather different from Beth's previous experience. Instead of braving the public areas, the police escort was ushered straight through an unobtrusive entrance to an underground parking area. From there, they were guided to a simple, comfortable waiting room, where they were given coffee and sandwiches. Their waiting was presided over by several men in suits, making sure they didn't leave, but saying little. A moment later, a medic arrived to check them over, and, to her surprise, a veterinary doctor for Evan. It was amusing to watch as the vet did all the talking without letting the wolf get a word in edgewise. She guessed that he wasn't used to treating patients who could talk back. Finally, one of the suits asked her to follow, leading her down a very familiar hallway to a very familiar interrogation room, complete with a very familiar occupant.

"Agent Bale," she said, dropping into the chair for the second time that day. "Well, isn't this a bit of *déjà vu*."

"Oh, believe me, Captain," Bale said, "the situation here has indeed changed." He steepled his fingers, glancing down at the piece of paper before him. "So, you didn't get any help from us, and decided to take matters into your own hands. Breaking and entering, theft, assault, multiple manslaughter... oh, and destruction of property." He put on a look of bland surprise. "What, were you going for a record? There's enough there for a life sentence or two. For you *and* Mr. Grant. It's not looking very good for you right now."

Beth had anticipated this. She offered a wry smile. "And yet we both know it's not that simple. An open and shut case like this, there would be no need for Investigative Services to get involved. That raises the question: what am I doing here?"

"An excellent question, to be sure. One that I think you already know the answer to."

She waited a calculated second, then pulled out a small memory stick from her pocket, setting it on the table. "You'd be amazed what our AI dug up on ABI's mainframe. Information that, I'm guessing, you guys couldn't get by any legal means. This will bring them down for you."

Bale smiled. "Your future is looking brighter already, Captain. If that info checks out, I think my superiors would be more than happy to make all of this go away for you."

Beth felt a flush of victory. But a small voice in the back of her mind reminded her that that hadn't been her main goal. *Maybe I'm being paranoid. But checking can't hurt.*

"What about my engineer?" she asked warily. "What happens to him?"

"Ah yes... Subject 112. Your Evan." Bale settled back in his chair with a sigh. "I'm afraid that might be a problem. No matter what we say, he still killed two people. The law says that he needs to be decommissioned and studied. I would strike that from the record right now if it was up to me, Captain, but I doubt my superiors will see it in the same light that I do."

Beth clenched her hands on the arms of her chair. *All that work for nothing? Ramirez dies for nothing? No!*

Bale's tone was sympathetic. "I'm sorry, Captain, but you have to see it from their perspective. They would need some serious motivation to bail him out and you're not exactly in a position to bargain with them."

Beth gritted her teeth. "That's where you're mistaken." Bale looked at her enquiringly. She had anticipated something along these lines, but she still didn't like what she had to do. In the end, however, she had no choice. "I can give them Dr. Phillips' carrier-virus. That's what everyone's been going spare to get, right? That's what started this whole mess. That's my damned bargaining chip."

"You got it back, then." It was a statement, not a question. "Why am I not surprised? You've been pretty busy, Captain. I won't ask how many other laws you broke to get it." Bale sighed, glancing down at his papers. "But that is one hell of an offer. I don't think my director will need any encouragement to take you up on that."

"Can you guarantee that?"

"Give us the virus and I give you my word that if he doesn't clear Subject 112, I will."

Beth nodded decisively. "Contact the LPD and ask for Chief Inspector March. Tell him that I sent you. He'll be holding on to it for me."

"You'll need to stay on-planet for a few days until everything checks out, Captain, but right now, you're free to go. I need to know something, though." He looked up at Beth, spinning the memory stick absently between his fingers. "This virus is worth a fortune. A couple fortunes, actually. You could have been set for life if you had sold it on the black market."

"All I care about is my crew," she said, answering the unspoken question. "They're my family, and they're worth more than all the money in the galaxy to me."

"I understand," Bale said kindly. "Good luck, Captain. I'll be in touch."

As she followed her guide down the hallway, she tried to stop from feeling that she had made a terrible mistake. She had, in essence, handed the Coalition a possible superweapon, capable of creating a very efficient form of genocide. And from what she had seen, they were not the most trustworthy keepers for such a technology. How many people might be killed, because she needed to save the lives of her own friends? Was it worth it? Could it ever be?

Just then, they arrived back at the waiting room. Over her escort's shoulder, she watched Evan nodding as the veterinarian explained something to him, pointing to his leg. Charlie sat slightly removed, with his arm in a sling, trying to brush sandwich crumbs out of his beard.

Yes, Beth decided, it was worth it. It had to be.

* * *

"Last night, a government raid on an Arkady Biotech Industries building revealed the shocking truth behind the supercorporation's success. Documents and photos recovered from the ABI mainframe tell a sordid story of the industrial espionage, corporate extortion and massive cover-ups that brought ABI to the forefront of biotechnical pioneering," a pretty, female news anchor announced, looking seriously out at the occupants of the café through the display screen on the wall. "ABI's CEO, Benjamin Arkady, as well as over a dozen members of his senior staff have all been charged as accessories to multiple murders—all concerning employees of competing companies—as well as facing various additional charges for their involvement in the biggest cover-up of the century." She scrolled down her datapad importantly, apparently ignoring the fact that there was a lot of century left to come. "Arkady has been placed under arrest, pending further investigation."

"Surprise number four, Arkady. I warned you," Hugin commented quietly, nursing her coffee. Evan made a note to ask her what she meant after the anchor was done speaking.

"During the events of last night, members of the Coalition's elite Investigative

Services discovered proof of illegal experimentation on sentients inside one of ABI's buildings known only as 'Compound 5'. This facility is the one that housed the famous Fletcher Project—the first successful attempt to market a biological AI." Here an out-of-date picture of a Fletcher's Wolf popped up in the upper left-hand corner of the screen. "These Fletcher's Wolves, as they came to be known, were evidently the victims of cruel testing and subjected to a battery of inhumane assessments and training techniques. This brutal treatment went on for at least sixteen years in conditions that make the average Coalition prison look appealing in contrast."

She paused for breath, glancing down again at the datapad in her hand. "Held primarily responsible for this atrocity, is Doctor Carson Morrow," a blurry clip of a silently ranting Dr. Morrow being muscled into a Coalition vehicle played behind the announcer, "one of the head researchers personally assigned to the Fletcher Project by Benjamin Arkady himself. He is currently being questioned by the Investigative Services, but he has promised to issue a public statement, quote 'when he is released.' I.S. Chief of Staff Scott Cole has refused to comment on Dr. Morrow's assertion."

"In related—and slightly happier—news," she continued, flashing a brilliant smile at the café, "the Coalition Board of Legislators has promised in a news conference held this morning to give top priority to reviewing the current laws governing biological AIs." A studious group of men in black suits appeared in the background. "Someone high up has seemingly taken quite an interest in the fortunes of these Wolves, because the wheels of the government have been well oiled and Dr. Emma Fletcher, the scientist originally responsible for creating the Fletcher's Wolves, has already been reassigned to the Project with what is being called 'significant government funding.' "

"You know her?" Grant asked, blowing on his enormous cup of very black coffee that he held carefully in his left hand. His right arm was still immobilized in a sling.

"Yes." Evan had let out the beginning of a *sir*, but managed to keep it behind his teeth. He smiled. That was progress. "Dr. Fletcher was always good to us. Sometimes she even snuck books in for us from the outside. That's how we got the idea of giving each other names."

"Sounds like a real bloody saint," Grant said sarcastically. "Provide reading material and you make up for turning a blind eye to torture. Why haven't these Coalition bigwigs who've taken 'quite an interest' just shut the whole project down, if it's as bad as you've been telling us?"

"It's a good thing they haven't, really. If the project was simply shut down, the Fletcher's Wolves wouldn't have much of a chance of surviving as a species. Our numbers are too small right now to be self-sustaining long-term. And besides, Dr. Fletcher would never let the project go back to how it was. She was fired because she tried to protect us from Dr. Morrow and the others. She's not like them."

"Mm." The security officer's eyes were glued to the screen again.

"According to records found on the ABI mainframe," the blond anchor continued, "Fletcher was coerced into leaving the project by Arkady when she failed to produce the results he wanted with a top-secret part of the biological aspect of the project known only as 'safeguards.'" Evan saw Hugin's face darken out of the corner of his eye. Out of the few sympathetic people Evan had met, she was the one most disturbed by the revelations of the past week. Every time the 'Pound or ABI was mentioned, she got a look in her eye that made Evan want to tuck his tail and slink out of the room. "In a brief conference with members of the press, Dr. Fletcher expressed anger at her former colleagues and a heartfelt desire to help the wolves, as well as a promise to turn the project around."

The announcer flicked her blond hair back over her shoulder and smiled confidently. "And so it seems that after all that they've gone through, the plight of the Fletcher's Wolves is finally receiving the attention it's been denied for over twenty years and their collective future is looking up. More details at 20:00. Up next: Could your datapad be killing you? See the truth behind the scare. This is Jean Archer, reporting live for Europe's Current Events Broadcast."

Grant turned his chair back around to face Hugin and Evan. "Well," he said, setting his cup down and leaning back in the chair, "that's that."

There was silence for a few minutes as Hugin and Grant sipped their coffee. It wasn't an uncomfortable silence; there had been many like it in the past day following the simple funeral they had held for Ramirez. It seemed as though they had all taken on a bit of the late procurement officer's laconic demeanor in his absence. There were four chairs around the table Hugin had chosen, and everyone was studiously ignoring the empty one. But Evan knew that no one wanted to move it, either. They had all been dealing with their grief in different ways. Grant seemed much quieter than usual and his almost permanent cheer seemed ready to crack at the slightest reminder of Ramirez. Evan had heard him crying quietly when Grant went into the procurement officer's room to tidy up the clutter of electronic parts.

Tavia, on the other hand, had claimed to be unaffected, saying dispassionately that all humans died sometime and that it would have happened sooner or later anyway. No one believed her, though.

Hugin was also subdued, but in a different way. She mourned for her friend, but she seemed to have a kind of peace with his death that Grant did not. When Evan had asked her about it, she had said that Ramirez had died how he would have wanted to and that if he could see her tearing herself apart with guilt again he would call her a sentimental idiot and tell her to get on with her life.

As for how Evan felt about it himself... that was a little more complicated. In the short time he had spent with the man, Ramirez had seemed downright hostile and, aside from confronting Evan the first night onboard the shuttle, hadn't said a single word to him. But something had changed when Ramirez came to break him out of the 'Pound,

Evan knew. Something had changed enough to make the previously unfriendly man throw himself in front of a bullet for him.

Why was that? Evan wondered, staring into his untouched cup. Just water for him. No use wasting money when he wasn't going to drink it anyway. He was already drawing stares without messily trying to lap water out of a cup. It was absurd, really. He was here, sitting in a modern, little café, when he should have been dead two or three times over. But he wasn't. Ramirez was dead instead. He flicked his ears in frustration. Why? It didn't make sense!

"It doesn't make sense," he repeated to himself.

Hugin and Grant looked up at him from their coffee.

"What doesn't?" Hugin asked.

Evan gestured at the empty chair. "Why he…" He trailed off.

Hugin sighed and glanced at the empty chair, resting her chin on her hands. For a few minutes, she just stared at it, lost in thought or memories. Just as Evan started to think that she didn't have an answer, she turned back, a sad smile on her lips.

"Because," she said simply, "that's what a family does."

Evan blinked.

"It's what I would do for either of you without a second thought." She grinned ruefully. "I know you weren't on the best of terms but sometime in the past few days he decided that you were one of the few people he was willing to die to protect."

"But why?" Evan asked again. "It doesn't make any sense. He hated me."

"I don't think we'll ever know exactly *why*, but you're wrong about the second part. He didn't hate you. I think he distrusted you at first, but something happened to change his mind."

He chewed that over. It was true; Ramirez's attitude toward him had certainly undergone a change when they had spoken in the hallway.

Whatever I did to win you over, though, it can never equal what you did for me.

"Thank you," he said, too softly for the others to hear.

"So," Grant said, breaking the silence in his usual manner, "will you be staying on with us, Evan?"

"I'm sorry?"

"Seems like you're going to start having some real options pretty soon." Grant gestured at the screen. "I was wondering if you were planning on hanging around the shuttle or if you'd decided to branch off on your own?"

"I'm not going anywhere on my own. I still belong to Captain Hugin."

"Not anymore," Hugin broke in, pulling a sheet of paper out of her jacket pocket. "This says that for the price of 6,000 credits, the ownership of Fletcher Project Subject 112 has been legally passed to an Engineering Officer Evan. No last name. Got the papers last night."

"B-but where did I get 6,000 credits?" Evan stammered, staring in shock at the paper Hugin set on the table.

"Consider it a gift. You've done some sterling work on our ship which deserves some compensation. And there are some things that all the money in the galaxy can't make up for," she finished quietly.

"So!" Grant leaned back in his chair, beaming through his beard. "Now that that's settled, you can do whatever you want, for once."

"Don't take this the wrong way," Hugin hastily interjected. "We're not cutting you loose, here. No one's going to tell you what you have to do. We'd all love for you to stay… but it's your life now."

My choice. This is what I've wanted my whole life. My choice. It's actually up to me. And now that the Coalition is taking an interest in us, things might start to change. It's a new world out there. Evan looked back and forth between Hugin's earnest concern and Grant's contented smile. *It's my life now.*

He grinned. "And there's no one I'd rather spend it with than my family, Beth."

Grant's smile exploded into a booming laugh. "I would hug you, but I think that would hurt both of us." Evan self-consciously touched the fresh bandages under his shirt.

"I guess we'll just need to settle for this," Hugin said, laughing. "Evan, I am officially signing you on as a paid member of our crew. Welcome back aboard."

The three spacers had drawn a good deal of attention from the clientele of the café with their assortment of bandages, firearms and unusual appearances, but the novelty had worn off and, for the most part, the other customers were too absorbed in the news or their datapads to notice the steady thumping of a grey-furred tail against a table leg.

Family… I have a family.

Epilogue

Deliver directly to Director Cole.

Nature of Report: Pending situations in galactic terrorism.

Author: Danvers, Sarah C, Chief Analyst, Counter-Terror Division

The purpose of this report is to apprise the Director of the rising terrorist activity seen in recent months, particularly in the sector of techno-terrorism. In the event that the Director is unaware, I will sum up the ideology behind these acts. Techno-terrorists believe that mankind's advances in technology are harmful to society, their claims ranging from a lazier workforce to opening a kind of technological Pandora's Box. Over recent years, we've seen a sharp upswing in this type of terrorist activity, particularly from the anti-AI sector.

The Director is already aware of the programming facility bombing last spring, and the sabotage of the starliner Konrad's AI that crippled the ship in the middle of open space a few months later. It is suspected that both of these acts were connected to the activist organization called Humans Against Artificial Life (HAAL). Investigation suggests that HAAL is funding and arming radical anti-AI groups, but we have yet to find any substantial proof. Connected or not, these acts of terrorism against AIs and other advanced technology are growing, both in number and in scope.

The reason I bring this to the Director's personal attention is because of the addition of a new factor; the Fletcher's Wolf. Up until the recent scandal involving Arkady Biotech, Fletcher's Wolves have mostly remained quietly in the background as a minor novelty. Now they are the subject of intense media scrutiny on every world. In the mind of a techno-terrorist, computers using AI are an abomination.

Recommendation and Conclusion: Authorize additional manpower to investigate HAAL and other activist organizations as they move to respond to this new threat to their ideology. Advise planetary police forces and other law-enforcement agencies on the nature of the threat, and pool resources with them to investigate and prevent further attacks. As far as the movement goes, techno-terrorism is still very much in its infancy, but simulations have suggested that activity will increase over the next year or so. They will spend this time preparing. With respect, I strongly recommend that we do the same.

Acknowledgements

Sean: Before starting on this project, the image of the solitary writer laboring alone in a darkened room was an illusion I had long held. Nothing could be further from reality. This book would have been impossible without a small army of guides and advisors, contributing without thought to the reward. First and foremost, I want to thank my family for their understanding and sacrifice, especially my parents Tony and Susan for their patience, wisdom, encouragement, and vehicular support. Also my sisters Mehgan, Brenna and Anna for listening to me babble about jumble of plot and character in my head. Your patient enthusiasm helped more than you know. I would also like to extend thanks to Emma Ciric, for always offering a useful perspective and heartfelt support, and whose hot pink font pinpointed so many typos with such blinding clarity. Thanks also to the multitude of friends, family and acquaintances whose names would be too numerous to list, who showed interest and enthusiasm for the project, and reassuring me the pursuit was a worthy one. At last, of course, my co-writer for coming up with the idea, and having the courage to go, and never settling for less than our best.

Acknowledgements

AJ: There are so many people who helped to bring this book from an idea to a reality, providing advice, encouragement, prayer, and occasionally a much-needed dousing with an ice-cold bucket of reality to remind me that I wasn't done yet (but now I am done—hah!). I wish I could mention all of the people who contributed by name, but the list is very, very long. You know who you are, and I thank you!

I would, however, like to mention to my family, and loyal reviewers. My father, whose knowledge was an indispensable tool in the editing process, and who tirelessly battled against the evils of misplaced commas, incorrect sentence structure, and dangling participles (oh my!); my mother, for being a faithful and loving listener whenever I was having a hard time; my sister, Erika, who was always ready to help me whip my bizarre ideas into shape, and for filling in whenever "Mrs. Hudson took my skull."

To all those who helped me edit the book, Sarah Beason, Maria Sergeant, Benjy Joung, Emma Ciric, and everyone else: thank you for offering your time and sanity to help make sense of our ramblings. We couldn't have done it without you!

Finally, I'd like to thank my co-author, for sticking with me through the good times and bad; through writer's-block, personality clashes, and the endless rewrites. Despite everything we went through, I know you had my back the whole time, and that means the world to me.